P9-EMO-268

CONCORD FREE
CONCORD
MA
PUBLIC LIBRARY

Blood Game

Blood Game

Iris Johansen

THORNDIKE
CHIVERS

This Large Print edition is published by Thorndike Press, Waterville, Maine USA and by BBC Audiobooks Ltd, Bath, England.

An Eve Duncan Forensic Thriller.

Thorndike Press, a part of Gale, Cengage Learning.

Thorndike Press® Large Print Basic.
The text of this Large Print edition is unabridged.
Other aspects of the book may vary from the original edition.
Set in 16 pt. Plantin.
Printed on permanent paper.

LIBRARY OF CONGRESS CATALOGING-IN-PUBLICATION DATA

Johansen, Iris.
Blood game / by Iris Johansen.
p. cm. — (Thorndike Press large print basic)
"An Eve Duncan forensic thriller."
ISBN-13: 978-1-4104-1992-7 (alk. paper)
ISBN-10: 1-4104-1992-4 (alk. paper)
1. Duncan, Eve (Fictitious character)—Fiction. 2. Serial murder investigation—Fiction. 3. Large type books. I. Title.
PS3560.O275B58 2009b
813'.54—dc22 2009025785

BRITISH LIBRARY CATALOGUING-IN-PUBLICATION DATA AVAILABLE
Published in the U.S. in 2009 by arrangement with St. Martin's Press, LLC.
Published in the U.K. in 2010 by arrangement with the author.
U.K. Hardcover: 978 1 408 45784 9 (Chivers Large Print)
U.K. Softcover: 978 1 408 45785 6 (Camden Large Print)

Printed in the United States of America
1 2 3 4 5 6 7 13 12 11 10 09

Blood Game

One

The woman was fruitful.

She had given to him, and he must give back.

Kevin Jelak arranged her naked body carefully on the grass. He brushed her long blond hair back from her face and closed her blue eyes, which were staring straight up at the sky. But he could do nothing about the twisted horror that was frozen on her face. She hadn't understood the honor he was doing her. Well, what could you expect? Nancy Jo Norris was only nineteen, and she didn't know what nightmares could attack a woman, the nightmares from which he'd saved her. He preferred to honor older, more experienced women, but the fever had been upon him, and he'd had to compromise.

The fever. You didn't realize how fortunate you were, Nancy Jo. I might have driven right past you if the torment hadn't been so intense and if I hadn't been forced to confine myself to such a small corner of the world.

The corner of the world that contained Eve Duncan. Wonderful, strong, tortured Eve Duncan. Eve knew about the nightmares. She had lived through them. She might pretend that she wanted life, but deep in her heart of hearts she only wanted the release he could give her. The release he must give her. He had known that she would be his final move in the game. But she had destroyed his prime source, and it was his duty to take the time and effort to single her out for attention right away.

He looked up at the crescent moon, sharp as a scythe in the night sky. "Eve, do you hear me?" he whispered. "Do you feel me?" Then he closed his eyes and tried to form a picture of Eve in his mind. Short red-brown hair, thin, strong body, intelligent face brimming with character. "You're not going to be easy. But I promise I will persevere."

In the meantime, he had this lesser woman, this Nancy Jo Norris, to do final honor.

He took the golden goblet that he had cupped between her folded hands on her breasts. "You're released, Nancy Jo. Take flight." He bent and kissed her lingeringly on the lips. She was already turning cool as her soul departed. "Have you forgiven me yet? Do you realize the gift I've given you?"

They were the questions he asked every time but to no avail. He must be patient. Someday, one of them would give him that reassurance.

Perhaps Eve Duncan . . .

One final duty that was always pure pleasure.

"Nancy Jo Norris." He lifted the goblet to his lips, his gaze once more on the night sky and the cold, sharp sliver of moon. "Gift to Gift."

He drained the goblet.

The crescent moon was bright and cold, tossing its icy glitter over the sleeping fields that bordered the highway leading toward the Atlanta airport.

Cold? Why had that word suddenly occurred to her, Eve wondered. She was on her way to pick up her adopted daughter, Jane, arriving from Paris, and until a few minutes ago she had been filled with warmth and excitement.

She was being foolish. She was still filled with that same love and excitement. This chill was only because it was the middle of the night and probably a carryover from the last few days Joe and she had spent in the swamp tracking down that monster, Henry Kistle. It had been a nightmare period when the serial killer had taken a little girl hostage to lure Eve to come after him. She could do nothing else when he had lied to her and told her that he was the one who had killed her little girl, Bonnie, all those years ago. The nightmare had taken on gigantic proportions when they discovered the island on which dozens of murdered children had been buried. Yes, that was enough to chill anyone to the bone.

Together with the realization that Joe Quinn was growing farther and farther away from her every minute she continued to search for the body of her murdered daughter, Bonnie. All the years of love and living together that might be coming to an end because she couldn't bear not to continue to try to bring her Bonnie home. Years ago, her child had been kidnapped and presumed murdered. When they later discovered that Ralph Fraser, who had confessed and been executed for multiple murders, was not the killer, she had started on the search to find the man who had taken her daughter.

And Joe had been with her through it all, giving her support and love. First as an FBI agent, then with the ATLPD, but always right beside her. He'd been there to pull her out of the depths of depression, give her encouragement when she'd decided to go back to school and become a forensic sculptor to help bring closure to other parents of children who had been lost. He had been her lover, her friend, her protector.

Until this last year, when he had grown weary and frustrated at the constant threat to Eve. That last danger from Henry Kistle might have been the final straw.

Don't think about it. Think about seeing Jane and the fact that Joe had not walked away from her yet. He'd been fine when she'd left home this morning. Maybe she could work out the —

Her cell phone rang. Jane.

"I'm on my way," she said when she picked up. "Was your flight early? I thought I had another thirty minutes."

"You probably have a hell of a lot more time than that," Jane said. "I'm in Charlotte, North Carolina. My plane had a mechanical problem and landed here. They're trying to put us on another flight. It looks like a two- or three-hour delay."

"Damn. Well, I'll come out and wait anyway."

"You will not. Go back home. I'll call you when I'm ready to board the flight."

Eve thought about it. "You're probably

right. I should be able to get back in plenty of time to meet you at baggage claim."

"Sorry. I didn't want to put you to this trouble. I know how exhausted you must be. Not a very good start for my visit."

"Any way I can get you is a good start."

"Is Joe with you?"

"No, I left him in bed. He was even more exhausted than I was. He was at the precinct last night trying to put names to those dead children we found in the swamp."

She was silent a moment. "But your Bonnie wasn't one of them?"

"No." She couldn't speak for a moment as she remembered the agony of that realization. "Lord, I was praying that I'd find her, Jane."

"I know. That's why I hopped on that plane to come home. I know you have Joe, but I want to be there for you."

"Yes, I have Joe." She had to get off the phone until she could regain full control. Jane could always read her. "And I'm going to be happy as a clam to have you home. Call me." She hung up.

She hoped she had Joe. Dear God, life without Joe would be empty and without texture or substance, as cold as that moon shining above her.

Coldness, again. She couldn't shake it off.

She got off the exit and turned around. She would go home to the lake cottage and Joe. She would hold him and let his strength pour into her. Then maybe, after a little while, the chill would go away.

The lights were on in the kitchen, Eve noticed as she drove up to the cottage. Joe must not have been able to go back to sleep after she'd left. He was probably having coffee and waiting for her to bring Jane home.

But he wasn't in the kitchen, although the coffeemaker was on. Cups, saucers, and creamer had been set on the table in readiness. He wasn't in the bedroom either.

What the hell?

Then she heard him coming up the porch steps.

A moment later he came into the house. He was wearing his brown robe and slippers, and his hair was rumpled. She had bought the robe last Christmas because she always loved him in brown. It made his dark hair appear almost caramel-colored and his eyes a shimmering tea color. Everyone was usually only aware of the toughness that he radiated, and that was still there, but the hardness seemed to be softened by the rich color.

She smiled. "Where have you been? I was

wondering what happened to you. I saw that the coffee was —" She stopped, her eyes widening as she saw his face. "What's wrong?"

"Nothing," he said curtly. "I went for a walk in the woods."

"At this hour? Dressed like that?"

"Why not? I couldn't sleep." He went to the coffeemaker and poured a cup of coffee. "There's no law against it. I guarantee it. Who should know better than a cop?"

His tone was almost brutally sharp, and he was avoiding looking at her. But he was too late; she had already caught that first glimpse of his expression. Joe was seldom pale, but his color wasn't good now. The skin looked as if it was pulled taut over his cheekbones, and his brown eyes were glittering and appeared a little wild. Wild? Joe was never wild. He could be violent and reckless, but it was always under control.

"Why couldn't you sleep?"

"How the hell do I know? Maybe I was dreaming of those murdered kids on that island in the swamp. That's what my life has been about, hasn't it? Murdered kids." He took a swallow of coffee. "Or maybe just one murdered kid. Your kid. From the moment I met you, it's been all about Bonnie. It's enough to drive anyone nuts."

She stiffened in shock. It was true, their lives had revolved around Bonnie's death and disappearance all these years, but his harshness came as a blow. She supposed it shouldn't have hurt since she'd been aware that Joe was nearing the end of his patience. He'd given all his strength and knowledge to try to give her what she needed, and having her constantly in jeopardy was tearing him apart. "You're right, of course. No one knows better than I do what I put you through. You have a perfect right to want to escape from me and the situation."

He suddenly whirled on her. "I don't want to escape you," he said fiercely. "You're the only woman I've ever loved. From the first time I saw you, I knew that I had to stay with you. When the FBI sent me down to Atlanta to investigate your Bonnie's disappearance and probable death, who the hell would guess that I wouldn't be able to leave you. You'd lost a sweet seven-year-old little girl who meant the world to you. You were fragile and tragic and yet so damn strong that it blew me away. I wanted to fight all your dragons and give you whatever you wanted."

"You have," she said unevenly. "Only it's been a one-way street. I haven't fought any dragons for you. You deserve someone who will do that."

"Screw it. I knew what I was getting into when we came together." His eyes were blazing in his taut face. "But I haven't been able to kill your dragon, and I started wondering tonight if it's going to devour me."

"Tonight?" He had not been like this when she had left him to go to the airport. She had been aware of a slight withdrawal, but his attitude now was full of violence and explosive tension. She could almost feel the disturbance whirling around him. "Did something happen while I was gone?"

"Of course not. I told you I just went for a walk." He set his cup down on the counter and turned away. "And I'm tired of being cross-examined. I'm fine. Drop it, Eve."

"So fine that you haven't asked why Jane wasn't with me when I came back."

He looked back at her. "Is she okay?"

"Yes, her plane had a mechanical problem and had to land in Charlotte. She'll call me when she's ready to board again."

"That's good. I'm going to shower, then make some phone calls and go into work early. I have paperwork to do."

"Don't you dare leave this room," Eve said fiercely. "Something's wrong. I know it, dammit. Tell me."

"If there's something wrong, I can handle it by myself. I can fight my own dragons." Joe's words were jerky as he strode toward the door. "I don't need help."

"Joe, for God's sake, *talk* to me."

He didn't answer. She watched the bedroom door shut behind him. He was closing her out, mentally as well as physically.

She felt the pain soaring through her. She had known trouble was on the horizon, but she had thought she'd have time to try to work her way through it. What the hell had happened to escalate the situation?

Her cell phone rang. Jane.

She took a few seconds to pull herself together before she answered the call. "I wasn't expecting to hear from you so soon."

"They managed to fix the other plane. I'm boarding now. Do you want me to get a rental car?"

"Don't be silly. I'm on my way. I'll meet you at baggage claim."

Jane was silent for a moment. "You sound funny. Are you okay?"

"Sure. I'll be even better when I see you. Bye." She hung up.

Trust Jane to read her mood even long-distance. She hesitated as she cast a glance at the closed bedroom door. No, she wouldn't go in and tell Joe she was leaving for the airport. The closing of that door had been firm and final. She would give him time and hope that those dragons he was talking about would slink away into the darkness.

She left the house and ran down the porch steps to the car. But her eyes were stinging with tears, and she had to wait a moment before she pulled out of the driveway. Her hands clenched on the steering wheel as she stared blindly out into the darkness.

Joe's pain was all about Bonnie and Eve's obsession with finding her daughter's murderer. The hunt that had gone on for years. It was hurting him. She couldn't expect him to have empathy. He had never had a child. They had taken Jane from foster homes when she was ten, and by that time, Jane had been wise beyond her years. She had become their friend, not their child. Joe had never had the wonderful experiences that Eve had known of raising a little girl. That was why he would never understand why Eve couldn't let it go.

Because the memory of Bonnie would never let go. That night before Bonnie was taken was as fresh tonight as if it had happened yesterday.

Bonnie running into Eve's bedroom in her yellow pajamas with the orange clowns all over them. Her wild red curls were bouncing, and her face was lit with her luminous smile.

"Mama, Lindsey says her mother is going to let her wear her Goofy T-shirt to the park tomorrow for the school picnic. Can I wear my Bugs Bunny T-shirt?"

Eve looked up from her English Lit book open on the desk in front of her. "It's not can, it's may, baby. And yes, you may wear Bugs tomorrow." She smiled. "We wouldn't want Lindsey to put you in the shade."

"I wouldn't care. She's my friend. You said we always had to want the best for our friends."

"Yes, we do. Now run along to bed."

Bonnie didn't move. "I know you're studying for your test, but could you read me a story?" She added coaxingly, "I thought maybe a very, very, short one?"

"Your grandmother loves to read you stories, baby."

Bonnie came closer and whispered, "I love Grandma. But it's always special when you read it to me. Just a short one . . ."

Eve glanced at her Lit book. She'd be up until after midnight as it was studying for that exam. She looked at Bonnie's pleading face. Oh, to hell with it. Bonnie was the reason Eve was working for her degree anyway. She was the reason for every action Eve took in life. Why cheat either one of them? "Run and choose a storybook." She pushed her textbook aside and stood up. "And it doesn't have to be a short one."

Bonnie's expression could have lit up Times Square. "No, I promise . . ." She ran out of the room. She was back in seconds with a Dr. Seuss book. "This will be quick, and I like the rhymes."

Eve sat down in the blue-padded rocking chair that she'd used since Bonnie was a newborn. "Climb up. I like Dr. Seuss too."

"I know you do." Bonnie scrambled up in her lap and cuddled close. "But since it's such a short book, can — may I have my song too?"

"I think that's a reasonable request," Eve said solemnly. The two of them had their little traditions, and every night since she was a toddler, Bonnie had loved to share a song with Eve. Eve would sing the first line, and Bonnie would sing the next. "What's it to be tonight?"

" 'All the Pretty Little Horses.' " She turned around on Eve's lap and hugged her with all her might. "I love you, Mama."

Eve's arms closed around her. Bonnie's riot of curls was soft and fragrant against her cheek, and her small body was endearingly vital and sturdy against Eve. Lord, she was lucky. "I love you, too, Bonnie."

Bonnie let her go and flopped back around to cuddle in the curve of her arm. "You start, Mama."

"Hushabye, don't you cry," Eve sang softly.

Bonnie's thin little voice chimed. "Go to sleep, little baby."

The moment was so precious, so dear. Eve's arms held Bonnie closer and she could feel the tightening of her throat as she sang. "When you wake, you shall have . . ."

Bonnie's voice was only a wisp of sound. "All the pretty little horses . . ."

Eve's head sank down to rest on the steering wheel. Get a grip. She couldn't sit here and wallow in the past. So her life right now seemed to be going down the tubes. She had to go on. She had to deal with the problem with Joe. She had to pick up Jane from the airport.

She lifted her head and started the car.

And she had to try to block out that bittersweet memory that was still echoing in her mind and heart.

All the pretty little horses . . .

"Dammit, I've missed you so much." Eve gave Jane a hug before releasing her. "How dare you look as beautiful as if you'd spent the night at a spa. After that international trip, you should be haggard and rumpled. I always am."

"I'm rumpled, but I got a new haircut in Paris that makes it look fashionable." She glanced at the revolving baggage carousel. "I think I see my duffel. I'll be right back." She sprinted toward it.

So much energy, Eve thought. Jane was the complete package: beauty, talent, and a loving nature that didn't preclude a streak of pure iron. She had graduated from college only two years ago and was already making her name as an artist in the galleries of the U.S. and Europe. It had been a blessing that Eve and Joe had been able to take Jane into their home when she was a street kid. She had enriched their lives then and now. It was a shining —

Her cell phone rang. Joe? she thought as she pulled her phone out of her handbag. Let it be Joe.

Megan Blair. She smothered her disappointment. It had to be important. Yet she still was wary to take the call. Megan's psychic gifts were undoubtedly genuine, but Eve had wanted to distance herself for a while. And why on earth was she calling at this hour of the morning?

"Eve, are you okay?" Megan Blair's voice vibrated with urgency as Eve picked up the call. "Dear God, I'm sorry. I didn't know that — Is everything all right with you?"

"What are you talking about?" Eve glanced at Jane, who was pulling her black duffel off the carousel. "Everything's fine. I'm just picking Jane up at the airport. She flew in from Paris tonight."

"Good. Someone's with you. Tell her not to leave you."

"I'll tell her no such thing. Why should I?"

"It's this damn facilitator thing. I thought you were safe. I was unconscious, so I thought the emotion wouldn't trigger anything."

"You're not making yourself clear, Megan."

"I'll try to slow down." She took a deep breath. "Remember I told you that I had this other gift. Gift? No, that's not the word. So far it's been mostly a curse. Anyway, when I'm experiencing extreme emotion, it's dangerous for me to touch anyone."

"Yes, I noticed you treated everyone as if they had the plague."

"It's because I facilitate. Whatever latent psychic gift the person I touch possesses becomes active. Mind reading, healing, finding . . . whatever. But that sudden freeing of the psychic talent can be too much for some minds."

"Madness. Yes, you told me all that. But you also said I didn't have to worry because you were in a coma when I touched you in the swamp."

"But it just occurred to me that I was still aware of those dead children that were buried on that island even then. That means that the coma wasn't deep enough. At least, I don't think it was. I just don't *know.*"

"Shh. You're upset for nothing, Megan."

"Don't tell me that." Megan was silent a moment. "Look, I know you probably didn't believe me when I told you about this weird facilitator stuff. You accept that I can hear echoes of what happened to those murdered children in the place where they were killed because you were there, you saw me going through it. But the other is too bizarre for you. Well, it's bizarre to me too. But I'm not going to let anyone be hurt by it if I can help it. I touched you. I held your hands. That's all it takes sometimes. Lord, I don't want to hurt you, Eve."

Jane was coming toward her, pulling her duffel bag, her brows lifted inquiringly.

"I'm not hurt," Eve said. "Nothing is going to happen to me, Megan."

"I hope not. But if anything strange does happen, don't be afraid. We'll work through it together."

"I don't think we're going to have to work through it. I feel perfectly normal, Megan. Besides, you said the danger period had long passed by the time I left you at the hospital."

"But that was before I realized that my emotional response was still active even though I was in that coma. The effect may have been delayed. Tell Jane to stay with you anyway. Just in case. Will you do that for me?"

"I'm not going to have her holding my hand, Megan. I'll be fine. If there's a problem, I promise to call you. Just try to relax."

"No way. Dammit, I know this all sounds crazy to you. Hell, it is crazy. But I can't let go until I know for sure that you've not been affected. I'll check back later." Megan hung up.

"What was that all about?" Jane asked. "You sounded very soothing. And why should I have to be holding your hand, Eve?"

"You shouldn't, that's the point." Eve turned and walked with her toward the exit. "I'm fine."

"And why doesn't Megan Blair think you're fine? She should know. She's a doctor, isn't she?"

Eve nodded. "ER. But she's not practicing right now."

"Too busy with this voodoo stuff?"

Voodoo. Yes, that was what Eve had thought when she had first met Megan. She had believed all psychic powers were crap and everyone who claimed to have them charlatans. But she had seen too much in that swamp while they were chasing that killer, Henry Kistle, to discount anything that Megan told her.

Except that last facilitator revelation. Eve still couldn't quite accept that possibility as reality. It was too bizarre, as Megan had said.

"I guess you could call it voodoo. But Megan isn't . . . I respect her, Jane."

"Then I apologize for being flip. Heaven knows, I realize that there's more out there than we can see or touch. It's just that someone like Megan Blair is outside my realm of experience. Where's your car parked?"

"Short-term lot." She started across the street. "I brought the Jeep. I was expecting more luggage, or maybe a canvas or two."

"No, I left everything in Paris. I'll go back, or they can send it to me." Jane's brow was furrowed. "Why did Megan think I should hold your hand? You told me Kistle was dead. There's no threat from him, right?"

"Right." Jane wasn't going to let it go, Eve thought. She was in protective mode, or she wouldn't have flown here from Paris just to be with Eve. "And there's no threat, period. Megan is just having second thoughts about something."

"What?"

Tell her, but keep it light. "She thinks I may go off my rocker." Eve made a face. "Or become a voodoo priestess myself."

"Not likely."

"That's what I told her."

"Why would she say something like that?"

Okay, just explain and then drop it. "I told you that Megan has certain . . . talents."

Jane nodded. "She can hear the dead under certain circumstances or, at least, echoes of what happened to them. Pretty creepy." She paused. "And hard for me to believe. Though I can see that you might be open to it."

Because Jane knew that the memory of Bonnie was still a major part of Eve's life. "It was difficult for me too. I thought Megan was like one of those psychic phonies who victimized me right after Bonnie disappeared all those years ago. It took a lot for me to admit to myself that Megan was the real thing. But I was with her when she located the grave of a little boy in the woods in Illinois. I saw her go into deep shock in the swamp here in Georgia trying to help us find Kistle and those children he'd killed."

Jane's lips quirked. "I imagine 'real' is rather an ambivalent term in cases like this. And did Megan's dead friends tell her that you had to be looked after?"

"No." She made a face. "It seems Megan has another talent. She said that she releases . . ." She shrugged. "She said that she's sort of a facilitator, that if she touches someone while she's in an emotionally charged state, it could trigger the release of latent psychic powers in the person she touches. According to her, some people can't accept that release. They go bonkers."

"Now that's bizarre."

" 'Bizarre' seems to be the word for the night," Eve said as she unlocked the Jeep. "Megan used it, I used it. Now you, Jane. Megan said that she understood how I'd fight accepting this facilitator effect. She's absolutely right." She slipped into the driver's seat. "Particularly since I seem to be a candidate for it, and I'm not feeling in the least bonkers. Nor am I sensing any splendid new mental powers."

"You don't need any more mental powers," Jane said as she got into the passenger seat. "You're probably the foremost forensic sculptor in the world. And you're the smartest woman I know."

"I'm not bad in the IQ department, but I can't say the same for my emotional acumen. I don't seem to learn from my mistakes."

"You're smart enough to hold on to Joe," Jane said. "That strikes me as positively brilliant."

"I've been lucky . . . so far." Her smile faded. "I have you, and I have Joe. And neither one of you is inclined to kick me out of your lives. That's pretty wonderful."

Jane was silent for a moment. "How are you and Joe getting along?"

She had known that question would be asked. "As well as can be expected considering that I have an obsession that dominates our lives." She looked away from Jane. "We really needed that Henry Kistle be Bonnie's murderer as well as the killer of all those other children on the island. Joe is . . . tired of it all. Who can blame him? Certainly not I." She smiled determinedly as she backed out of the parking place. "But he'll be glad to see you. You're like a fresh breeze every time you whisk into our lives."

"And how is your work going?"

"I just finished up a forensic sculpting job

a few days ago. Joe said I may have to work on the skulls of one or two of the children we found buried on the island in the Okefenokee Swamp if we can't get an ID. I'll do whatever it takes to bring them home."

Jane nodded. "Since you couldn't bring your Bonnie home."

"I still have hope. In fact, I have two more names that may pan out. Paul Black. Kevin Jelak. I'll have to follow up as soon as I learn more about them." She could see Jane gazing at her in wonder, and she smiled crookedly. "Yes, I know that I just got through dealing with Henry Kistle. But he wasn't the right one. He couldn't help me bring my Bonnie home. So I have to go on. You see? I *am* obsessed."

"Maybe." Jane's hand covered hers on the steering wheel. "But it's one I can understand. It's a beloved obsession, Eve."

Eve was touched. "Good heavens, that sounds like a movie."

Jane chuckled. "And I embarrassed you. Sorry. I must have picked up a few melodramatic flourishes in Paris."

"You didn't embarrass me." Jane could say anything she wanted to Eve. She was just glad to have her here beside her. As a successful artist, Jane's life was busy these days and, as Eve had said, she whisked in and out of her life, leaving only lingering affection and wonderful memories. Eve wouldn't have it any other way. The last thing she wanted was to interfere in Jane's life or hold her back.

And she couldn't pull her down into the darkness that seemed to be approaching Eve right now. So push away the darkness, try to keep the conversation light. "But tell me about some of the other things you picked up in Paris. Anyone tall, sexy, and interesting?"

Two

Joe came out on the porch as soon as they pulled up in front of the cottage. He was fully dressed in khakis and a white shirt.

Eve tensed. Let it be better. Let Jane make a difference.

"Joe!" Jane jumped out of the Jeep as soon as Eve turned off the engine. She flew up the steps and into his arms. "Dammit, it's good to see you."

"It's good to see you too." His arms tightened around her. "Though you should have stayed in —"

"I heard all that from Eve," she interrupted. "So be quiet." She took a step back. "I hear you were fighting alligators and trying to —" She stiffened as she looked up at his face. "Joe?"

He turned quickly to Eve. "I put fresh coffee on. I'm going to go in and get my phone, then I have to leave."

"Whatever you say." Eve slowly got out of

the Jeep. Joe was in the shadow, and she couldn't see his face, but she could see Jane's expression. She didn't like what she was seeing. "I hoped you'd stay for a cup of coffee. I stopped at Dunkin' Donuts."

"Thanks, but I don't have time. I have to get to the precinct." He moved back toward the door. "I just wanted to stay and see Jane before I left. I'll get my phone and take off."

Jane took a half step forward after him. "Joe, wait. I want to —"

But he had disappeared into the house.

Jane whirled to face Eve. "I thought you said everything was okay."

"I didn't say okay." She climbed the porch steps. "I said as good as could be expected. Nothing to be alarmed about." But she was alarmed and had to hide it from Jane. Not an easy task. "And he does have work to do at the precinct. What are you getting bent out of shape about?"

"He was . . . stiff. His face was — And he didn't look at me."

"I'm sure he didn't mean anything by it. Look, maybe you need some time alone with him. I'll go inside and set out the doughnuts. You catch him when he comes out. Okay?"

Jane nodded. "I have to make sure. It's not like Joe to treat me like that." She sat down on the porch swing. "I'll be in right away."

Eve nodded. "Take your time. I'm not going anywhere." She went into the house and straight to the kitchen. Give Jane her chance to talk to Joe with no interference. Maybe she'd be able to make him tell her why he was behaving in a way that was scaring Eve. She couldn't believe their problems would impact Joe's relationship with Jane. It had to be something else. But Jane would make sure that everything was straightened out. She wasn't shy about taking matters and relationships into her own hands.

Lord, she was glad to have her home again.

Jane jumped to her feet the minute Joe walked out on the porch. "Okay," she said. "What the hell is wrong with you, Joe?"

"I don't know what you mean." Joe looked away from her and out at the lake. "Nothing is wrong with me. Eve and I have had a rough patch for the last few weeks. She probably told you about it on the way from the airport."

"She told me that the serial killer who she'd thought might have killed Bonnie hadn't done it. She told me that you'd found a virtual killing ground of children on that island in the swamp that he had murdered." She paused. "She didn't tell me that you'd withdrawn from her like this. She downplayed it. But you didn't even look at her. And not only her. Have I done something lately to make you angry with me?"

"How could you? You've been in Paris at your art gallery."

"Maybe you think I should have been here and supporting Eve. I did try, Joe. She wouldn't have it."

"I'm not blaming anyone for anything." Joe's smile was forced. "Look, we just have to work through this." He checked his wristwatch. "And it's time I got to the precinct and did some work on cleaning up that case. We still haven't identified all those bodies."

"And you won't tell me what's wrong," Jane said bluntly. "You're running away. Don't bullshit me, Joe. You and Eve practically raised me. I know you."

"Do you?" He started down the porch steps. "Then you know that I'm a cop and when I have a job to do, I do it. I'll call you and Eve later and tell you what time I'll be home." He could feel Jane's troubled gaze on him as he got into the driver's seat. As he started the car, he saw Eve come out of the house and stand beside Jane on the porch. Two strong, intelligent women, the two women he loved most in the world.

And because of their strength and intelligence he had to avoid them like the plague right now. He didn't need them focusing that keen intelligence and perceptiveness on him. They might see something he didn't want anyone to see.

He waved as he backed the car out of the driveway.

He'd be okay. It had only been the stress and strain of the years of searching for Eve's little girl that had sparked that hallucination earlier this morning. He wasn't nuts. As long as he recognized the problem, then it was no problem at all. There would be no more hallucinations.

There would be no more ghostly visits from Bonnie.

"Why didn't you tell me, Eve?" Jane watched Joe drive down the road. "I've never seen him like this. I know you've been having problems, but Joe was almost . . . distant."

"I couldn't tell you what I didn't know," Eve said. "He was fine when I left to pick you up at the airport." No, not fine. Joe's and her relationship was strained, and the failure to find Bonnie on that island and bring closure to the agony of the years of searching had not made it any better. But he hadn't been the stiff, almost remote man who'd greeted Eve and Jane when they'd returned to the lake cottage. "Yes, we're not absolutely on the same page, but we're working through it."

"Are you?"

She shrugged. "We're trying. We may not make it. If we don't, it will be my fault. I have to find Bonnie, but that's my obsession, not Joe's. I don't know why he doesn't just walk away from me."

"Yes, you do. He loves you. You're his center," Jane said. "And he won't walk away from you."

"He came close this time," Eve murmured. "I told you, he needed for me to find Bonnie. He wants it over, Jane."

"You said you were working it out. As long as there's hope, he's not going to give up." Jane gave her a hug. "He said that you were going through a rough patch. Maybe that's all it was this morning, just a reaction to that horror on the island. I don't know how in hell you survived."

"We had Megan. She was the one who almost didn't survive. She went into shock and was in a coma for hours."

"So you told me." She slid her arm around

Eve's waist and led her back into the cottage. "Though some of the things you told me are pretty hard to believe. Come on, let's have a cup of coffee, and we'll talk it out."

"I can't make you believe in her, Jane. I thought Megan was a phony, but she's not." Her lips curved in a sad smile. "I guarantee that she doesn't want to be able to hear those dead children. She can't help it. She heard them, and she led us to that island. It could have killed her. She said she doesn't know much about how that psychic talent works. She only became aware she even had any psychic abilities very recently."

Jane poured coffee into Eve's cup. "You're right. I'm having a few problems with this Megan business. I have a tendency to think that you only *wanted* it to be true." She paused before she added deliberately, "Because then she might be able to help you find Bonnie."

"I wouldn't ask her to do it." She took a sip of her coffee. "Lord, I hope I wouldn't ask her. I know what it would do to her." She gazed at Jane across the table. "She thinks I'll ask her someday. She's already told me that she won't do it. That it would be worse for me to really know the details of how Bonnie died."

"My respect is growing for her. She may

be right," Jane said. She held up her hand as Eve opened her lips. "I hope with all my heart that you find Bonnie. But I don't want you to find a new stock of nightmares along with her."

Eve was silent a moment. Even Jane could see the dangers that Megan had told her about. Eve could see them, too, but to find Bonnie . . . To bring her home . . .

"Eve . . ."

Jane's expression was full of love, full of understanding, full of concern. "Listen, Eve. I'd like to say I know how you feel, but there's no way anyone could." She reached across the table and took both of Eve's hands. "When I was a kid, I was even a little jealous that you could love Bonnie so much. I never wanted to take her place. I just wanted to find a way to take away your pain. But I knew I never could." She shook her head as Eve opened her lips to speak. "And when I grew older, I began to understand. To lose a child . . . I probably won't fully realize what that means until I have a child myself. But even if I can't feel what you feel, I want you to know that I'm with you until hell freezes over."

"I know you are." Eve could feel her throat tighten with emotion. "And I bless the day we found you." She smiled with an effort. "Enough of this. You haven't been home a few hours, and you're already worried about Joe, worried about me, and trying to solve all the problems in the world. Now, forget about us. Tell me about your work. Are you working on a new painting?"

"No, I've been too busy doing public-relations stuff with the gallery." She made a face. "You know how I love that. I'm not meant for —" She stopped as Eve's phone rang. "Answer it. You don't really want to hear about my trials and tribulations with the media."

"Yes, I do. You're not getting out of it." She glanced at the ID. "It's Montalvo."

Jane's brows rose. "Montalvo's still on the scene?"

"Yes, but he's under control." As much as anyone could control him. She punched the button. "I'm very busy, Montalvo."

"Why do you always greet me as if I was on the attack?" Luis Montalvo's voice was amused. "When you know I only want the best for you."

"I'm having coffee with Jane. What do you want, Montalvo?"

"Ah, your Jane. The beautiful Jane MacGuire. I didn't know she was back in the country."

"She just flew in from Paris."

"Then I won't keep you. I just wanted to tell you that I received word from one of my investigators that he'd come up with the possible location of Kevin Jelak."

She stiffened. "What?"

"Well, at least, the general location. He traced a credit-card receipt to Garsdell, Alabama."

Alabama. Just across the state border. "So close . . ."

"Maybe too close. I was wondering what he was doing on your doorstep. And why now?"

"I was thinking just last night that I would have to try to find him and Paul Black."

"I knew that would be your next move the moment you found out that you'd tracked down the wrong killer. That's why I made a few phone calls. It's a very slim lead, nothing that you can get your teeth into . . . yet."

"Then why didn't you wait until you had something more promising?"

"Because I'll always give you what you want, not what I think is good for you. That's how Quinn and I differ." He paused. "How is Quinn?"

"As disappointed as I am that we didn't find Bonnie."

"Then I'm sure you'll share the news of this new opportunity on the horizon."

"Yes, I share everything with Joe."

"Lucky man," Montalvo said. "But I'd wait a little while before you break it to him. He may need a period of adjustment."

"Your concern is touching."

"I am concerned. I told you that I was going to be Quinn's new best friend. After all, he did save my life."

"Yes, he did."

"And I'm truly grateful." His tone was sincere. "But I have to balance my obligations toward you and my duties toward my new best friend. It may be quite a challenge. Perhaps you'd better put Quinn on the phone so that I can tell him myself."

"He's at the precinct."

"Then I'll have to rely on you to tell him later," he said. "I'll let you know as soon as I hear something more. Or maybe I'll call my new best friend."

"You're gritting your teeth," Jane said, as Eve hung up the phone. "Montalvo always gets a definite response from you. Though not always positive."

"Seldom positive. Always disturbing," Eve said. "He said that he's possibly located one of the other men who are on the suspect list for Bonnie's murder."

"Possibly? Is he dangling a carrot in front of you?"

"Maybe. But he wouldn't lie to me."

"You trust him?"

"Yes." Montalvo was brilliant, complicated, dangerous, and sometimes ruthless, but he was not a liar. Their relationship was complex, and she would just as soon he disappeared from her life. Yet in many ways he understood her better than anyone else. Montalvo had been an arms dealer in Colombia when Eve had first met him. He had searched for a long time for the body of his wife, who had been murdered, and had brought Eve into his search in return for the names of the three men who could have killed her Bonnie. Since she and Montalvo had suffered a similar loss and a similar obsession, that bond was hard to overlook. "I trust him. But every time I turn around, he does something that takes me off guard."

"Such as?"

"He says he wants to be friends with Joe."

"What?" Then Jane started to laugh. "He's joking. Right? Joe is jealous as hell of Montalvo. He'd as soon cut his throat as look at him."

"No, he's not joking."

Jane studied her thoughtfully before she gave a low whistle. "What a crafty bastard. And what a great way to insinuate himself into your life."

"Yes. But it's not going to work." Or maybe it would, Eve thought. Joe had saved Montalvo's life, and that made a difference to Montalvo. Her opinion was similar to Jane's, but in the end no one really knew Montalvo but Montalvo. "But at least he's still feeding me information."

"Jelak." Jane nodded. "What do you know about him?"

"Nothing much. Only that he was one of three men who Montalvo's investigators thought might have killed Bonnie. He lived here in Atlanta at the time she disappeared but moved and dropped from sight all those years ago." Her lips tightened. "But I'll know a hell of a lot more soon."

"Through Montalvo?"

"If I have to tap him." She finished her coffee. "But I meant Joe. I'll call him and ask him to check out that credit slip in Alabama." She leaned back in the chair. "Now why don't you go to bed and get some sleep? You must be exhausted."

"A little tired." Jane got up and started to clear the table. "And I don't think that even this coffee is going to keep me awake." She took the creamer over to the refrigerator. "I doused it with milk to weaken the caffeine." She put the creamer in the refrigerator. "Though I would much rather have had it

—" She stopped, her gaze on the lower shelf of the refrigerator. "What the hell is that?"

"What?"

"That cup. It's gold or brass or . . . It's pushed way in the back and I almost didn't see it. The light caught it and . . ." She squatted and reached inside the refrigerator. "I think there's something in it."

"I don't know what you're talking about." Eve stood up and crossed the kitchen. "The only thing I use is Tupperware, and that's definitely not gold or brass. And for the last couple weeks we haven't been cooking or storing —" She stopped as she saw the object Jane was holding. "What is it?"

"That's what I asked you."

The gold cup in Jane's hand was really a goblet that looked like something from a medieval feast. It was intricately carved with script and scenes that appeared to be taking place in some ancient dining hall.

"I never saw it before," Eve said flatly.

"Joe?"

"I'll ask him. But it's not his style. He's not a collector, and this appears to be something you'd see in a gift shop at a castle. Or one of those art magazines that sell medieval movie memorabilia."

"I don't think so. It's nice work, not cheap." Jane was turning the goblet. "Beautiful carving. I can't make out quite what it —" She lifted the cup to her nose. "It looks like a sort of dark red paste, dried . . . but it smells . . . coppery."

"Copper?" Eve took the goblet and looked down at the dark red contents. A chill was going through her. She had smelled that scent before, and it was hard to forget. She lifted the goblet and smelled it. Definitely copper. The muscles of her stomach clenched as she tried to keep from being sick.

Jane was watching her expression. "Is it what I think it is?"

Eve looked down at the cup. Beautiful goblet. Shimmering and full of artistry and scenes of times gone by. Yet all she could think about was the dark red contents staining the goblet.

"Blood." She quickly set the goblet on the counter. "It's full of blood."

"You're sure?" Jane asked.

"Yes, blood coagulates very quickly, but this goblet must have been full to the brim of liquid at one time."

"What do we do?" Jane asked. "You're sure you've never seen it before?"

Eve shook her head. "No." She added dryly, "I don't generally keep goblets of blood on hand." She swallowed. "And it's scaring the hell out of me. I feel . . . violated. How did it get in my house?" She forced herself to look back at the cup. "As for what we do, first we should find out if that blood is human."

"And like you, I'm wondering how it got here," Jane said.

Eve nodded. "Joe and I were both away from the cottage for those days we were down in Okefenokee Swamp. It would have had to have happened then." She added, "But I know Joe set the alarm before we left."

"You can get around alarms. And my dog, Toby, wasn't here. You said Patty is still taking care of him?"

Eve nodded. "I'm glad he wasn't here. He may be half wolf, but I think the golden retriever dominates. He doesn't have the killer temperament."

Jane nodded. "There's something very creepy about the idea of goblets of blood. Sort of vampirish. Shades of Béla Lugosi."

That comparison was too close to what Eve had been thinking. "You would have to bring that up. As far as I remember, he didn't use goblets. He took his blood straight from the victim."

"Whatever." Jane glanced away from the

goblet. "I suppose it could be a practical joke or something. Your profession could make you a target for that kind of thing."

Eve shook her head. "I'd like to believe that but I don't. It's too . . . ugly."

"Absolutely. I want to get rid of it," Jane said. "Let's send the damn thing away and get the blood analyzed. And I want someone from the department out here to protect you. Do you call Joe or do I?"

"I'll do it." Eve dialed Joe's cell. It rang five times before voice mail picked up.

She frowned as she slowly hung up. "No answer. But he has to be on his way to the precinct. Maybe he's on a call. I'll try again in a few minutes." She moved toward the bedrooms. "In the meantime, let's go through the house and see if we come across any more charming mementos."

"The crime scene is in the woods along Lake Allatoona. Near Kellogg Creek," Detective Gary Schindler told Joe when he called him on his cell.

"Why me?" Joe asked. "I'm still working the Kistle wrap-up."

"The captain wants you on this one. Hell, she's going to want everyone on this one. It's my day off, and they called me at home and told me to get my ass out there. The victim is Nancy Jo Norris, and the media is going to be all over us."

"And who is Nancy Jo Norris?"

"Daughter of Senator Ed Norris. She was a sophomore at the University of Georgia and only nineteen years old."

"Shit."

"Yeah. Pretty kid. The forensic team should be there by the time we get there."

"I'm on my way." Joe hung up and turned right toward the freeway. It was just as well that he wasn't going directly to the precinct. In his present frame of mind, paperwork would have driven him nuts.

Nuts. Not a comfortable word to use right now after what had happened before dawn this morning. Hallucinations were definitely signs of instability. Seeing the spirit of Bonnie Duncan verged on insanity.

Screw it. There was nothing wrong with him. He'd been under stress for months, years, and it had all been connected with Eve's daughter, who had disappeared all those years ago. This latest disappointment in trying to find both Bonnie's killer and her body had tipped the balance, and he'd had a few moments of disorientation. It would never happen again.

And it had probably had something to do with working with Megan Blair to find Kistle. All that psychic stuff had seemed too damn authentic. Now he was back in the real world, and he'd be just fine as soon as he could shake off that —

His cell phone rang. Eve. He hesitated before he answered. It had been crystal clear she had been aware of his disturbance this morning. How could she help it? Not only had he behaved irrationally, but they were too close not to be conscious of every nuance of each other's feelings. That was why he had practically fled the cottage. There was no way he was going to worry her about that weird hallucination.

But he couldn't ignore her call.

"Everything okay?" she asked when he picked up. "I couldn't get you."

"I got a call to go directly to a crime scene at Lake Allatoona."

"Then I won't keep you." Eve paused. "Jane found something sort of macabre on a shelf in the bottom of the refrigerator. A very intricately carved gold goblet. You don't know anything about it, do you?"

"What? Hell, no. What's macabre about it?"

"It has blood in it. I don't know if it's human blood. Would you send someone out to pick it up for testing?"

Joe tensed. This was the morning for

weird, but blood was real and more chilling than any hallucination. "As soon as I get off the phone. And I'll send someone out to watch the place. Be careful until he gets there."

"Oh, I will. I don't like any of this. Particularly now that Jane's here," Eve said. "The goblet had to have been placed there while we were at the swamp. It could just be some nut who read about me and my work and wanted to freak me out. But whoever did it was able to get around the alarm system. I'm calling the alarm company and getting them to come out and go over it and make sure it doesn't happen again." She paused. "Montalvo called. He said that his investigators traced a credit-card receipt for Kevin Jelak to a town across the border in Alabama."

"Montalvo didn't let any grass grow under his feet," Joe said sarcastically. "Kistle is barely dead, and he's scrambling to keep you on the hunt."

"Montalvo wouldn't manufacture evidence," she said. "It's just a strange coincidence that Jelak is suddenly making an appearance."

"I don't believe in coincidences." He turned down Kellogg Creek. "I'll check out this Kevin Jelak lead." He paused. "I was a little curt with you this morning. I'm sorry. I guess I'm a little on edge."

"More than a little. Are you ready to tell me why?"

He ignored the question since there was no way he would tell her what she wanted to know. "Call me if you have any more problems."

"I hope I don't," Eve said dryly. "We've had quite enough to start off the day. It's barely eight in the morning." She hung up.

Yes, the day had started with explosive disturbance and was continuing in the same vein, Joe thought. From the moment he had gotten out of bed at five and put the coffee on while he was waiting for Eve and Jane to get home from the airport. But that memory of what had come after was rushing back to him and he was trying to keep cool and calm.

Everything had been normal until he had gone out on the porch. He had been gazing out at the lake and thinking about Eve.

See.

Hear.

Open.

What on earth was happening to — ?

"Hello, Joe."

He whirled toward the porch swing,

A little girl was curled up on the swing. "I've wanted to come to see you so many times, but I couldn't do it. I'm so happy I can do it now."

In the dimness of the porch she was only a blur, but she couldn't be more than seven or eight. The nearest house was miles away. How had she gotten here? "Who are you?" he asked. "You shouldn't be here. Where's your family?"

"Coming. But you're my family, too, Joe. You closed me out for so long, but something . . . happened. You're open to me now."

Hear. See. Open.

"Yes, that's right, Joe."

"No, it's not right. None of this is right. You should go home. Your parents must be worrying."

She shook her head. "You know that won't happen. You know who I am."

"The hell I do." The dawn rays were gradually banishing the pool of darkness surrounding the swing, touching the little girl's curly red hair and small face with light. He couldn't take his eyes off her. This was crazy. Yet he didn't feel crazy. He felt a weird sense of . . . peace. "Who are you?"

"It's going to be all right, Joe. I promise you."

"Who are you?"

The sunlight was now surrounding her as

had the darkness before, revealing the Bugs Bunny T-shirt she was wearing.

"Why, Joe." Her luminous smile lit her face and reached out to touch him, embrace him, enfold him in love. "I'm Bonnie."

Madness.

That sense of peace vanished, and he had turned and run down the porch steps in a panic.

It wasn't real. It was a hallucination. It was all craziness, and there was no reason for him to feel this — His heart was beating hard. Why was he afraid? Not of that little girl in the swing. She wasn't real.

Insanity. The breakdown of the mind was the enemy, that was why he was in this panic. He had always been so sure of what was real and what was fantasy. It was the bedrock of his character and now that bedrock was shifting, crumbling.

He'd forced himself to look back at the swing on the porch. No little girl with a luminous smile. He'd felt a little of the tension leaving him. He was still shaken and alarmed, but the first panic was gone. He'd known it was only a momentary aberration and would never be repeated.

Just as he was sure of that now, hours later, as he drove toward Lake Allatoona.

There had been no ghostly visit from Eve's daughter. Stress, the strain of the last days, and imagination had combined to make him lose it for a couple minutes. But now he was back to doing what he did best, and even the thought of Bonnie was fading.

A few minutes later, he pulled over behind the medical examiner's van. Back to his reality. Not pleasant. Often grim.

Today he welcomed it.

He got out of the car, ducked under the yellow tape, and made his way toward the bank where Detective Gary Schindler was standing.

"Nasty." Schindler turned to face Joe as he approached. He nodded at the body of the girl a few yards away surrounded by the forensic team. "She was just a kid."

"Naked. Do we know if she was raped?"

"Not yet. She was wearing jeans and a red University of Georgia sweatshirt. Her clothes are piled over beneath that tree. Very neatly. Her body and hair are arranged neatly too." He was silent a moment. "Ritual killing?"

"Could be." Joe took a careful step forward to get a closer look. Poor kid. Her eyes were closed, but her expression was twisted with horror. "Her throat was cut."

"Again, very neatly," Schindler said. "One

neat swipe of the jugular, or so the M.E. said. Her wrists have rope burns. She must have been tied down before or during the killing."

"Not enough blood for that kind of wound."

Schindler nodded. "Oh, there was blood. The bastard cleaned her up so that she'd be all pretty. Except for the goblet. He left traces in the goblet."

Joe's gaze flew to his face. "Goblet?"

"Her right hand." Schindler pointed. "It's half under her body, but there's some kind of gold or brass goblet in her hand. I think it has carvings on it. We can't move it until forensics gets finished, but you can see the blood on the inside of the cup. That's why I was leaning toward a ritual killing."

Joe stiffened.

Gold cup, intricately carved, Eve had said.

Joe squatted to get a better look at the goblet in Nancy Jo Norris's hand.

The gold glittered in the early-morning sunlight. He couldn't make out what they were but there were definitely carvings on the goblet.

Shit.

THREE

Eve watched the police car with the young officer who had picked up the goblet go down the drive, passing the other police car parked on the road.

"There, it's gone." She turned to Jane. "Now will you go to bed and get some sleep?"

"Yep." Jane gave her a hug and turned toward her bedroom. "It made me uneasy. No, it scared the hell out of me. The thing just reminded me of an Aztec or Mayan sacrificial cup. Not the most soothing thought to lull one to sleep. Now it's in the hands of the police, and we're doing something about it. Joe will get to the bottom of it."

"Yes, we can count on that." Eve watched Jane go into the bedroom and shut the door. She knew what Jane meant about the uneasiness. She'd had the same reaction when she'd seen the goblet.

Forget it. She couldn't do anything about it now. There was a guard on duty. The alarm-company inspector would be out in a few hours to make sure the alarm could not be tampered with again. Keep busy. Check the mail. Check her e-mail to see if there were any requests for her to work on any of the children found on the island in the swamp. She reached for the pile of letters on the coffee table.

Her phone rang. Megan, again.

"I'm fine, Megan," she said as she picked up. "I know you're concerned, but I'm not experiencing any —"

"What about Joe Quinn?"

Eve froze. "What about him?"

"How much physical contact did he have with me while I was unconscious?"

"You were in shock and ice-cold. On the way back to the dock, he held you in his arms to warm you."

"Damn."

"Megan, you were unconscious. According to what you told me, this particular gift doesn't usually work unless you're fully aware and in a high emotional state."

"Usually. I don't have that much experience with it. I just don't know. But I told you, I could hear those murdered children even while I was in a coma. That means every part of my mind was still keyed up and functioning. Maybe that facilitation effect was functioning too."

"If it was working, then maybe Joe and I are immune."

"God, I hope so. Your Joe isn't behaving differently?"

"No. He's working on a case now. I talked to him on the phone a few hours ago." Eve tried to smother the sudden flash of anxiety that made her hand tighten on the phone. "Okay, he was a little . . . stiff with Jane when she first came. Maybe a little emotional with me. But he's been through a hell of a lot in the past few days. I'm not willing to ascribe a slight difference in behavior to your voodoo."

"Would he talk to you if he had a problem that was off the normalcy scope?"

"He talks to me." But Joe was the ultimate realist. Would he even admit to himself that he was experiencing something neither real nor acceptable to him? And he hadn't been able to talk to her this morning about what was troubling him.

"But you're not sure," Megan said shrewdly. "Not in this case. I don't blame you. I don't blame him. None of the usual rules apply. You question your sanity. That's the first reaction. After that, I imagine it's up to the individual."

"Megan." Eve had to say it. "I believe that you heard those dead children. It was very difficult for me to come to that conclusion. As you said, it breaks all the rules. But I can't believe in this facilitation business. I know you do, and I respect you, but I think you must be mistaken."

"You said that very diplomatically," Megan said. "It's only what I expected." She was silent a moment. "We've become friends, Eve. I hoped you might trust me in this. It's lonely carrying this by myself."

"We are friends. Friends don't always agree."

"That's true." She added, "But friends also protect each other, and I have to keep trying to do that. I have to protect you, and I have to protect Joe Quinn." Her voice vibrated with intensity. "Even if I had no personal feelings for you, I have a responsibility. I won't let either of you be destroyed by something I did, something I am. Promise me that you'll keep an eye out for anything out of the normal?"

"Of course."

"And promise you'll call me. Don't keep it to yourself."

"I'll call you."

"Good. I know that was hard for you. You

prefer to keep things to yourself."

"And you don't?"

"Sure. We have a good deal in common. Maybe that's why I feel so close to you. Good-bye, Eve." She hung up.

Yes, and that was why she felt close to Megan, Eve thought as she hung up. They both had a past that cast shadows on their present and had fought through nightmare pain. She hadn't wanted to tell Megan that she doubted her. Megan was her friend, and that friendship was a rare and special thing in Eve's life. She led a very solitary existence except for Joe, and, of course, Jane. Megan had almost exploded into her life while they were searching for the remains of a little boy, and they had formed bonds that would be hard to break.

Eve went out on the porch and down the steps to the lake path. Why was she fighting Megan so hard in this? Megan had shown her bizarre and chilling things that had rocked her to her core. Yet Eve found she couldn't take that final step and swallow all that business about her touch releasing latent psychic gifts. She had rejected it almost instinctively. She should have at least —

"You were afraid, Mama."

Bonnie.

She glanced at the tall pine tree beneath which Bonnie was sitting cross-legged. Same Bugs Bunny T-shirt, her mop of red curls was shining in the sunlight, and her smile was warm and bright. Eve felt a rush of love so intense that she couldn't speak for a moment. "And how do you know that?" she asked lightly. "There aren't many things that I'm afraid of, Bonnie."

"Because you're not afraid of being hurt or dying. Because you think you'd be happier with me." She shook her head. "But I keep telling you that can't happen. We will be together but not for a long time. You have to stay and take care of Joe and Jane. They need you."

"Lecture number fifty-six."

Bonnie chuckled. "More than that. You just don't listen, Mama."

"You're either a ghost or a dream. Why should I listen?"

"Because you love me. Because you know I'm right."

Yes, she loved her. From the moment she had given birth to her, Bonnie had been the center of her life. When her little girl had been taken from her, she had thought her life was over. Then these dreams of Bonnie had begun to come to Eve about a year after she had disappeared. Dream or spirit? During those first years, telling herself these appearances were only dreams was a safety net and kept her certain of her own sanity. Nowadays, she didn't really care whether her daughter was a dream or a ghost. She was real to her, she was here. "You always think you're right, young lady."

"Because I am. Especially where you're concerned, Mama."

"And why do you think I'm afraid?"

"Because of Joe. You're afraid for Joe." The tiniest frown wrinkled her brow. "I'm afraid, too."

"Why?"

"He's not like you. I love Joe. I was so happy . . . But he's not like you."

"What are you talking about?"

Bonnie looked at her. "You're afraid because Joe may be different. Megan scared you."

"Don't be silly."

"Joe is like an anchor for you. He is what he is. You don't want him to be changed."

"Everybody changes. That's what life's all about. You learn to love the changes too."

"What if Joe doesn't love the changes? I went away, but I don't think she will."

"Megan? Look, Bonnie, this psychic thing is completely without —" Her cell phone rang and she reached in her pocket. "It's Montalvo."

■ ■ ■ ■

Bonnie didn't answer.

Eve didn't have to glance at the pine tree to know that Bonnie would no longer be there. Disappointment sharpened her voice as she answered the phone. "What do you want, Montalvo?"

"In what order?" Montalvo asked. "No, I can tell by your tone that you're not about to indulge me that way. I called to tell you that there was another credit slip for Kevin Jelak issued at a gas station in Calhoun, Georgia."

Calhoun. That was a town not too far from Chattanooga. "He's coming closer. What was the date on the slip?"

"Yesterday."

"He's leaving a trail. It's stupid of him to use a credit card that can be traced."

"Maybe he doesn't know that we know about him."

"Maybe he doesn't care. Maybe he wants us to know he's heading this way." She gazed out at the lake. "Why now, Montalvo? It's strange that he should appear right on the heels of Kistle's death. All these years, and we heard nothing from Jelak. Did those investigators of yours stir him into action?"

"Possibly. I'm expecting a report on him later today. They're tracing his background through the credit-card application. I'll let you know." He paused. "Is everything all right with you?"

A gold goblet stained with blood.

"Everything is fine."

"I don't believe you, but I'll let it go. I'll call you when I have anything of interest to you." He hung up.

It didn't surprise her that Montalvo would sense her disturbance. He knew her very well. Too well.

She turned and moved back toward the cottage. She would finish going through her e-mail, then maybe take a nap while Jane was still asleep. She'd had only a few hours' sleep before she'd had to go pick up Jane at the airport.

As if she'd be able to relax, she thought ruefully. Her mind was skipping from Jelak to Megan's worried questions about Joe, to that damn goblet. Everything was swirling around her, leaping closer, like a tornado, hovering, then touching down.

And Bonnie was the eye of the tornado, calm, loving, a shimmering orb that vanished as the storm overtook them.

She glanced back at the pine tree where Bonnie had been sitting and remembered those last cryptic words.

I went away, but I don't think she will.

Uneasiness, again.

She impulsively reached in her pocket for her phone and dialed Joe. She wanted to reach out, touch him.

"I was just going to call you." His tone was curt. "I've been busy as hell. This crime scene is a media circus. We have to cordon off the entire area to keep the journalists from sneaking past the tapes."

"Why?"

"That's right, I didn't tell you. The victim is Nancy Jo Norris. Her father is Ed Norris. He's flying down from Washington now, and we have to get the forensic investigation done and Nancy Jo moved to the morgue before we have him coming here and causing more uproar from the media. I'll be late getting home." He paused. "After I leave here, I want to stop by the precinct and take a look at that goblet. We should have a preliminary report on the blood by that time."

"Nancy Jo Norris." Eve felt sick. "I saw a photo of her in the newspaper last month. She was playing soccer in some tournament. She was smiling, and she looked positively radiant."

"That's one of the reasons the media is

hyped. A 4.0 student, popular, good at sports, on the student council . . . and a daddy who might run for president someday."

"Poor girl. Everything to live for . . ." She shook her head. "I'd be out there on top of you too. Any clues as to who did it?"

"One." He paused. "Schindler thinks it may be a ritual killing."

"What do you think?"

"Maybe. I'll talk to you about it when I get home tonight. Do me a favor. You and Jane stick close to the cottage today. Is the squad car there?"

"Yes, he's parked down the road." She was silent a moment. "I thought I might be overreacting. You're really worried about that goblet."

"Damn right. And you're not overreacting, Eve. Just stay close to the house, okay?"

"Okay. Jane and I have some catching up to do anyway."

"I'll be home soon as I can. By the way, why did you phone me?"

Joe was so blessedly normal Eve felt foolish that she had yielded to the temptation to call him. "I just wanted to talk to you. Is everything all right with you?"

He didn't answer directly. "Why wouldn't it be?"

"No reason. I'll see you tonight." She hung up. Lord, she was relieved. He sounded much better than he had earlier. She had told Megan that she and Joe talked, but she had slid away from telling Joe about Megan's call. He would have just laughed and made some kind of derogatory comment about Megan's voodoo.

You were afraid, Mama.

But there's nothing to be afraid of, baby. Joe is doing just fine.

"I'm on my way back to the precinct," Schindler said as he watched the M.E. vehicle pulling away from the curb carrying Nancy Jo Norris to the morgue. "You too?"

Joe nodded. "Right away. I want to take a look at that goblet they pulled from her hand." He was moving toward Johnson, who had placed the goblet in a clear plastic bag and was sealing it. "I won't be long."

"Better not. They're going to want our reports in a hurry. Everything is going to have to be in a hurry. The captain will need answers."

"She's not going to get them. Forensics is swearing that the killer didn't leave much for them to work with. He cleaned up the site.

"Except maybe that goblet . . ." Joe took

the plastic bag from Johnson and held it up to the light. The sun was going down, but the rays pierced the plastic, and he could make out the carving. It looked like an ancient dining hall, a long table at which sat several men. All the men had goblets sitting in front of them, and one man was standing with a goblet raised in his hand.

"I've got to get that to the lab, Quinn," Johnson said. "My boss has been on my ass for the last hour."

"I know. The big push." Joe handed the bag back to him. "I'm pushing too. Get it done fast, Johnson." He turned away. "And I want a report every step of the way."

He started for his car, then turned and looked back at the place by the river where they'd found Nancy Jo Norris. The chalk outline gleamed in the fading light. Too neat for a murder —

What?

See.

Hear.

Open.

He stiffened. What the hell?

There were four uniformed officers guarding the taped-off crime scene. Forensics had gone. Two TV trucks were down the street. The words hadn't come from there.

See. Hear. Open.

He moved slowly toward the trees beyond the place where Nancy Jo Norris had been murdered.

See. Hear. Open.

He was now in the twilight shadows cast by the trees. He stood still, listening, waiting for it to come again.

"I don't like it here. It scares me."

He whirled to the left and saw her.

She was standing only a few yards away. Long blond hair, jeans, red University of Georgia sweatshirt, a face that he'd been staring at all day, blue eyes wide with fear and bewilderment.

"Who the hell are you?" he asked hoarsely.

"I'm Nancy Jo. Who are you?"

Joe felt as if he'd been kicked in the stomach. He could feel the small hairs rise on the back of his neck. Get a grip. There had to be an explanation.

"You're some relation to the dead girl? A sister?"

"I don't have a sister. Dead girl." She whispered, "You're talking about me, aren't you? I don't understand. How can that be? Why?"

"How did you get here? Why didn't the policeman on duty stop you at the tape?"

"I've been here all day, watching you." She shuddered. "You kept talking about that girl as if she was me. She's not me. She used to be, but that was before he —"

He had to stop this craziness. Get everything back to reality. "You're saying that she's not Nancy Jo Norris? Then who is the victim?"

"Victim." She closed her eyes. "Yes, I was a victim. I've been trying to run away from it. But he made me a victim. He took away my life. And my blood. He took my blood." Her lids lifted to reveal blue eyes glittering with tears. "Why? It's not right. It shouldn't have happened. Not to me. I didn't do anything bad."

Either he was crazy, or this girl was a crackpot. He hoped to God it wasn't him. Regardless, he had to respond to the situation as if he was thinking and acting normally. It was his only salvation. "I think you'd better come along with me. We'll need to question you about your relationship with the deceased and how you came to be here."

"He brought me here, you idiot." The tears were suddenly gone, and her fists were clenched at her sides. "He attacked me from behind in that parking garage at Perimeter Mall and stuffed a handkerchief over my face. It smelled . . . sweet. Like the anesthetic I had when they took out my appendix. I went out like a light. Then he brought me here and slit my throat. Now what are you going to do about it? You're a cop, aren't you?"

"I'm Detective Joe Quinn." He paused. "And you're obviously having delusions. You need help. Will you come with me?"

"You're saying I'm crazy, dammit. I'm not crazy. He was crazy. Do you think this is easy for me? I'm scared, and I don't know what to do. They keep telling me I have to come away, but I think they're wrong. I do need help. But I don't need it from you. I'll find my father or maybe one of those policemen over there."

"By all means." He turned. "I'll go and send an officer to you. Stay here." He walked quickly away. Not too quickly. He wasn't running away, he assured himself. He was just resolving a difficult situation. He glanced over his shoulder. She was still standing there, waiting.

Shit. Admit it. Of course he was running away. Not only from Nancy Jo Norris but what it said about his sanity that he was seeing her.

He stopped as he reached the officer standing at the tape. "Would you go and take that woman into custody, Officer Millbran? We need her for questioning."

"Yes, sir. Which woman?"

"Who do you think?" He nodded. "The woman over there in the red sweatshirt."

"Right. I'll go find her." Officer Millbran sprinted toward the trees.

Find her? She was standing there in full view waiting for him.

The officer ran right past her into the trees.

A shudder went through Joe's spine. He hadn't seen her, he realized. Millbran had been only a few feet from her, and he hadn't seen her.

She was looking as bewildered as Joe felt. But she couldn't be feeling the same panic. Because he was imagining it all. She wasn't real. Another hallucination.

He tore his gaze away from her. He turned on his heel and strode blindly toward his car.

What the hell was happening to him?

Joe kept his gaze away from the trees, staring straight ahead, his hands clenched on the steering wheel. He wouldn't wait for Officer Millbran to come back and tell him that there had been no woman in a red sweatshirt. He had no desire to see the young man's confusion or hear his excuses. And he most certainly didn't want to have to lie to him. He would deal with this problem himself, as he did everything else.

But he had never had a problem like this, one that could affect every facet of his life. If he wasn't careful, he'd find himself in a straitjacket in the booby hatch. One episode he could lay to stress. This second occurrence was a sign that he was definitely off-kilter.

No! He would not accept that as truth while he was functioning perfectly normally in every other way.

He started the car and pulled away from the curb. He would continue on as if nothing had happened until he could figure out what he was going through. In the meantime, he would stop at the precinct and take a look at the goblet Eve had discovered in the refrigerator and compare it with the goblet found in the hand of Nancy Jo Norris.

Then he would go home to Eve and Jane. It seemed strange that this morning he had only wanted to get away from them. After what had happened in the woods, he supposed he should be even more afraid that they would notice something wrong with him. Somehow that wasn't the case. He was willing to risk them tearing down his protective barriers in exchange for the love and comfort he knew they'd give him.

In the end, pride and ego didn't mean a damn. Love was the only thing that mattered.

■ ■ ■ ■

"Patty Avery's on her way over with Toby," Jane said as she came out of the bedroom. "She called me on my cell and told me to stay put. She said that she never got to see me anymore, and she was going to make damn sure that she at least had a cup of coffee with me before I took off again."

"It's true," Eve said as she put the coffee in the coffeemaker. "Joe and I see more of Patty than you do. She's a godsend when we need someone to take care of Toby when we have to leave on a trip. She's been a good friend to us as well as to you."

"She was my best friend in high school, and I thought that we'd drift apart, but she wouldn't let that happen," Jane said as she got the cups down from the cabinet. "Patty is a virtual steamroller. She told me once that she didn't have that many friends, and she couldn't afford to lose one." She frowned. "Heaven knows she has enough on her plate without taking care of Toby. How is her grandfather doing?"

"Not well. He's always been a bastard and his physical condition is deteriorating and he takes it out on Patty. She can't do anything that pleases him. That's why she keeps herself busy doing anything that will keep her close to home. She cooks, studies the stock market, repairs cars. Toby is a blessing. She said she wishes she could keep him permanently."

"He's a sweet boy. I miss him." Jane smiled. "After I finish this Parisian exhibit, I'm going to take him home. I like to leave him here because he can get more exercise but he's no spring chicken. We need to be together."

Eve nodded. "He's been with us a long time. When Sarah Logan first gave him to you as a pup, I had my doubts about a dog that was half golden retriever and half wolf, but he's very affectionate." She tilted her head. "And I think I hear Toby and Patty in the driveway. There's no missing the sound of that souped-up engine she put in her Camaro. I'm surprised she doesn't get a ticket."

"Are you saying you wouldn't have Joe try to fix it?" Jane asked teasingly.

"You know better than that. He'd never fix a ticket." She grinned. "Though he might ask the officer just to give her a warning. He says she's a wonder. He admires her mechanical ability tremendously." She added soberly, "And her strength and endurance."

"Yes, he would be able to recognize those qualities. He sees them every day." Jane headed for the door to the porch. "Did you talk to Joe while I was napping?"

"Yes. He sounded . . . better. But he said he might be late."

"That doesn't matter." She opened the door. "Patty! It's about time you —" She staggered backward as Toby launched himself at her. "Okay, boy." She hugged him fiercely. "I missed you too. I think your face is a little whiter. But it's very becoming." She pushed him down as she turned to Patty. "And you look gorgeous." She gave her a hug. "That long black braid looks very exotic and Old World."

"It keeps the hair out of my face," Patty said. "I'd cut it but my grandfather would have a tantrum and I like to keep the peace. That's the name of the game right now." She came into the cottage. "Hi, Eve. Wonderful to see you." She turned back to Jane and flipped her single braid back over her shoulder. "Now give me a cup of coffee and tell me what's happening to you in the real world. I have a lot of catching up to do."

Jane MacGuire was young, Jelak thought.

Perhaps not quite as young as Nancy Jo Norris, but all the vigor and bloom of youth was there in the strength and lithe beauty of her body as she hugged her friend. Young, but fully a woman in contrast to the petite woman she was greeting, whose round baby face made her look almost childlike.

Jelak lowered his binoculars. He had hoped to get a glimpse of Eve Duncan, but she hadn't come out to greet the woman who had obviously delivered the big dog to them. He was planning to get here earlier, but he had slept too deeply after he had taken Nancy Jo's gift. The blood first made him dizzy, then drugged, and, when he woke, strong as thunder, strong as Samson. He could feel that strength soar through him now, along with a faint regret. He'd wanted to see Eve's face, dammit. He had seen her only in newspaper photos and on TV since he had left Atlanta all those years ago.

Instead he had been given a bonus he hadn't expected. Jane MacGuire. There was no question that she would be a beacon to draw Eve Duncan. He would probably need it. That police car parked down the road would keep him from getting near her. Well, not keep him from acting but make it more difficult.

She must have found the goblet he had given her.

Did it frighten you, Eve? I hope it did. Fear is good. It conditions you mentally and makes the blood run faster . . . and sweeter.

It had been a risk to give her the goblet before the act, but she was very special. She had to anticipate, to know it was coming toward her. But now he had to deal with the difficulties that the warning brought. He had no problem with overcoming complications. He always found them interesting. He might just have to swerve around them and go another route to get to Eve.

A route called Jane MacGuire.

"Detective Quinn."

Joe turned as he was walking into the precinct to see a tall, handsome man in his early fifties hurrying toward him from the captain's office. He recognized that broad, intelligent face though it was now haggard and ravaged with pain. "My sincere sympathy, Senator Norris. I can't tell you how sorry I am that —"

"I don't want your sympathy. I want to know what you're doing about finding my little girl's murderer." His lips tightened with pain. "Though she's not a little girl, is she? But that was all I could think about when I was looking down at her in that morgue. My little girl . . ."

"We're doing everything we can. I just came back from Allatoona. I'm going to check the preliminary reports now."

"Your captain says you're the best," Norris said. "I hope she's right. I'll find a way to crucify you if you drag your feet. I lost my wife six years ago. It's just been me and Nancy Jo since then. Now she's gone too." He turned away. "I'm going out to Allatoona now. I want to see the place where she was killed."

I'll find my father.

The words of that imaginary woman in the woods came back to him. Now Nancy Jo's father was trying to seek a connection with his daughter by seeing where her life had ended. "I have to warn you, the media is still camped out there."

"I don't give a damn."

Joe watched him stride out of the precinct. Poor bastard. You never knew what was going to come out of the fog and hit you. Norris had everything a man could hope to possess: money, a brilliant career, a child he loved. Take away the one most important ingredient, and he'd found out how empty the rest could be.

Like Eve and her Bonnie.

Don't think about Bonnie. He had enough of a nightmare being forced to come to terms with Nancy Jo Norris.

He turned and strode down the hall toward forensics.

Four

"I brought Chinese," Joe said as he walked into the cottage. "I know I should have called first. Have you eaten?" He set the bag down on the kitchen table. "Where's Jane?"

"Out for a walk. Patty dropped Jane's dog off a few hours ago." She held up her hand as he opened his lips. "And we know Toby is gentle, but he doesn't give that appearance. No one is going to bother her with Toby near."

"I'm glad you're sure. I'm not."

"And I called one of the officers in the squad car and asked him to follow her. And, no, we haven't eaten dinner yet. We ate a late lunch and thought we'd wait for you." She began to unpack the cartons in the bag. "Did you get a report on the blood in that goblet we found?"

"Human blood. Type A negative."

"I was afraid of that." She threw the empty bag in the trash. "A warning of some sort?"

"I have no idea. It's a definite possibility." He got plates down from the cabinet. "Do you remember the carving on the cup?"

"How could I forget? I stared at the damn thing for a couple hours while I was waiting for it to be picked up. Some kind of medieval dining hall, nine seated men and one standing with a goblet in his hand. Unusual."

"Not that unusual. We found one that was identical to it in Nancy Jo Norris's hand."

She went rigid. "What?"

"Same carving." He was getting out the cutlery. "They're checking the blood now. But the blood wasn't Nancy Jo's. She was B positive."

"Dear God. If it wasn't her blood, then it had to come from another victim. You're saying her murderer is —"

"I don't know." He suddenly whirled and threw the cutlery on the table. "Dammit to hell. I don't know *anything.*" In two strides he was beside her, and she was in his arms. "It's all crazy." His voice was muffled against her hair. "Just hold me, okay?"

"Okay." Her arms went around him with fierce protectiveness. "What's wrong, Joe?"

"What could possibly be the matter? Other than we have a ritual killer who seems to have picked you as a victim? Everything is just fine."

There was something very wrong. There was an element of desperation in Joe's voice Eve couldn't remember ever hearing before. She had known from the moment he walked through the door that she'd been wrong in thinking that whatever had been bothering him had gone away. "It will be fine. It's not as if we haven't dealt with —"

"I've never dealt with this." He pushed her back and turned away. "It's crazy."

Crazy. That was the second time he had said that word in the past few sentences. Eve felt a sinking sensation as she stared at him.

You'll call me if he doesn't behave normally, Megan had said.

But she couldn't believe that Joe's behavior had anything to do with all that Pandora business. As she had told Megan, that was too far a reach for her.

He had a perfect right to be upset. He was a very protective man and he was worried about her.

Upset, not desperate.

And he didn't want to admit that he was feeling that desperation. He seemed to view it as an admission, a loss of control.

All right. Handle it his way. He had come home to her. Now she had to be patient and let him come the rest of the way.

"Yes, it's crazy." She began to spoon the rice out on the plates. "I guess we'll have to try to make sense of it. You'd better call Jane before this food gets cold."

"Whew." Eve was panting as she rolled away from Joe to her own side of the bed. "That was . . . interesting."

"Did I hurt you?"

"No. It was just intense. Nothing wrong with that."

The sex that night had been explosive and completely draining. Desperation again. She had an idea that demand hadn't been about any carnal need. "A little different . . ."

She felt him stiffen beside her. "Different? What the hell do you mean different? I either hurt you or I didn't."

"You didn't. I told you. It was damn well incredible." As sex always was with Joe. She rolled closer and tucked her head in her favorite place in the hollow of his shoulder. "Stop being so defensive."

He relaxed. "Sorry. I told you, I'm a little on edge."

"I noticed." She was silent a moment. Okay, go for it. "I didn't tell you. Megan called me twice today. She was pretty upset."

"More psychic mumbo jumbo?"

"You're being very scathing. You told me that you believed her when she told you about hearing those dead children."

"I also told you that I wouldn't go to her on another case." He kissed the top of her head. "I'm a little too pragmatic. There have to be reasonable explanations. It's the way I live."

"Megan is an ER physician. What's more practical? But when she had to face the fact that she had this so-called gift, she had to come to terms with it." She paused. "But she's having trouble with this other facilitating gift she says she has. It's erratic, and she doesn't understand it."

"Then I'm sure I wouldn't either," he said flatly. "Let's drop it."

He didn't want to talk about anything to do with psychic gifts, Eve realized. "Okay, I just wanted to tell you that Megan was full of warnings because of what happened in the swamp. Remember that she didn't want to be touched? She said that sometimes if she touched someone, it released latent psychic talents in them. Some people can't adjust. She was afraid for me because I touched her." Don't mention that she'd included Joe in the warning. It might cause him to instinctively reject it. Let him draw his own inferences. "I told her I was fine and that I'd contact her if there was a problem."

He didn't speak for a moment. "She thought you'd hear dead people like she does?"

"She said it depended on the person. She said it might cause them to read minds or be a healer or be able to make flowers grow. Any special talent that might be within them." She cuddled closer. "And I told her that I found all of this a little hard to swallow."

"Of course." His tone was absent. "Totally ridiculous."

"Nothing about Megan is ridiculous. It's just out of my realm of experience, so I can't imagine it."

"I can imagine it." He added with sudden roughness, "And I find it ridiculous as hell."

"Don't get upset about it."

"Why not? It's bullshit. Dead children speaking from the beyond, corpses walking around. It's *bullshit.*"

"I'll tell her that when she calls again. She'll probably agree with you. But it's the bullshit she has to live with."

"Well, I don't have to live with it." He sat up and swung his legs to the floor. "I can't sleep. I'm going to call the M.E. and see if he has a report on the Norris autopsy."

"It's almost midnight."

"They'll still be there. We're working around the clock on this one." He shrugged on his robe. "Ed Norris will have his aides on our ass every step of the way."

"Do you want company?"

"No, stay in bed. This shouldn't take long."

Eve watched him leave the room. She had done her best. She didn't know if that would be good enough. It was like trying to walk along a precipice blindfolded. For the first time in their relationship, she had no idea what he was thinking. And it was only guesswork that it had something to do with Megan's facilitator talent. She was grasping at straws. She could only allow him his space and hope that he would work it out for himself.

Damn, it was hard.

What was she complaining about? If it was hard, then it was only a tiny portion of the hell Joe had gone through for her over the years. From that initial meeting after Bonnie had been taken, he had tried to shoulder every burden, ease every pain. Yet when he had first come into her kitchen that first morning, she'd been bitterly resentful.

■ ■ ■ ■

There was a discreet knock on the kitchen door. "Ms. Duncan. FBI. I rang the front doorbell, but no one was answering. May I come in?"

Because she'd ignored the bell. She turned back to the stove. "Yes, I suppose you may."

She heard the door open behind her.

"I can understand why you wouldn't want to answer the bell. I've heard the media has been harassing you. I'm Special Agent Joe Quinn. FBI. I wonder if I could have a few words with you."

She glanced over her shoulder at him as she turned the omelet in the pan. Dark blue suit, square face, brown eyes, maybe twenty-six or -seven, good-looking. Young, too young. Why hadn't they sent her someone older, with more experience? "Questions? I've answered millions of questions. It's all in ATLPD's records. Go ask them."

"I have to make my own report."

"Red tape. Procedures." She scooped up the omelet and put it on a plate. "Why didn't they send someone right after it happened?"

"We had to wait for a request from the local police."

"You should have been here. Everyone

should have come right away." Her hand was shaking as she picked up the plate and put it on a tray. "I suppose I'll have to talk to you, but I have to take this omelet to my mother. She hasn't gotten out of bed since Bonnie disappeared. I can't get her to eat."

"I'll take it." He reached out and took the plate. "Which room?"

She wasn't about to argue. Let him do something, anything. He hadn't done what was important. He hadn't found Bonnie. "First door at the top of the stairs."

She took the pan to the sink and started to wash it. Keep busy. Don't think. Keep moving.

"She started to eat," Quinn said as he came back in the room. "Maybe it was the shock of seeing a stranger."

"Maybe."

"And how are you eating, Ms. Duncan?"

"I eat enough. I know I can't afford to lose strength." She started drying the pan. Slowly. She was desperately afraid of running out of something to do. "What do you want to know, Agent Quinn?"

He looked down at his notes. "Your daughter, Bonnie, disappeared at the park over a week ago. She went to the refreshment stand to get an ice cream and didn't return. She was wearing a Bugs Bunny T-shirt, jeans, and tennis shoes."

"Yes."

"And you didn't see anyone suspicious loitering anywhere nearby?"

"No one. It was crowded. I wasn't expecting anyone to be —" She drew a deep breath. "No one suspicious. I told the police that I wondered if maybe someone had seen what a sweet kid my Bonnie was and taken her away. Maybe someone who had lost a child and only wanted another one." She stared at his face. "And they only looked at me the way you're doing and made soothing noises. It could have happened that way."

"Yes, it could." He paused. "But the odds are against it. I'm not going to lie to you."

"I know that. I'm not a fool. I grew up on the streets, and I know all about the scum that's out there." She looked wonderingly up at him. "But I have to hope. She's my baby. I have to bring her home. How can I live if I don't hope?"

"Then hope." His voice was hoarse. "And I'll hope with you. We'll explore every way we can to find her safe and alive. There's nothing I won't do. Just stick with me and give me a little help."

She believed him. The intensity in his expression was overwhelming. Suddenly he didn't look like the young man she'd assumed him to be when he'd walked into the kitchen. He looked hard and mature and fully capable.

"Of course I'll help." She glanced away from him as she put the pan in the cupboard. "I'm afraid, you know," she said unevenly. "I'm afraid all the time. My mother gave up and just went to bed, but I can't do that. I have to keep fighting. As long as I'm fighting, I have a chance to find Bonnie."

He nodded. "Then we'll fight together. I'll stay with you until we get through this." He paused. "If you'll let me."

Together.

She suddenly felt a little less lonely. Nothing could ease the aching fear, but to share it was somehow comforting. She slowly nodded. "I think that would be very kind. Thank you, Agent Quinn."

But how could she have ever dreamed how long Joe would have to stay with her to get her through that search for Bonnie, she thought as she stared into the darkness. He had been everything to her during that period when her life had been pure hell: friend, brother, a constant support when her world was falling apart around her. He'd marshaled everyone to search for Bonnie, then kept Eve sane when the realization had come that her daughter was dead, murdered, and buried away somewhere Eve might never find her.

Yes, she owed him more than he'd ever know. No matter what was wrong in Joe's life, she had to help him put it right.

It was all bullshit, Joe thought as he switched on the coffeemaker. Forget it. There weren't any ghosts. No mystic psychic powers.

So he'd believed in Megan for that brief period in the swamp. He'd come to his senses after he'd come back to Atlanta.

Until he'd thought he'd seen Bonnie Duncan. Until Nancy Jo Norris had paid him a visit.

And if those had been hallucinations, then he was left with the realization that he was going off his rocker. He'd trot to the department's psychiatrist and let the bastard talk soothingly to him about work-related stress and how he should take time off.

He couldn't take time off. It was his work that kept him balanced.

Some balance.

At least, it kept him busy and full of purpose. He reached for his phone and dialed the M.E.

"Tim Brooks."

It was one of the M.E.'s assistants. Joe had talked to him before. "Quinn. Is the autopsy finished?"

"Hell, no," Brooks said sourly "This one

will take days. Every test in the book."

"What's the preliminary?"

"Loss of blood due to the severance of the jugular."

"Anything else?"

"Presence of ether and fiber fragments in the nostrils. He evidently knocked her out before he killed her."

Joe stiffened. "Ether?"

"You heard me. Look, I've got to get back. You know I shouldn't talk to you before we get a final."

"Thanks, Brooks." He slowly hung up.

He attacked me and stuffed a handkerchief over my face. It smelled sweet. Then he brought me here and slit my throat.

Nancy Jo's words during his hallucination earlier today.

But why would he have had that particular detail in that hallucination?

Guesswork from a hundred similar cases?

But there was no case similar to this one. God help him. He was becoming increasingly convinced that was true. And if it wasn't guesswork, he was left with a choice.

Go to see the department shrink or jump headfirst into the river of no return?

He spun on his heel and strode toward the bedroom.

■ ■ ■ ■

Eve watched Joe drive down the road before she reached for her cell phone and dialed Megan's number. Megan answered after three rings. "I'm sorry to call this late. Did I wake you?"

"That doesn't matter. I told you to call me if you needed me." She paused. "And do you need me?"

"I might. Joe may be on his way to see you. I thought I'd prepare you."

" 'May'? You don't know?"

"He said he'd found out something from the Medical Examiner's Office that he had to check out. It could be the truth or at least part of the truth. It's a rough case, and we may be personally involved. But I have a hunch that whatever he has to check out, he wants to do it with you."

Silence. "You're telling me that Joe Quinn is behaving . . . irrationally?"

"I'm telling you that for the first time since I've known him, Joe is doubting his —" She took a deep breath. "There's no one more solid or confident than Joe. That's not what I'm seeing right now. I don't know if it has anything to do with you or not, but I tried to steer him in your direction. It was the only thing I could think to do."

"You didn't talk to him?"

"Dammit, he would have backed away from me. If he is having any kind of weird reaction, it's not the kind of thing he would admit, much less discuss. He calls it all bullshit. I did my best. It has to come from him." She paused. "I'm worried. I feel helpless. If he does come to you, help him, Megan. Please."

"You don't have to ask," Megan said. "I'll do what I can, though I don't know what that will be. But I can tell you that it doesn't always turn out badly."

"You mentioned insanity and death. I'd say that's pretty bad."

"But it may have something to do with the strength of the individual character."

"Well, Joe has plenty of that. And it may not have anything to do with you. I just had to hedge every bet."

"I'll let you know." Megan hung up.

Eve gazed out at the lake. Had she done the right thing? She had guided Joe toward Megan even though she wasn't sure that she believed that Megan's talent was at the bottom of Joe's problem. She had been afraid to do anything else.

She could only hope that there was a solution and that Megan would find it.

■ ■ ■ ■

Megan turned to her uncle as she hung up the phone. "We may have a visitor, Carey. Better put on the coffee while I throw on some clothes."

"At this hour? Who?"

"Joe Quinn."

He frowned. "What the hell? After all the sarcastic bull he was throwing at you down at the swamp? I wanted to sock him."

"So did I. But you can't blame him for being cynical about me. Sometimes I don't believe in this psychic crap either." Her lips twisted. "Or wish I didn't believe it. It would make life easier." That was the understatement of the century. "And I don't have any right to blame him for anything now." She whispered, "I may have hurt him, Carey."

"The facilitating thing?"

"Eve thinks he's not behaving normally. And that would be hard for her to admit. She's very protective of him."

"I don't remember him needing protection. You were the one being attacked."

"And that cynicism would make it even more difficult for him . . . if something did happen." Megan turned and headed for her bedroom. "Maybe Eve's wrong. She wasn't sure. Maybe it's something else."

Joe Quinn rang the doorbell forty minutes later.

His gaze raked her up and down as she opened the door. From the top of her dark hair to her feet. "You're dressed. Were you expecting me?" His lips twisted. "Maybe some psychic premonition?"

"I don't have premonitions. I have only two psychic talents of which I'm aware. That's more than I want. Come in, Joe." She stepped aside. "We might as well go into the kitchen and have a cup of coffee."

"I don't want to sit down and have a cozy chat. That's not why I'm here."

"No, there's nothing cozy about you at the moment." She doubted if that word would describe him at any time. He was all hard, lean strength and keen intelligence. "You're angry, and you want to strike out at someone. Be my guest. I probably deserve it." She turned toward the kitchen. "But we'd better pretend to be on good terms. My uncle is very defensive, and you're not on his list of favorite people."

"That doesn't bother me." He followed her into the kitchen. "I can handle him."

"If you do, you'll have me to deal with. He's my only family, and I'm defensive too."

She sat down at the table and gestured for him to sit down across from her. "I tried to tell him you have a right to be angry, but he's not buying it."

He sat down but his posture was as stiff as his expression. "And why should I be angry with you?"

"Because I may have done you harm." She poured coffee into their cups from the carafe on the table. "Have I?"

He didn't speak for a moment. "I don't believe all that stuff you told Eve. It's something from a sci-fi movie."

"More like a horror film." Megan shrugged. "And not only for me." She looked up to meet his eyes. "Is it, Joe?"

His lips lifted in a sardonic smile. "Are you reading my mind?"

"No, your body language." She lifted her cup to her lips. "Tell me, can you read minds now? Did I do that to you?"

"Hell, no."

"Good. I imagine that would be a nightmare."

"Don't you know?"

"I'm an amateur. I'm new at this. I do know that I caused that in one man. He went insane."

"I'm *not* insane." His lips were tight, his eyes glittering.

"But you've been wondering."

He didn't speak for a moment. "I've had a few doubts. But I came to the conclusion that I either accept that you may not be the charlatan I thought you were, or I accept the fact that I may be heading for the funny farm. I find the former far more palatable. So I'm here to ask questions. So far, you're not being very reassuring."

"Tough. I don't think you want re-assurance. You want answers. I may not be able to give them to you, but I'll try to help you find them. Ask your questions."

"Ghosts. You hear the dead. Do you see them?"

Her cup stopped on the way to her lips. "No, and I never considered them ghosts. More like echoes of what happened at a given time and place." She gazed at him for a moment before she put the question to him. "Do you see them?"

He didn't answer for a moment. "Maybe." He scowled. "Damn, that was hard to say."

"Do you know who they are?"

"Bonnie. I thought at first that I was having a hallucination because of the stress of the years of trying to find her."

"How many times have you seen her?"

"Once."

"Then you could be right."

"I wasn't trying to find Nancy Jo Norris, and I saw her."

"The girl who was murdered? I saw the story on the evening news." She frowned. "How do you see them? Is it just a fleeting glimpse?"

"No, they talk to me. Like you, like anyone." He started to stand up. "I'm done. I'm getting out of here. I sound like the nutcase I probably am."

"Wait. Why did you come? What tipped the scales and made you think that maybe I could help you?"

"Nancy Jo told me that the man who killed her had grabbed her from behind, held a handkerchief over her nose, and knocked her out. The autopsy showed she'd been dosed with ether. It was slim evidence, but I grabbed at it."

"I would have done the same," Megan said. "And that's not so slim."

"Yes, it is. I'd say it's wishful thinking, but I don't like either option."

"But you've already accepted one of them, or you wouldn't be here."

"Any port in a storm. If you did this to me, can you undo it?"

She shook her head. "I think you're stuck with it. But I'll try to find out."

"For God's sake, don't you know?"

"Dammit, I told you. I'm new at this. I didn't even know I had any so-called psychic talents until a few months ago. I'm certainly no authority, for heaven's sake. But I'll call my friend Renata Wilger in Munich, and see if she knows someone who can help you."

"Another psychic voodoo priestess?"

She shook her head. "Not really. Renata is a distant cousin, and she's sort of an agent for a family business. But she has contacts."

"What family? It sounds like the Mafia."

"No. It's the Devanez family." She hesitated. She'd have to tell him. She owed him the whole truth. "It's a very old family and some of the members have certain . . . talents."

"A whole family of freaks? What the hell am I getting into?"

"Look, I know this is difficult for you. Well, it's not easy for me." She didn't blame him for being impatient. Her explanation would probably not make it any more acceptable. "I found out I was a member of the Devanez family at the same time I learned I was one of these 'freaks' you're talking about. The Devanezes were originally landholders in southern Spain. In 1485, they fled Spain to escape the Inquisition. The local peasants had gone to their priests and accused the family of every form of witchcraft from predicting the future to shape changing. Some of it was sheer superstition, but there was no doubt the family had certain talents. The family scattered to practically every corner of the civilized world and went into hiding. But Jose, the head of the family, believed in strength in Unity, and didn't want the family to lose contact with each other. He created a ledger that listed names, addresses, even talents, of family members, and sent it out of the country with his brother, Miguel. Since then there's always been a keeper of the ledger who visits around the world and keeps track of the family." She paused. "And problems that we might be having because of any gift we might have."

"And Renata Wilger can contact this damn keeper of the ledger and find me help?"

"Renata *is* the keeper of the ledger." She added quietly, "And she's my friend. She'll do whatever she can."

"I *hate* having to rely on you, or her, or anyone else." His tone was edged with frustration. "I don't *want* this. I'm clutching at straws. I don't want anything to do with your mumbo jumbo."

"Then walk away from me. Go to a psychiatrist. I'm sure that he'd tell you that after a few hundred sessions you wouldn't see any more spirits. Or maybe you'll just learn to ignore them."

He was silent. "Do you think I'm imagining them?"

"No, I think you're too hardheaded to imagine anything." She made a face. "I think I zapped you."

He shook his head in disgust. "It just shows how far gone I am that that statement fills me with relief."

She got to her feet. "I'll call Renata. I need someone a hell of a lot more knowledgeable than I am to tell you what to do. I don't even know where to start."

"I'll tell you where to start," Joe said. "I want you to come with me to Allatoona."

Her eyes widened. "Why?"

"I want you to tell me if you hear Nancy Jo Norris and what she tells you about what happened to her. As long as I'm able to extract information from a victim, I might as well make use of her."

"Very professional. Is that all?"

"No." He hesitated, then said bluntly, "This weirdness scares the hell out of me. I don't know how to handle it. I want company."

FIVE

Joe flashed his badge at the police officer on guard duty at the Allatoona crime scene. "We're just going to have a look around. We won't be long." He nodded for Megan to go ahead. "I see the TV trucks are still here."

The officer nodded. "They're hoping to shoot some more footage of Senator Norris. It was like a circus here a few hours ago. They were on him like bees after honey."

Not a good simile. There had been nothing honey-sweet about Ed Norris. His bitterness had been machete-sharp. Who could blame him?

He caught up with Megan. He pointed to the chalked outline. "That's where we found her."

"I don't think that's where he killed her," Megan said. "It feels . . . wrong."

"Why? Do you hear anything?"

She shook her head. "Nothing. It just isn't right. Where did you see her?"

"In those trees. It was dusk."

Now it was dark, and the shadows of the trees made the darkness seem heavy, forbidding.

"Sad. She's so sad," Megan murmured. "She's beginning to understand."

Joe turned to look at her. "Echoes?"

"No. Yes. I don't know. Something different." She moved toward the trees. "I think that's where she died. Not there by the lake. Is that possible?"

"Yes, we'll know when we get the forensic report." He followed her into the darkness.

He could feel the tension beginning to grip him. Stupid. He was looking straight ahead, afraid to gaze to the right or left. Afraid of what he'd see.

"It's suspected of being a ritual killing," he said. "The bastard could have killed her here, stripped her, and carried her out to the bank for his ceremony."

"I think that's what probably happened." Megan's gaze was traveling around the woods. "There's . . . fear here."

"Then why can't you hear her?"

"I don't know. Maybe I don't want to hear her. Or it could be I'm still numb from listening to the children on that island in the swamp. Perhaps they're getting in the way."

"That's a lot of 'maybes.' "

"It's the best I can do." She glanced at him. "You asked me to come here, but I'm not helping much, am I?"

"No. I wanted you to hear her. I wanted you to give me some wise revelation that would prove I'm not completely bananas." He shrugged. "But you did the next best thing. She hasn't made an appearance. You may have scared her off. That's pretty valuable too."

"Then may we leave now? This sadness is overpowering."

"I guess we might as well." He gave another glance around, then started to turn to go. "To tell you the truth, I have to admit I'm relieved that —"

"Don't you dare leave me."

"Oh, shit."

Blond hair, red collegiate sweatshirt, blue eyes blazing at him. Nancy Jo Norris stood at the edge of the trees, blocking their path.

"What is it?" Megan was gazing at Joe's face.

"The resident spirit of the wood." He had to be flip because he was feeling that same sense of panic he'd felt before. "You don't see her?"

"No." Her gaze was following Joe's to the place where Nancy Jo stood. "Nothing."

"Stop ignoring me," Nancy Jo said. "Of course she can't see me. No one can see me. Not even Daddy. I tried and tried to talk to him, and he didn't hear me, didn't see me. I reached out and touched him, tried to hug him, and he didn't even feel it." She was blinking back tears. "He was hurting and I wanted to help him but he couldn't feel me."

"I can't solve your problem, Nancy Jo," Joe said. "I don't know anything about this." He turned to Megan. "Do something."

She shook her head. "She's your ghost. I can't even hear her echoes. You'll have to deal with her."

Nancy Jo was glaring at Megan. "Is she some kind of ghost hunter? Is that why you brought her?" she asked bitterly. "I used to watch TV shows about ghost hunters. My roommate, Chelsea, and I used to make fun of them."

"So did I," Joe said. "I'm not laughing now."

"Neither am I," Nancy Jo said. "I don't care if she's a ghost hunter or not. I wish she could see me. I'm so lonely."

"Why are you still here? Isn't there some light or something you should be walking toward?" Damn he sounded stupid. But how the hell did you talk to a ghost?

"I don't know. They keep telling me I have to leave, that I'll be fine once I go."

"Who are 'they'?"

She shook her head. "I don't know. I can't listen to them. I have to stay here. It shouldn't have happened. I wanted to live. He had no right to take it from me." She shuddered. "Do you know what he did? He drank my blood. My blood is in him, feeding him. I can't stand the thought of that. It makes me angry. He shouldn't be alive when I'm dead."

"Look, if it will help, I'll promise you that I'll catch that bastard."

"I don't believe you. You just want me to go away. I won't go away."

"I'm a cop. It's my job to find who killed you. It doesn't matter if you go away or not. I'll still get the job done."

She studied his face. "I don't think you're lying to me. But I have to be sure that he doesn't live. He stole my blood. He stole my life."

"I can't do more than give you my word. Go off and do what 'they' say and let me get to work."

"You're pissed at me."

"Hell, yes. I feel sorry for you, I want to help you, but you're making my life damn miserable. Yes, I'm pissed at you."

"I guess that's better than being afraid of me. People are supposed to be afraid of ghosts."

"I had a few moments."

"That's too bad." She added defiantly, "But since you seem to be the only one who can see or hear me, you're stuck with me."

"The hell I am."

"You have to help me." Her voice vibrated with intensity. "I can't do it by myself. I would if I could." She hesitated, then said, "My father is angry. If you don't find this monster, Daddy is going to do it himself. How do I know that he won't kill my father too?"

What could he say to that? Joe thought in frustration. He could argue that she should leave revenge to him, but what about protecting the one you love? He could understand that motivation with all his mind and heart. Shielding and caring for Eve had been the rule that had driven him all these years. He was becoming more involved with Nancy Jo with every word she spoke.

Involved with a ghost? What was he thinking? " 'If'? I will find him, and your father will stay out of the picture."

"I hope so."

"I'm going now." He held up his hand as she started to speak. "I can't stay here having séances with you. I have a job to do."

"But I want to help you. I need to do it."

"Then tell me who did this. Do you have a name?"

She shook her head. "He said he was my savior. He said I should be grateful. He kept saying 'Gift to Gift.' "

"What did he look like?"

She didn't answer.

"What did he —"

"I'm trying to remember. I was so scared . . . Gray eyes, short, close-cut dark hair. White at the temples. A Roman nose, sort of hooked."

"Tall. Short?"

"Medium. But he was burly, strong, biceps like a weight lifter."

"Car?"

"I only caught a glimpse of it after I woke up. It was parked at the edge of the woods." She frowned, thinking. "It was a big car. Light-colored. I think it might have been a Lincoln Town Car."

"New? Old?"

"Old. I don't think the new Lincolns are that big." She shook her head. "I only had a glimpse." She closed her eyes. "And I was so scared."

"I can see that you were. But you're doing well."

"Thank you." Her lids opened, and she tried to smile. "After all, I have to please you. You appear to be the only game in town."

Joe again felt that strong surge of sympathy. She wasn't much younger than his Jane. He wanted to reach out and — Hell, he couldn't even do that.

I'm so lonely, she had said.

"I'm going to leave now. I'll come back if I have any more questions."

She nodded. "I don't know if I can come to you. I don't know how it works. I'm going to have to experiment." She looked at Megan. "She's not afraid of me. You can bring her with you if you like."

"That's up to her. I thought she might help." He started to turn away, then said, "The knife. Was there anything different about it?"

"The knife . . ." Her teeth sank into her lower lip. "I'm afraid to —"

"It's okay. You don't have to remember."

"Yes, I do. My heart was beating so hard. I was trying to get out of the ropes. He held up the knife and showed it to me. He said 'Gift to Gift.' Then he sliced across — Blood. I'm bleeding. He has a cup, and he's pressing it to my throat. What's he —"

"Enough," Joe said curtly. "You've said enough."

"No, you want to know what it looked like. But it's hard to get past the pain." She was breathing hard. "It's a dagger. It looks . . . black in the shadows. The handle has some kind of carving. A man with a knife. A man with a goblet. Or maybe I'm getting mixed up.

My blood is . . . I'm getting weaker . . ."

"Stop it, Nancy Jo. Enough."

She nodded jerkily. "Too much. Go away. I don't want you to see me this way. I don't want anyone to know how scared he made me. I think he liked it."

"He probably did. Most serial killers enjoy a feeling of power."

"So clinical. You're going by the book. Generic-case types. Well, he wasn't generic," she said fiercely. "He was a monster who drank my blood. Go away and don't come back until you've found him."

"Right. Whatever you say." He wheeled and strode toward the edge of the woods.

"Conversation over?" Megan was hurrying to catch up with him. "Are you going to tell me what it was about? I only heard your side."

"She's lonely. She wants to keep her father from being a victim if he goes after her killer. She wants revenge against the bastard who slit her throat, and then drank her blood." He was walking fast, carefully not looking back at the woods. "And for a dead girl, she seems very much alive and very human. She's not tough like Jane, but I kept thinking that if Jane hadn't grown up on the streets, she might have turned out like

Nancy Jo. Same determination, same affectionate nature."

Megan was silent until they reached the car. "Then you're convinced that she's not a figment of your imagination?"

"Hell, no. I don't know if I'll ever be certain. But I'm operating on that assumption since I can't do anything else. I made my decision that I refuse to believe I'm crazy and that leaves only the option to accept and use this damn thing that's happened to me."

"You're quite a man, Joe Quinn," Megan said quietly. "I don't believe many people would handle all that's happened to you this well." She paused. "I'm sorry, Joe. I tried my best not to hurt anyone."

"Your best wasn't good enough." He opened the car door for her. "But I'm going to let you make amends. I don't know a tinker's damn about this spook business." He shook his head. "Who the hell does know anything? Does our friend, Renata?"

"When I called her, she said she'd look into it and get back to me."

"Then she'd better get back to you quick. I have questions to ask."

"You may have to find out the answers yourself. After all, you're the one who can talk to them."

"I'm not going to go along with that. Nancy Jo didn't seem to know much more than I do." He got into the driver's seat and started the car. "And one of the questions is why you didn't hear any echoes."

"I've been thinking about that," Megan said. "Echoes come from empty spaces. Maybe there would be no echoes if the spirit hadn't passed on and left the place where the death had occurred. Nancy Jo is refusing to go anywhere, so she leaves no lingering echo."

Joe was silent a moment. "What about Bonnie? You said that you heard no echoes from Bonnie on that island. Could she have been killed on that island, and you didn't hear an echo because she refused to pass on?"

"It's possible. I hope so. Then I wouldn't feel guilty about not doing what Eve will probably ask me to do." She looked at him. "You're going to have to talk to Eve about seeing Bonnie."

"Do you think I don't know that?" His hands tightened on the steering wheel. "But not yet. Bonnie is the center of Eve's world. Hell, every day revolves around her. I've got to get a handle on this mess before I bring her into the picture. That could open a whole new can of worms."

Megan nodded. "I can understand how you'd hesitate. I'd be very careful the way I let Eve know I'd seen her daughter." She glanced back out the window. "I'll help you get all the information you need. I'll come when you call me. But Eve's my friend, and I won't let you keep this from her for long. She's worried, and it's not fair."

"I didn't expect anything else." His tone hardened. "But you owe me, Megan. You let me do it my way."

"I'll try. But you'd better start breaking it to her about Nancy Jo right away."

"Then find me information so that I don't sound like a complete idiot," Joe said sarcastically. "I think you'll agree that she'd be a little worried if she thought I was going around the bend."

"I'll call Renata again when I get home."

"And I'll tell you everything that Nancy Jo told me about her death. I'll even sketch out a rough picture of the cup that her killer used in his ritual. You can fax it to your friend, Renata, in Munich."

She nodded. "I don't know if that will help, but it can't hurt." She paused, then repeated, "Tell Eve about Bonnie, Joe."

"I'll do what I think best. And since you seem to want your own way in this, you can make one more call while I'm driving back to the lake. You call Eve and prepare the way for me. Tell her that, thanks to you, I have a new soul mate in Nancy Jo Norris."

From the porch, Eve watched Joe park the car and walk up the driveway. Dawn was just beginning to pearl the skies, and she couldn't see his expression, but he was moving quickly, his strides full of leashed emotion.

As she must leash her own emotions. She was confused and scared and feeling completely inadequate to handle this development. But she had to find a way to help him and not let her emotions get in the way.

He stopped on the top step and looked at her. "What a hell of a mess. Do you want to cut and run?"

"No." She went into his arms and buried her face on his chest. "Did you cut and run anytime during all these years with me? We just have to find a way to get through this."

"Preferably without putting me in the booby hatch. That must have occurred to you."

"It did not." Her arms tightened around him. "I didn't really believe Megan's facilitating stuff until she told me that it had happened to you. But you're a rock. I've never known anyone as strong and steady as you are. If you tell me that you saw Nancy Jo Norris, then you did."

"I saw her. I talked to her." He pushed her away and gazed down at her. "Now look at me and let me see your face."

She stared him in the eye. "You're not going to see anything but love and trust. You're a rock."

He gazed at her for a long moment. "My God, you're making me believe it."

"Good. Because now I can tell you how pissed I am that you didn't tell me what was bothering you before this."

"I had reasons."

"Not good enough. You wouldn't have been in that swamp searching for Henry Kistle if it hadn't been for me. Megan would never have touched you. Whatever happens to you, happens to me too. You should have let me share."

"I don't think sharing is going to be an option in this case. Megan couldn't see or hear Nancy Jo."

"Then I'll find another way to help you." She kissed him. "Just don't close me out again. It scared me."

"I hate to damage my reputation as a rock, but I've been a little upset myself." He buried his face in her hair, and said hoarsely, "Lord, I'm lucky."

"Yes, you are." She hugged him again. "You have me and Jane . . ." She deliberately made her tone lighter. "And a brand-new soul mate." She stepped back and drew him toward the door. "But I have to admit I hope you don't widen those acquaintances to any great extent. It could be very confusing." She glanced at him as they entered the house. "Now do you want to try to get some sleep, or are you too wired?"

"Sleep." He slid his arm around her waist. "I want to hold you and tell you about Nancy Jo. I'll share what I can." He was walking with her toward their bedroom. "I know that Megan has convinced you that she has this gift, but this is different. I'm still amazed that you'd accept the idea so readily."

Because she had lived with the spirit of her Bonnie for years, she thought. Dream or ghost, there had never been a doubt that spirit existed. Should she tell Joe that was her reason?

No, Joe had begun to feel resentment toward Bonnie during these last years and wanted Eve to give up the search. How could she bring up Bonnie now and tell him she hadn't trusted him enough to share those visions with him? She had just told him he should have shared his problems with her. Later. After they had fought their way through Joe's battle.

"Not exactly readily. But if you say it's so, then I believe you." She frowned, thinking about it. "But I'm wondering if the reason you saw Nancy Jo is that her killer has some connection with you . . . us. You said the goblets were similar. The one Jane found in the refrigerator had to be some kind of threat."

"Or a calling card."

"Pretty macabre calling card."

"His whole modus operandi is macabre," Joe said.

"So do you think that you're only going to see victims of killers with whom you have contact?"

An undecipherable expression flitted across his face. "I don't think it's going to be that easy."

"Why not?"

"That pool is too narrow. I'm not that lucky."

"How can you be —"

"Drop it," he said curtly. "I can't be sure of anything, so stop speculating. Maybe when Megan pulls one of her psychic buddies out of her hat, then I'll know more."

Eve shrugged. "I'm just trying to put the pieces together. It seemed reasonable." She made a face. “As reasonable as anything else. It’s an entirely new ball game, isn’t it?”

“There may be new rules, but I’m going with standard operating procedure. I have a killer I have to catch, and I’m going to do what I always do. It’s the only way I can keep it together.” He glanced at her. “I’m trying to track down Jelak’s steps. It’s too close a coincidence that he shows up at the same time that we find this goblet in the refrigerator.”

“You think it was Jelak who killed Nancy Jo?”

“As I said, I have problems with coincidence.”

“So do I,” Eve said. “Montalvo said that his investigators are trying to find out more about him.”

“I was planning on calling him later in the day.”

She gazed at him in surprise. “You were?”

“Not willingly. But that murdering bastard invaded my home. That goblet was a direct threat. I’ll use anyone who can help me get him.” He opened the bedroom door. “Even Montalvo.”

Munich, Germany

“Mark, come over here and look at this.” Renata Wilger took the fax off the machine as her cousin crossed the office toward her. "I think I've seen it before." She handed him the drawing of the goblet. "Fiero?"

Mark examined the fax closely. "Fiero," he confirmed. "Megan sent it?"

"It's in connection to another problem." She took the fax back. "Which I don't think is going to turn out to be as big a problem as this will be.

"At least we have a tentative location." She glanced at Mark. "I'm going to call Seth Caleb and tell him." She made a face. "I'm not looking forward to it."

"You can handle him."

"Because he lets me handle him. I'd be curious to see how he'd react if you weren't around. He respects you because you're an ex–Israeli agent and thinks of you as a fellow hunter."

"Yet you're the one who hires him to do the hunting." Mark smiled. "And he respects you too. He told me once that there's always room in the world for firebrands. They make life interesting."

"Really?" She was always conscious of a cool wariness when she spoke to Caleb. That was fine with her. She had no desire to get any closer to him. She wondered if anyone ventured into that territory. Somehow she doubted it. "It probably wasn't a compliment. With Caleb, you can never tell if there's an edge." It shouldn't matter. It was her job to deal with all kinds of people to keep the family safe. Caleb was just another wild card who had to be made aware he couldn't have things all his own way. She crossed to the desk and picked up her phone.

She dialed Seth Caleb and got his voice mail. "Renata Wilger. I'm sending you a photo attachment on your phone. Call me back." She hung up.

She leaned back against the edge of the desk and waited.

Two minutes later her phone rang.

She smiled as she checked the ID. Seth Caleb. She picked up the call.

The question came sharp as a dagger. "Where?"

Megan's cell phone rang at four that afternoon. Renata.

"Did you find someone who can help Joe Quinn?" Megan asked when she picked up. "I feel so damn helpless. I *did* this, Renata."

"Yes, you did. But you didn't do it deliberately so stop obsessing about it."

That was typical of Renata — blunt, crisp, and to the point. "You're the one who should be able to dig up someone with that same psychic talent. Help me."

"I'm working on it." She paused. "But right now I'm more interested in that fax you sent me with the drawing of the goblet. How accurate is it?"

"As accurate as I could make it without seeing the goblet myself. Joe Quinn is a detective and has a trained eye. It's probably pretty close. Why?"

"I showed it to my cousin Mark. He was very interested, and we thought we recognized it. I got on the phone and made a call. We're going to send someone to Atlanta to do a more in-depth investigation."

"Because of the goblet? I don't care about the goblet. I want someone here to give me some insight into how to do something that will make sense of this albatross I've hung around Joe's neck."

"This may be more important. At least, more urgent to us. We think he may have done injury to one of the family members. The man we're sending is Seth Caleb, and I told him to contact you. He may or may not do it. The bastard usually does as he likes."

"I don't care what he does. I want answers, Renata."

"You'll get them. But this is important. You know we can't let anyone hurt the family. It could cause unpleasant chain reactions among the others. They already feel like victims and it's sometimes hard to keep them from striking back. You should understand. You're part of the family, too, Megan."

"The only thing the family has done for me is give me a talent that's made my life a nightmare. Is this Seth Caleb an agent or some kind of peacekeeper?"

" 'Peace'? No way. He doesn't know the meaning of the word."

"Then why are you sending him?"

"Because he'd come even if we didn't send him. The moment he heard about the goblet, he told us he was going. But he's smart and experienced, and that may be enough to keep us out of trouble." She didn't wait for Megan to reply. "I'll phone you as soon as I find out anything else that may interest you." She hung up.

Anything else? Renata had told her nothing that had interested her, Megan thought in frustration. She didn't want this Caleb to explode on a situation that was already tense and bewildering. All she wanted was to be able to handle the problems she had now.

Okay, look at it from a positive angle. If Nancy Jo's killer was found, then she might disappear, and one facet of Joe's problem might vanish with her. Maybe this Seth Caleb was a bright shining light that would make everything better.

Only Renata had not made him sound like a bright shining light. More like a loose cannon.

She could only hope.

"Where the hell have you been?"

Joe turned to see Ed Norris striding out of the captain's office. The senator's eyes were swollen and rimmed, and he looked as if he hadn't slept. He probably hadn't, Joe thought. You didn't sleep when you were going through all the fires of hell. "Good afternoon, Senator."

"Do you always wander in at two in the afternoon?" Norris demanded. "Well, you'd better change your ways while you're on my daughter's case. I want you here by eight in the morning and working a full day."

"I'll work as long as it takes to get the job done," Joe said. "I don't always punch a time clock."

"Convenient."

Joe was trying to hold on to his patience. He felt sorry for the poor bastard. "Sometimes."

"Not on Nancy Jo's case."

To hell with patience. "Look, I wasn't here this morning because I went back to the crime scene last night and didn't get home until dawn. I don't know why I'm telling you because I don't give a damn what you think. I answer to the captain, and she won't cave because a senator starts pressuring." He added, "And it would help us if you'd stay away from Allatoona. You can't do anything but stir up the media and get in the way."

"I had to go there. I needed —" His lips compressed with pain. "But those reporters were all over me. I suppose if I'd thought, I would have known they — But I didn't think." He took a deep breath. "I don't seem to be doing a good job of that lately. Except about Nancy Jo. I can't seem to think of anything else but her." His expression darkened. "And that son of a bitch who killed her. I have to get him, Quinn."

"Let me do my job. She wouldn't want you to be involved."

"Involved. I am involved. How can I —" He stopped. "Have you found out anything more?"

"We think that she may have been taken at a parking garage at Perimeter Mall. I've sent someone to ask questions of the attendants and check security video cameras."

"Why Perimeter Mall?"

"We've checked with her roommate, Chelsea Burke, and she told us that your daughter was going shopping there. Her roommate was planning on going with her, but she had an exam the next day."

"If she'd gone with Nancy Jo, he might not have been able to grab her . . . Such a little thing to make a difference."

Joe nodded. "Such a little thing." He started to turn away.

"Wait." Norris was silent for a moment. "I have to be kept in the loop. I'll make it worth your while if you come to me first with any break in the case."

So that he could go after the bastard himself. Nancy Jo had been right on the money.

"I'm sure the captain will keep you informed on the investigation," Joe said. "If you'll excuse me, I need to make some calls."

"If you change your mind . . . Why did you go out to Allatoona again? Did you think you missed something?"

"No, I didn't miss anything." He paused. "But I have a hunch she was killed in the trees, not on the bank. I asked forensics to check it out. We should know in a few hours."

"Why would you think that? You may be wasting time. He could be getting away while we 'check' out your hunches."

"Or we could take a step closer," Joe said. "I'm trusting my instincts. I'll let you know if I'm right."

He could feel Norris's gaze on his back as he walked away from him. This case was going to be a headache in more ways than the obvious. Norris was going to be on his ass every minute of the day, and how much of what Nancy Jo had told Joe could he attribute to "instinct"? If he'd been forced to tell Norris that he had asked that the security tapes at the parking garage be scanned for a large light-colored Lincoln, he would have had a hell of a time explaining.

Well, he would just have to dance around the truth and try to avoid Norris as much as possible. It wouldn't be easy considering the fact that Norris was hurting and angry and wanted to be in on every detail of the investigation. He couldn't blame him. Joe would have felt the same in his shoes. Nancy Jo was definitely right in worrying about her father.

Damn, that last thought about Nancy Jo had come out of nowhere and been perfectly natural. As if he was accepting her as a living, thinking force.

He quickly edged away from that realization. Instead, he had to concentrate on the case, on the man who had killed Nancy Jo, try to find a link between Jelak and the killing.

And that meant he had to bite the bullet and call Montalvo.

SIX

"I just talked to Quinn," Montalvo said, when Eve picked up the phone. "I was going to call him anyway but it was gratifying that he made the first move."

"I don't know why. It doesn't mean anything except that he wants to solve this case."

"And wanted it enough to come to me for help. I'm not saying that it flattered my ego. I'm saying that the antagonism can't be quite as strong as it used to be if he could bring himself to do it. It bodes well for our being able to work together." He chuckled. "The first step in our burgeoning friendship."

"The circumstances are different right now. I wouldn't count on anything when we manage to catch this killer."

"I never count on anything. I just work at making it happen."

"Is that what you called to tell me?"

"No, I called to share what I told Quinn."

"Joe will tell me."

"But I want to do it first. I don't want you to have to wait."

"That's not the way to feed a burgeoning friendship."

"I have to strike a balance. Do you want to know or not?"

"Of course I want to know. What did you find out about Jelak?"

"It's sketchy right now. I've been trying to build a picture but so far all we have is based on credit-card information. We've traced the trail back to Illinois." He paused. "He checked into a motel outside Bloomburg three weeks ago."

She stiffened. "Bloomburg? That's where we got on the track of Henry Kistle. You say he was there?"

"According to Visa."

"Kistle and Jelak? Is there some kind of connection between them? Did Kistle stay there?"

"No, he rented a flat in town. We can't be sure, but so far there doesn't appear to be any contact between them."

"Then why was he there? There must have been a reason." She was trying to work it out. "I suppose they could have been partners. They left Atlanta about the same time after Bonnie's death."

"But I had in-depth reports on Kistle. There was no mention of Jelak in any of them."

"But you weren't looking for any mention of Jelak. Why would you? Why would he suddenly pop up in Bloomburg if he didn't have some kind of history with Kistle?"

"If I knew that, I wouldn't still be digging, and Quinn would be looking upon me as if I were a brother."

"Brother Cain, maybe."

"Very good." Montalvo laughed. "But I don't mind the comparison. That was a very interesting relationship." He added, "But Jelak had one other credit charge in Bloomburg than the motel. He took out a weekly membership at Gold's Gym. But he only went there twice."

"A gym?"

"I thought it a little peculiar too. Particularly since one of the times he went there was when we were all in town trying to hunt down Kistle."

Peculiar and chilling, she thought. The idea of Jelak's calmly going about his life to that extent, probably only miles from where she had stayed, without her having any idea of his presence. She had been totally focused on Henry Kistle, having no clue that there was another, maybe even greater, threat standing in the shadows. "And you told Joe this?"

"Every bit. But I was only a few steps ahead of him. He told me he was getting an order to trace back Jelak's credit info as far back as he'd held the card. He should be receiving a report anytime." He paused. "I asked to see the report. After all, turnabout is fair play. To my surprise, Quinn agreed. I suppose I thought he'd want to close me out."

"Not with Jelak. He's too close."

"How close, Eve?" he asked softly. "What aren't you telling me?"

She hesitated. But, as he'd said, turnabout was fair play. "You heard about the murder of Nancy Jo Norris? There was an object left here at the cottage that was meant to be a threat. It was connected to the girl's murder. Why would her killer be targeting me? The coincidence was too strong when we knew that Jelak was in the area."

He gave a low whistle. "Much too strong." He was silent a moment. "And I don't like it that he was near your cottage. I'm going to send Miguel out to keep an eye on it."

"I don't need Miguel. I have a police car parked practically right outside my door. And I have Joe."

"Who is busy trying to find Jelak," Montalvo said. "I'll think about it. I may still send Miguel. If you won't let me come?"

"No."

"I didn't think so. I'll call you when I know anything else." He hung up.

All she needed was Montalvo hovering around the cottage, Eve thought as she hung up. Things were tense enough between her and Joe, and Joe was always on the verge of an explosion when Montalvo was around.

"Montalvo again?" Jane came out of the bedroom. "You always have the same expression after you finish talking to him. He usually manages to annoy you." She plopped down on a chair. "Or stir you."

"He wants to send Miguel to protect us."

"Oh, that young friend of Montalvo's?" She smiled. "I remember Miguel. I met him in Bloomburg. I liked him."

"And he liked you. If I recall, he was smitten."

"He's just a kid, and he likes women. And he has no discrimination." She tilted her head. "You must have told Montalvo about our goblet. He's worried about you."

"That's part of it." She had not told Jane anything about Joe's visit to Megan's last night or the personal turmoil that was tearing him apart. Only Joe had the right to confide in her. But she couldn't keep her completely in the dark. "But Joe believes that Jelak may be Nancy Jo's murderer." She paused. "And that means the goblet was probably left by Jelak."

"Holy shit." Jane's eyes widened. "What's happening? You said that was a ritual killing."

"We don't know. We're trying to trace Jelak's past and find out what we have to deal with," she said. "He was in Bloomburg at the same time we were. But not with Kistle. He was standing on the sidelines and watching. He even went to a gym while he was there."

"Creepy. A health nut?"

"Maybe." She suddenly remembered something Joe had told her about Nancy Jo's description of her murderer. "But Nancy Jo's killer had huge biceps, like a weight lifter's."

"How do you know? Was there a witness?"

"Sort of. But if Jelak was a fitness addict, it would explain how he felt compelled to work out at a gym."

"What do you mean? 'Sort of'?" Jane said. "You're not telling me everything."

Eve should have known that Jane would pick up on any discrepancy. "I'm telling you everything I can. Ask Joe."

"I will." Jane rose to her feet. "This time I'm not going to be left out in the cold." She held up her hand as Eve started to speak. "I'm not blaming you. I trust you. You have to have your reasons. I'll just find out what's happening on my own." She gave Eve a quick hug. "But right now I have a dinner date with Patty. We're going to an Italian restaurant near her house. She doesn't want to be gone too long." She made a face. "Or she'll catch hell later from her grandfather."

"Charming." Eve hesitated. "Go ahead. But I'm going to call Joe and have a police car over at Patty's to follow you home."

"I can take care of myself, Eve," Jane said. "You know Joe taught me the fine art of self-defense when I was just a kid. I can do anything from karate to sharpshooting."

"So I'm a worrywart," she said. "You notice I'm not trying to make you stay home. I know better. But I just want to make sure that you have a little extra protection."

"Whatever." Jane smiled as she went out on the porch. "I'll probably be home by ten. If my plans change, I'll give you a call." She waved and ran down the steps. "Bye. See you later." She stopped as she looked up at the darkening sky. "It looks like a storm is coming, doesn't it?"

"Yes." Eve gazed out at the lake, which was already being whipped by the wind. "I think you're right. It's on its way."

Huge raindrops were striking his cheeks as Jelak sprinted deeper into the trees where he'd hidden his Lincoln. He didn't mind. Storms made his heart beat harder and filled him with exhilaration. All the precious gift blood from Nancy Jo Norris was pounding through his veins.

He hadn't expected his opportunity to come this quickly. Jane MacGuire was leaving alone, and the police car would remain to protect Eve and the cottage. He had crept close to the cottage and bugged both cars last night. Even if the woman had a slight head start, he'd be able to locate her.

But it was going to be hard to keep from taking her gift immediately. His hunger was growing, burning, and Jane MacGuire would be able to sate it. The blood that ran through her would be strong and full of life. He could always tell . . .

You weren't enough, Nancy Jo. But the blood you gave me will give me the strength to reach out and grasp what I need.

That's how the game is played.

Gift to Gift.

■ ■ ■ ■

Joe didn't get home until close to seven that evening. It was still raining, and drops were running down his face after he got out of the car and ran up the porch steps.

Eve handed him a towel as he came in the door. "It's a real gully washer, isn't it? You can hardly see. I hope it quits by the time Jane leaves the restaurant."

"You shouldn't have let her go." He dried his face and hair before tossing the towel on the counter. "The rain may be the least of her worries."

"I can't keep her penned up." Eve turned back to the stove. "You know that, Joe. We just have to make her as safe as we can. I had the police officer who is following her call me from the restaurant. So far, so good." She turned the slow cooker off. "I made a Mexican stew. It's hot enough to chase the chill away." She made a face. "Which is good in more ways than one."

"Yes." He glanced at the small skull set up on the pedestal across the room in her work area. It appeared very fragile surrounded by all the high-tech cameras and monitors that comprised her lab. "You've started to work? Who sent you the skull?"

"Your captain. It arrived about an hour ago. It's one of the children on the island. A little boy. After all the publicity in the past few days, you'd think they would have been able to ID him."

"Most of those kills were a long time ago. What are you calling him?"

"Matt." She always named the skull she was currently working on. It seemed less impersonal, and she needed that connection. These murdered children who had just been tossed in the ground filled her with immense sadness. The skulls sent to her were those of children who were completely unknown to the local police departments. They had to have a starting place before they could begin DNA testing and matching. It was her job to take the skull and build a close enough resemblance so that it could be photographed, published in the media, and, hopefully, be recognized by friends or relatives. She took down two bowls from the cabinet. "Long time or not, I would have been calling nonstop if I knew there were unidentified bodies in those graves."

"Not everyone is you, Eve. Some people have managed to move on."

"I know. I'm happy for them." She shrugged. "Maybe when I do finish Matt, they won't thank me for stirring up the memories again."

"They'll thank you. Closure is a great gift." He sat down at the table. "I wish I could give it to you." He paused. "I called Montalvo today."

"I know. He phoned and filled me in."

"I thought maybe he would."

She gazed at him a long moment. "You're not angry."

"I won't let myself be angry. I can't afford it, any more than I can afford jealousy. You and I have gone way past that point, haven't we?"

"I suppose we have." But his cool assessment and realization of the situation was not like that of the emotion-charged man she had known lately. It made her feel uneasy. "He said you'd agreed to let him in on anything you found out about Jelak."

"I will." He picked up his spoon. "I had the sheriff in Bloomburg go into Gold's Gym and get a description of Jelak. About five-foot-nine, Roman nose, dark hair with white sideburns, very muscular."

"Nancy Jo," Eve whispered.

"Yes, he fits her description. We have a very observant ghost." He lowered his gaze to the stew. "You said I was a rock. Well, the rock gets a deeper crack running across it every time something like this happens. I just have to hold on and keep it from shattering." He lifted his eyes to her face. "But I *will* do it, Eve."

"I know you will." She sat down across from him. She could feel the strength and determination he was emitting as if it were a living force. Those qualities had never changed. From the time she had met him all those years ago, he had been a bastion of strength. She remembered breaking down and clinging to him in those weeks after Bonnie had been taken. Even at that time, she'd had moments of feeling safe and treasured in a barren world.

He should have seemed more vulnerable now. His brown hair was damp and a little mussed. His tea-colored eyes were older and a little weary. His face was thinner, the bones more pronounced. He didn't look vulnerable. He reminded her of the portrait of a gladiator she had seen in a gallery she had visited with Jane in California. The man had been leaning against a sun-baked wall, relaxed and at rest, but the leashed strength had been clearly visible, only waiting to break free.

Very close to breaking free.

"What are you thinking?" Joe's gaze was studying her expression.

"You're changing." She tried to smile. "I

have a tendency to cling to you as I first knew you. But you're not that man, any more than I'm that poor broken woman."

"Some things never change."

"But people do. Lately I told someone that everyone changes, and you just have to adjust." She held up her hand. "Oh, it's not because of this weird business of Megan's. Well, maybe a little of it because it's an experience, and experiences cause aftereffects. You've probably been changing all along, and I didn't want to see it. All I let myself see was that you were tired of the search for Bonnie."

He met her gaze and repeated, "Some things never change."

"But we have to explore what those things are." She drew a deep breath. "But not now. That's putting a little too much pressure on you for it to be fair." She lifted her spoon to her mouth. "So did you find out anything more about Nancy Jo's murder?"

"The Perimeter Mall security camera on the level where Nancy Jo left her car was smashed. We managed to find a picture of a light gray Lincoln Town Car that exited about that time."

"License plate?"

"Conveniently covered with mud." Joe finished eating and leaned back in his chair.

"She seems to have been a random victim. Poor kid."

"Why?" Eve shook her head. "For her blood? The whole thing is sick."

"Gift to Gift." Joe said. "And why was Jelak trailing behind Henry Kistle? I wouldn't be surprised if the paper trail we're doing on him leads us back to Kistle's stomping grounds."

"It doesn't make sense. Have you traced his early years here in Atlanta?"

He nodded. "It's pretty skimpy. He grew up in College Park in a foster home. His mother was a whore on crack and left him to fend for himself for most of his early years before DEFACS took him away from her. He was in trouble with the law from the time he was eight or ten. When he was seventeen, he beat up one of his teachers and was thrown into jail. The man almost died. After that, Jelak was in and out of prison for the next eight years." He paused. "We went back into some of the trial-court records and found something interesting. At one point during a routine search of his apartment, the police found a sizable collection of vials containing blood."

Eve's eyes widened. "And?"

"Nothing. A few were animal and the rest human. Jelak claimed that it was only a hobby, and he'd stolen the human blood from a blood bank downtown."

"And the police didn't pursue it?"

"It dropped between the cracks. No proof. And he was going to jail for another robbery within a few weeks anyway. They probably thought they'd have time to investigate the vials later." He added, "During the last time he was serving time, he told his cellmate that he was the one who had killed Bonnie Duncan."

"Yet according to his records he wasn't a serial killer during those years. Why Bonnie?"

"He could have been lying. Bonnie's death caused a media storm. A man who was as much in love with power as Jelak might have wanted the cachet of a kill that important. Anyway, two months after he got out of prison, he left the city."

"No connection with Henry Kistle at that time?"

"Maybe. Criminals network and every scumbag in Atlanta probably either knows or knows of most of the others. They left the city at approximately the same time. He could have known where Kistle had gone." He shook his head. "I don't know." He glanced at the clock. "Isn't it time Jane got home?"

"She said ten. It's not nine yet." But talking about Jelak had prompted in her the same anxiety that Joe was feeling. Keep busy.

She got to her feet. "I'll wash up these dishes. Then I thought I'd start the measuring on Matt."

He nodded, his gaze on the rain pounding on the windows. "I'll give her a little while longer. Then I'll go after her."

"She has that squad car following her."

"Which is the only reason I'm not going after her right now." He stood up. "I'm going out on the porch to call the precinct and check and see if anything new has come in on Jelak."

"The porch? It's still pouring outside."

"It's not blowing." He headed for the door. "And the rain doesn't bother me."

Dammit, it wasn't working out, Jelak thought in frustration.

That bastard in the cop car was trailing Jane MacGuire too close for him to get near her.

Son of a bitch. He had thought that luck was going to be on his side. He had made his plans to edge her off the road on her way home.

But then that cop car had shown up at

the restaurant.

Rage was tearing through him. It was Eve Duncan who had done it. He knew it. She had wanted to protect her young charge and called on Quinn's cop friends to do it. Damn her.

He had wanted the gift to be clean and powerful, and she was keeping him from doing it.

He tried to control himself. It could still be clean and powerful, but he had to make a few adjustments to his plan. He would take MacGuire later rather than immediately. But he could not bear to remain in the background too long. He knew himself and he must have satisfaction and a certain amount of triumph.

Otherwise the burning would be too strong and would lead him to make mistakes.

So plan. Turn this small defeat into a glorious victory.

The haze of anger was gradually ebbing away as he pulled away from the curb.

He could barely see the cop's taillights through the rain as he slowly drove after him. The bastard was still sticking to her as close as glue.

Guard her. It won't do you any good. I'll get her and make everyone who gets in my way pay.

Do you hear me, Eve?

"What are you doing out here, Joe?" Jane ran up the steps, shaking the dampness from her hair. She reached down to pat Toby, who had rolled over on his back in silent invitation. "As if I didn't know."

"Any trouble?"

"Not a bit." She turned and waved at the police officer in the squad car who had just pulled into the driveway and was turning around. "Bye, Charlie." She watched him drive away. "Except that I got wet running out to Charlie Brand's patrol car at the restaurant and convincing him to come in and eat dinner while he was waiting for me. He's a nice guy. We had coffee with him after Patty and I finished dinner."

"Very cozy."

"And he's not married. I think he liked Patty. She doesn't get out much to meet people these days. I thought this was a golden opportunity to have her get to know someone besides nurses and therapists. Those are the only people her grandfather will let in the house." She grinned at Joe. "Besides, I like cops."

"Good. Because you're going to have one with you or behind you for the foreseeable future."

Her smile faded. "The goblet of blood. Is it Jelak?"

"More than likely."

"He's after Eve?" She nodded slowly. "And you think he may use me to get to her."

"There's a slight possibility that I might want to make sure you're safe as well."

"That goes without saying. But it's Eve that we have to worry about." Jane frowned. "You know I'll be careful. I'd never risk Eve. She may be your center, but she means more to me than anyone in the world."

He was silent a moment. "What about Mark Trevor? I haven't heard you mention him lately."

She said warily, "What about him? I haven't seen him recently. He's busy. He globe-trots all over the world. I'm busy. I have a career. We agreed that it might be best not to incur any additional obligations."

"Because you're afraid to trust any relationship."

"Maybe." She smiled. "I trust Eve. I trust you . . . when you don't act weird as you did when I first arrived here. Are you going to tell me what that was all about?"

"Probably. Someday." He reached out and touched her cheek. "Don't take chances,

Jane. Not now. Not ever. You're too important to us." He turned on his heel. "There's a gun in a case on the top shelf of the closet. Take it with you when you go out from now on."

"I will." She watched him go into the house before she turned and gazed out at the thick veil of rain. It was like being cocooned behind her own private waterfall. She used to love sitting out here in a rainstorm when she was a teenager. Sometimes she and Eve would sit on the swing and talk for hours.

Precious times.

Precious memories.

Someone was watching.

She was suddenly shivering.

Nonsense. If she couldn't see through this veil of rain, no one else out there could see her. It was Joe's talk of Jelak and warning her against taking risks that had spooked her.

Maybe.

She had always trusted her instincts, and they were sending up skyrocket signals now.

She took a step closer to the porch railing, then stopped. If there was a threat out there, she didn't want to confront it blindly. It was enough to be on her guard and perhaps mention it to Joe to follow up tomorrow.

Joe believed in the power of instinct. He would understand.

Jelak smiled with satisfaction as he lowered the infrared binoculars. He hadn't been able to see more than a flash of body heat on the porch, but it comforted him to know that he was still in contact, in control. Every instinct told him that it was Jane MacGuire, and she had moved toward the edge of the porch as if wanting to confront him. "I want to confront you too," he murmured. "But you shouldn't be so defiant. If I had a rifle, I could take you down right now."

But he didn't like guns. He always carried a Glock pistol because of the convenience, but he seldom used it. He preferred the might of his muscles and the clean stroke of his knife to claim the gift.

"Do you feel me, Jane MacGuire?" he murmured. "You're standing so still I think you must. I was angry with you, but it's going away. As soon as the rain stops, I think I'll take a gift in your honor. Anger makes the hunger burn, and I have to keep up my strength." He rolled the window of the car up and leaned back in the seat. "It will be difficult, but I'll find a suitable —"

Fear.

No!

His heart was pounding, jerking, panic racing through him.

It was out there in the darkness, coming toward him. *He* was coming toward him.

He had to get away.

His hand was shaking as he started the car, backed up, and stomped on the accelerator.

Closer. He was closer.

His tires were skidding in the mud as he raced through the forest.

Get away. He had to be stronger before he could face him. More blood. More power.

He'd reached the road leading north to the highway.

How had he found him? The village of Fiero was a world away, and he'd been careful for years not to do anything that might trigger a search. The goblet? Possibly. Before this, he'd used the goblets very sparingly so that there would be no connection.

It could be his imagination. The fear was ebbing the farther he went from the cottage. He could barely feel that sense of impending threat.

It wasn't his imagination. He'd felt that same fear all those years ago. He'd run then as he was running now.

But he was stronger now and would become even stronger after the next gift. He should strike boldly and show himself the master of the game.

It was time to stop running.

Skid marks in the mud.

Seth Caleb's lips tightened grimly as he knelt and checked the tire marks. Deep, tires spinning, lurching; Jelak had peeled out in a panic. Seth had hoped to track him down before he'd become aware that he was on the hunt. But the bastard had clearly known there was a threat near.

Caleb muttered a curse as he got to his feet.

Okay, he'd lost him tonight, but Jelak wasn't going to give up Eve Duncan. When she had killed Kistle, it had placed her as a prime and immediate target in Jelak's game.

All Caleb had to do was take control of the game and change the rules.

1:35 a.m.

The woman was sitting in a chair in the living room talking on the phone. She was laughing, and there was a flush of color on her cheeks.

Jelak drew closer to the window. Good. It was always better to take them when they were at the height of emotion. Joy or terror, it didn't really matter.

Now all he had to do was get in the house or get her out. It would be difficult to get her out in this storm. He'd probably have to go in after her.

But she was standing up and going toward another room.

Time to make a move.

You can't go to bed. I have to have your gift. He's coming closer, and I'll need your strength to fight him.

He moved silently away from the window and down the stairs, carefully avoiding the hanging baskets decorating the porch.

The rain had not lessened, and he could hear distant thunder as he carefully opened the gate to the backyard. The lamplight from the house glowed cozily from the windows.

Light was always the enemy.

First came darkness, then came fear.

Seven

"Look, I know it's early but I'm just acting as an intermediary, and he wants to see you right away," Megan said, when Eve picked up the phone.

"Who wants to see me?" Eve punched up the volume on her phone as she sat up in bed and glanced at the clock: 5:40 A.M. "And why should he need an intermediary?"

"Seth Caleb. Renata says he's a distant relation and that he may know something about those goblets. He saw the fax with the goblet and immediately flew in from Edinburgh. He called me at eleven last night and asked, no, told me to call you and tell you that he was going to come to see you. He wanted to make sure that you knew he was here to help and not one of the media."

"We'll be glad to talk to anyone who can tell us anything about Jelak."

"I thought you would. But Caleb impressed me as being a little . . . I just thought I'd warn you. Renata said that he was a law unto himself and would have come whether we wanted him or not."

"You've warned me." She glanced at Joe, who was sitting up and listening. "And when should we expect him?"

"Seven." She paused. "And he said to tell Joe Quinn that he should check the west side of the lake about two miles away from the cottage."

She stiffened. "What?"

"He said the rain would have washed out most of Jelak's tire prints, but there might be something he could use."

"You're saying Jelak was in a car parked outside the cottage last night? We had the police scour all the immediate area after we found that goblet."

"Caleb said the car was set way back from the lake and well hidden."

"If Caleb knew that, then he must have been out by the lake last night too."

"Presumably. For a rainy night, those woods must have been pretty crowded." Megan added, "That's all I know. But evidently he figured it was a strong enough card to get your attention."

Eve threw back the covers. "Oh, it got our attention."

Joe was already out of bed and throwing on his clothes.

"What else can you tell me about Seth Caleb?" Eve asked. "Does Renata trust him?"

Megan hesitated. "I think she trusts his motives. I'm not sure that she'd trust his way of handling the situation. I'd say treat him as an unknown factor."

"Great. That's all we need." Eve got out of bed. "I can hardly wait to meet him. Thanks for calling, Megan. I'll let you know just what kind of unknown factor he turns out to be."

"Do that," Megan hesitated. "Is Joe all right?"

"Joe is fine. He's working hard and nary a glimpse of Nancy Jo. I'll call you later." She hung up and said to Joe, who was ready to walk out the door, "Did you hear? Two miles away on the west bank. The car was far back, away from the lake."

Joe nodded. "I'm on my way."

And she'd be right behind him, Eve thought. Two miles was much too close for comfort, and the idea of Jelak hovering out there like a vulture was frightening.

Five minutes later she was walking out the door.

"Joe told me that we're going to have a visitor." Jane got up from the swing. "And that we might have had one last night."

"What are you doing up?"

"I wanted to talk to Joe before he left this morning." She started down the steps. "And I was having trouble sleeping."

"Why did you want to talk to him?"

"It's not important now. The situation has resolved itself." She looked out at the path. "Do you think he was staking you out or that he followed me home?"

"I have no idea. Perhaps both." She started down the steps. "Maybe this Seth Caleb will be able to tell us."

"He was here." Joe was kneeling beside a deep rut in the ground when they reached him. "Whether it was Jelak remains to be seen. But the car had some weight to it. It was big."

"But you won't be able to get an impression?" Eve asked. "The print's almost washed out."

"But there's a better one in the brush that was partially protected by the trees. I have a chance of getting a decent one." He shook his head. "When he drove out of here, he was in a hell of a hurry. There are skid marks all over the place."

"Panic?" Jane asked.

"Maybe." Joe got to his feet and reached

for his phone. "But why? Our guys who are watching the cottage were nowhere near here. I wish to hell they had been. He was too damn close. I'm going to have the area searched again and then have all the cars checked for bugs. We might as well go back to meet this Caleb and try to get some answers. I'm going to phone and get a team out here to check those tire prints and try to identify the car."

"It's a Lincoln Town Car built in the nineties. Jelak always likes the luxury models."

Eve whirled to see that the man who had spoken was standing only a few yards away from them. She hadn't even heard him approach.

"I'm sorry. I didn't mean to startle you. I'm Seth Caleb. I believe you were expecting me." He smiled. "I knew you'd be out here checking my story. I thought that I'd come to meet you." He studied Eve. "You must be Eve Duncan. Yes, I can see why Jelak would target you. Even if you hadn't killed his host, you're a prime piece."

"You make me sound like a slice of meat."

"No, that's not what I meant. I was referring to a game piece." He inclined his head. "And you're definitely worth his attention. Intelligence, sophistication, and experience. How could he resist?"

"I don't know what you're talking about." Megan had said that she'd gotten the impression that he might be abrasive, but there was nothing abrasive about this man, in Eve's opinion. He was dark and sleek and cool, and that smile was charged with megawattage. High cheekbones, a faint indentation in his chin, threads of gray at his temples, full, beautifully shaped lips. He had a slight accent. Scottish? Italian? She couldn't determine the origin. "Yes. Megan called to tell us that you'd be here." She met his gaze. "She didn't tell us what you were doing out here last night, Mr. Caleb."

"I preferred to do it myself." His glance shifted to Joe. "You're Joe Quinn?"

"I'm Quinn," Joe said. "And I'm about to ask those questions and a hell of a lot more."

Caleb nodded. "But you're probably blaming yourself for not realizing that Jelak was so close to her. I think he changed locations frequently and made sure he was far out of range. He probably has a trunkful of electronic equipment to keep tabs. I'd bet that he was in these woods for at least a week or two."

Eve shook her head. "We know he was in Alabama a few days ago."

"False trail. Alabama is a quick trip. Jelak has been setting you up since he knew that he might lose Kistle."

"The goblet of blood in the refrigerator," Jane said. "That was part of the setup?"

"A gesture of bravado. To show that he could do it." Seth gazed at her for a moment. "I'm surprised he hasn't made a more meaningful gesture."

He meant Jane, Eve realized with a chill. Jane's blood, Jane's life. "We take care of our own." She whirled on her heel. "Come back to the cottage. We have some talking to do. I want to know everything you know, Caleb."

"I wouldn't be here if I didn't intend to let you help me." He gave a mocking glance at Joe. "You have certain advantages that I don't. The police usually do have a slight edge."

"We're more interested in you helping us," Joe said coldly.

"Oh, I will. Never doubt it. I'll keep Jelak away from you." He smiled. "I know this demon, and he knows me."

" 'Demon'?" Jane asked. "Monster, maybe. Not demon."

"We are what we think we are," Seth said as he followed Eve down the path. "Haven't you discovered that yet?"

"May I have a cup of coffee?" Seth Caleb

asked as he entered the cottage. "I've been up all night, and I could use the caffeine."

"Why were you up all night?" Eve went to the coffeemaker and turned it on. "Megan says you called her late last night, but that was obviously after you'd lost Jelak."

"I had some other calls to make checking what we knew about Jelak's background before he came back to the States. I don't know everything yet, but I'm close." He glanced around the cottage. "Cozy." His gaze fell on the pedestal that held the skull on which Eve was working. "For the most part."

"Before Jelak came back to the States?" Joe asked. "What are you talking about?"

"I first ran across Jelak in Fiero, a small town outside Venice, Italy. That was over ten years ago." He looked at Jane, who had dropped down on the couch. "He'd just killed a girl about your age and was on the run. Her name was Maria Givano. She was young, beautiful, and full of life. He was still experimenting at that time and wasn't sure how much blood he'd require to help him become what he thought was his destiny." His tone was without expression. "So he kept her in a cellar for three days, keeping her alive, but slowly draining her of blood. When she died, he left her there and moved on to another town." He added. "Another woman. A little older, more experienced. Youth could feed him, but that wasn't what he was looking for in the long run. He was discovering that there was an element in a more mature, intelligent woman's blood that could enrich him. As I said, he was experimenting."

"What the hell do you mean?" Joe asked. "Feed him? You make him sound like a vampire."

"Do I?" He smiled crookedly. "As I said, you are what you think you are."

Eve turned to look at him. "You're saying that Jelak thinks he's a vampire?"

"Oh, yes. Well, he's not quite reached that exalted state, but he's working on it," Caleb said. "You must have suspected as much."

"Not really. It's too weird." Eve remembered the joking reference she and Jane had made to vampires and Béla Lugosi when they had first found the goblet. "Joe said that Nancy Jo Norris's murder was a ritual killing, but that doesn't mean — Why would he think he was a vampire?"

He shrugged. "Maybe he liked the idea. From what I could find out about his early years, he would have embraced the concept. Power. Death. Darkness. Everything incorporated in one entity." He added, "I think he went to Italy to find his roots and he would have twisted those roots to be anything he wanted them to be."

" 'Loots'?" Jane grimaced. "Why go to Italy? Why not Transylvania? Isn't that supposed to be vampire home ground?"

"So all the melodramas tell us. As a matter of fact, he did go there first. Then to Spain, and finally Italy." Caleb crossed the room and held out his hand for the cup of coffee Eve had poured. "It seemed that he preferred the Latin version of bloodsucker."

"This is too wild," Jane said. "You can't expect us to believe you."

"I can't blame you if you don't." He looked down into his cup. "But you have to accept what I'm telling you if you want to bring him to his knees."

"I don't want to bring him to his knees," Joe said. "I want to put him behind bars and throw away the key."

"Then I hope I get him before you do." Caleb's smiled without mirth. "Because I do want him on his knees. It's the best possible position for me to cut the son of a bitch's head off. Let's see how fast *he* bleeds to death."

Eve felt a ripple of shock go through her as she stared at him. Cold ferocity. He meant every word. "That sounds very personal."

"Does it?" He lifted his cup to his lips. "I guess that's because that's what it is to me. I followed Jelak halfway across Europe before I lost him. He left a trail of blood behind him everywhere he went. He preferred women's blood, but he'd take children if circumstances prevented him from getting the nectar of choice."

"Why were you following him?" Jane asked. "Are you some kind of policeman?"

"Hell, no." Seth glanced challengingly at Joe. "Ask him. I think he has my measure. Don't you, Quinn?"

Joe nodded slowly. "You don't give a damn about legalities. You're an outlaw. All you want to do is kill."

"You can't say I tried to hide it." Caleb smiled recklessly. "And I think you'd just as soon kill Jelak as jail him. You're something of an outlaw yourself, Quinn."

" 'Outlaw' is a little too vague for me," Eve said. "Just what do you do, Caleb?"

"I have private means, but I occasionally help the Devanez family out with problems. I have certain skills that they find useful."

"What kind of skills?"

"I'm a hunter." He paused. "Like you, Quinn. Only I'm not bound by pesky rules and laws."

"Why?" Eve asked Caleb. "Why is it personal?"

He didn't speak for a moment. "I was very fond of Maria Givano. She was barely alive when I found her in that cellar. She told me what he'd done, what he'd said, how he'd left her when he'd had enough." His lips tightened. "And then she died. Yes, it's damn personal with me."

"I can see how it would be," Jane said quietly. "I'm sorry."

"Not as sorry as I am. Nor as sorry as he'll be." Caleb finished his coffee in two swallows. "Now can we get down to the business of finding him?"

"I'm already working on it," Joe said. "I don't need you."

"Yes, you do." He glanced at Eve, then at Jane. "You need to keep them safe. He wants Eve Duncan, but he'll take the girl to show he can do it. And to draw Eve to him."

"And how do you intend to prevent that from happening?"

"He'll be more cautious if I'm around. He has a certain respect for me." He glanced at Joe. "But, of course, you could say screw caution and just use them as bait."

"No, I don't think that we'll do that," Joe said.

"I didn't think that was an option."

"You're damn right it's not."

"Respect?" Eve had fastened on that word. "Those tire marks indicated panic rather than respect. Why was he trying so desperately to get away from you?"

He shrugged. "As I said, we know each other very well." He turned back to Joe. "He'll be making a move very soon. He'll be angry with himself for running and want to prove his strength."

"What kind of move?"

"Blood. That's always primary for Jelak." He paused. "If he feels a lack, then he goes back to the well."

"Any well in particular?"

"The victim of choice isn't always possible. Then he goes after whatever he can get."

"Like Nancy Jo Norris?" Jane asked.

He nodded. "From what I've heard, she was probably a random. He saw her and thought she might do as a fill-in."

"So he slit her throat," Joe said harshly. "She was only nineteen, dammit."

"And Maria Givano was twenty." Caleb studied him. "You're angry. I wouldn't think a detective would be quite so involved. Why?"

"You mean your friend Renata Wilger

didn't tell you why I'm involved?" Joe asked sarcastically.

"No, Renata prefers to keep me at a distance unless it's family business."

"I wonder why," Eve murmured.

"I can be . . . difficult." Caleb added to Joe, "But then I imagine you can be too."

"You bet your ass I can," Joe said. "And I'm not hearing everything that I —" His phone rang and he glanced down. "The precinct." He picked up. "Quinn."

Eve stiffened as she watched his expression. Grim. Very grim.

"I'll be right there." Joe hung up and turned to Caleb. "I believe we may have your fill-in. A woman was found in Piedmont Park an hour ago. Throat slit. Naked. All the earmarks of a ritual murder."

"Who?" Eve whispered.

"We don't know yet. She's brunette, in her twenties." He headed for the bedroom. "I've got to shower and get over there."

"I'll go with you," Caleb said.

"You will not. This is my case. Stay out of it."

"I might be able to help."

Joe looked back over his shoulder. "And you might get in my way. I don't trust you worth a damn. I've got enough problems without having to worry about Megan

Blair's weird pack of relations."

The door closed behind him.

"I may have a few problems with your Joe Quinn," Caleb murmured. "He appears a little resistant."

Jane snorted. "You don't want to have problems with Joe. He'll take you down, Caleb."

"Will he?" He tilted his head. "Interesting. But I don't have time to explore those possibilities." He turned to Eve. "If you can persuade him, you might try to do it. I'm your best chance of getting Jelak before he damages anyone close to you."

"Joe will use you if he thinks you can help," Eve said. "And nothing I can say will alter that. He does what he thinks is right." She paused. "He might have been more likely to accept your help if you'd had a chance to fill in Jelak's background a little more."

He smiled. "Or maybe not. He seems very much opposed to associating with weirdos like me."

"He has his reasons. And are you a weirdo?" Eve asked.

He was silent a moment. "I have my moments." His smile faded. "But I'm no danger to you. Unless you get in my way."

"That's not very comforting."

"I'm not here to comfort you. I'm here to kill Jelak. Of course, that may be a comfort to you too."

"And why did you think you might be able to help Joe at that crime scene?"

"I can feel Jelak when I'm close to him."

Eve's brows lifted. "Really?"

"Oh, yes." He suddenly whirled toward Jane. "You believe me, don't you?"

"I believe that it might be possible," Jane said warily. "Actually, that's only a step beyond primitive instinct. A lot of people have . . . feelings."

He smiled. "Like you?"

She didn't answer. "How certain are you that you'd know if Jelak was near?"

"Absolutely. As long as there aren't too many people around to cause interference. I have problems in the middle of cities and with apartment buildings." He shook his head. "But I'm not going to argue with your Joe about letting me come. I doubt if Jelak would be lingering about in Piedmont Park. He's not the usual serial killer, who needs the kick of watching his victim found. He got his kick when he took the blood."

"Kick?" Eve asked. "What do you mean?"

"He thinks that the blood of a fresh kill makes him stronger, jump-starts his energy quotient." He shrugged. "This kill probably had little effect on him. It was more for show, and he'll be hungry for something more substantial."

Jane grimaced. "You make him sound like a cannibal."

"There are similarities. Cannibals also devour their victims to absorb their strengths."

Eve stiffened. "Is that what he's doing? He thinks that the blood he takes will transfer the strength of those poor victims to him?"

He nodded. "That's why he tries to be selective. Every kill is a step that moves him a little closer to the end of the game. But if the victim is particularly strong or intelligent, then it's a giant step."

"Game?" Eve repeated. "This is a game to him?"

"Of course. The quintessential game. The one that started in Fiero all those years ago and won't be over until he reaches what he considers his zenith." His lips tightened. "Or I kill the son of a bitch."

"You evidently haven't managed to do that in the last ten years," Jane said dryly. "I want to know more about —"

"I'm out of here." Joe was shrugging into his jacket as he came out of the bedroom. "I'll call you when I know something, Eve."

He glanced at Seth Caleb. "Don't disappear, Caleb. Before I see you again, I'm going to know everything there is to know about your background. I'm not through with you."

"No, you're not," Caleb said. "You have no idea how far you are from being through with me. I'll give my cell-phone number to Eve." He headed for the door. "In the meantime, I'll make a few calls myself and try to pin down where Jelak might be likely to show up next." He smiled. "And I'll be more generous than you about sharing information."

"I'll share when you prove that you can give me more than a bunch of vampire crap," Joe said as he headed for the door. "Jelak is a murderer, nuts maybe, but not anything more." He opened the door. "If you can give me any details about how we can use that particular craziness to catch him, then we'll talk again."

"My, my, you weren't listening. I never said he was a vampire," Caleb said. "Just a wannabe."

"Whatever." The next moment, Joe was going down the porch steps.

Caleb reached in his jacket and handed Eve a card. "My cell number. Call me if you need me."

"I won't need you."

"You can never tell. Or if you want to talk or ask me more questions. I'm entirely open to you."

She stared at him for a long moment before shaking her head. There was no telling what was behind that bland expression that seemed to hide a thousand secrets. "There's nothing open about you, Caleb."

He smiled. "You're right, of course. But I'd make the effort for you." He turned. "Good day, ladies. I'm sure I'll see you soon."

Eve turned to Jane as Caleb left the cottage. "What do you think?"

"About Caleb?" Jane was silent a moment. "He's a powerhouse. He tries to keep it under wraps, but every now and then we get a glimpse."

"Joe doesn't think he's keeping it under wraps." Eve paused. "Joe might have been more receptive if Megan hadn't been involved. He's been very tolerant about a lot of things, but pulling this vampire hunter into the mix is a little tough on him."

"Van Helsing Caleb isn't," Jane said. "And he keeps insisting that Jelak isn't a vampire." She shivered. "But this blood stuff gives me the creeps. That poor woman in Piedmont

Park. She probably didn't know what —" She broke off, her eyes widening. "Piedmont Park. Oh, my God."

Eve's gaze flew to her face. "What?"

"Patty's house is across the street from Piedmont Park."

Eve went rigid. Dear God, please no. "It's a big area, Jane."

"She's dark-haired and in her twenties. Isn't that the description of the victim?" She moistened her lips. "I had dinner with Patty last night. I went to her house. What if I led him to her?"

She didn't know what to answer. It could have happened. "Call her."

"I'm doing it." Jane was already dialing her cell. "Answer," she murmured. "Answer me, Patty." She hung up. "Dammit, it went to voice mail." She jumped to her feet. "I'm going over there."

Eve nodded. "I'll go with you. What about the home phone?"

Jane was dialing as she walked out the door. "Disconnected."

Not good, Eve thought. She'd had the faintest hope until then. But Patty's grandfather was an invalid. Why would the main phone be disconnected? "Let's go."

They saw the first signs of police activity

four blocks from Patty's house. Squad cars and a forensic van were parked near the trees several hundred yards from the entrance. Small crowds of curiosity seekers were hovering, edging closer.

"Joe should be there by now," Eve said. "Maybe I should call him. Maybe it's not Patty."

"He would have just gotten there. He might not know yet. And we're almost at her house," Jane said. "She didn't answer the phone. I want to see for myself."

Patty's house was a small cottage with cheerful geraniums in pots hanging on the wraparound porch. The garage door was open, and Eve could glimpse a disassembled car just inside.

"That's the car Patty is working on," Jane said as she parked. "She's teaching herself how to install new brakes. With the new cars, it's hard to do without special factory equipment. She said that she —" Jane stopped and took a deep breath. "I'm yammering. I'm scared, Eve."

"Me too." Eve got out of the car. "Come on. Let's just do it." She climbed the steps. "Ring the bell."

"I don't have to." Jane's gaze was fixed on the door. "It's ajar."

A slender crack of light was issuing from

the edge of the door.

"Oh, shit," Eve whispered. She slowly reached out and pushed the door wider.

"Patty!"

It was a scream that almost shook the rafters of the house.

"What the hell?" Jane threw the door open and ran into the hall. Eve was right behind her.

"Jane?"

They whirled around to see Patty standing in the doorway behind them, a bewildered look on her face. "What are you doing here?"

Relief soared through Eve. Thank God.

"Patty!" Another shrieking yell.

Patty grimaced. "Excuse me. I have to see what he wants. You'd think he'd be able to wait. I've only been in the backyard for a few minutes or so." She hurried past them toward the back of the house. "I'm coming, Granddad. Do you need something?"

"You wouldn't care if I did." The man's voice was whining. "You'd leave me here to rot."

"You know that's not true." Patty had disappeared into the room. "What do you want?"

"My juice needs refilling. And you know I don't like to be left alone."

"I'll get it for you right away."

Patty reappeared in the hall carrying a carafe. She crossed her finger over her lips for silence and motioned them to come with her. "Sorry about that," she said, when they'd reached the kitchen. "He's not in the greatest mood. I didn't want to expose you to that waspy tongue of his."

"Why do you put up with it, Patty?" Jane asked.

"I owe him. He wasn't always like this. When I was a kid, I remember him as being . . ." She made a face. "Well, he was never sweet, but he took me in after my parents broke up, and he did the best he could. It was only when he got sick that it got bad." She went to the sink and rinsed out the carafe. "You don't want to hear this. Why did you come to see me?"

"We just wanted to make sure you were all right," Eve said. "You weren't answering your cell phone."

"I didn't have it. Granddad pitched a fit when he heard me talking on it last night, and I had to give it to him to pacify him."

"Why was he angry?"

She grinned over her shoulder. "I was talking to Charlie Brand. He called me and asked me to dinner tomorrow night."

"Charlie?" Jane smiled. "Good. I knew he

liked you."

"And I like him. We talked about fifteen minutes before Granddad pulled the plug."

"You shouldn't have let him take your phone," Eve said. "He had no right."

She shrugged. "It's easier to let him have his way. It makes him feel as if he still has power. One of the sad things about getting old and sick is that everyone seems to have power but you. I usually just let him keep it for a little while, then pick it up on one of my trips into his room."

"You're more patient than I'd be," Jane said. "He still has it?"

"I didn't need it. It was storming, and Granddad wanted me to sit with him. We had a blackout last night. We must have lost power."

"Is that why your house phone wasn't working?"

"Probably. I was out in back when you came, trying to check the ground line from the pole." She frowned. "It looks sort of funny. I have to get a better look at it as soon as I get Granddad settled again."

"Leave it to the power company," Eve said.

"I'll be careful. I just want to make sure it's not some simple connection that I could do myself."

"Patty!"

"Coming," she called. "I'd better get his juice back to him."

"We'll go," Jane said. "We just wanted to make sure you were okay."

"Why shouldn't I be?" Then she nodded. "Oh, all those police cars down the street. I was wondering. Something nasty?"

"Something very nasty," Jane said. "Promise that you'll take your phone back from your grandfather so that you can reach us."

"Sure."

"And keep your doors locked and be very careful."

Patty gave a low whistle. "It must be pretty ugly. It has to have something to do with the reason Charlie was tagging you last night."

"Right." She paused. "I was afraid I might have pulled you into it. That bastard could have seen you with me."

"And that would make me a target?"

"We don't know," Eve said. "But we have to assume it's a possibility."

"So you ran to my rescue." She suddenly smiled. "Next time, could you send Charlie? I might as well get something out of this."

Jane chuckled. "I'll ask Joe to pull some strings." Her smile faded. "If your grandfather will let him come around. Are you going out to dinner with Charlie?"

"Hell, yes. I pick my battles. I know you think I'm a wimp, but I take what I need."

"That doesn't appear to be very much," Jane said dryly.

"My choice, Jane," Patty said quietly. "In the end, we all have to decide what we're willing to give up for payback. We all have parents or grandparents or children who will need us. Agonizing decisions sometimes. You have to weigh the memories and the debt against what's being taken from you."

"Yes, your choice." Jane gave her a quick hug. "But it wouldn't hurt to let someone help. Call me if you need me."

"Only if you promise to send Charlie." She made a shooing motion. "Now get out of here. Granddad can't walk very far, but if he gets mad enough, he'll stomp in here and give us all hell."

"We're going," Eve said. "Good-bye, Patty. Be careful."

"Within reason. I can take care of myself. Granddad does a good enough job of keeping me a prisoner without my helping it along." She was heading for the fridge. "Bye. Give Toby a hug for me."

Jane didn't speak until they had reached the car. "Damn, I was scared." She frowned.

"I wish she was more frightened. She didn't seem too worried. She thinks she can handle anything."

"If she can handle that old man, she may be right." They were passing the entrance to the park. "There are two media trucks there now. All hell will probably be breaking loose anytime now."

"It already broke loose." Jane was silent a moment. "Can we get surveillance for Patty?"

"We'll try. We have to show cause. Once the media publishes details, I'm sure everyone in this neighborhood is going to want police protection." She smiled. "But Patty had a good idea. Why don't you call Charlie Brand? I'm sure he'd volunteer."

Eight

Joe called Eve after noon that day. "The victim is Heather Carmello. Age twenty-five, prostitute, throat slit, naked."

"Footprints?"

"Clean as a whistle. How the hell he managed it in all that rain and mud is a wonder." He paused. "There was no goblet at the scene."

"And what does that mean?"

"Beats the hell out of me."

"But you still think it's Jelak?"

"Hell, yes."

"Jane and I were afraid the victim might be Patty Avery. Jane thought that she might have led Jelak to her last night. Is there any way we can get a house watch?"

"Maybe, not from the department. I can hire someone." He added, "I'll look into it later. I've got to tie this up and get back to the precinct. Do you need anything?"

"No."

"Then I'll answer the question you didn't ask. No, to my profound relief, Heather Carmello has decided to stay dead. No ghostly appearance."

"That's good . . . I guess."

"No guess about it. And you can do me a favor and call Seth Caleb and get him to come back and answer a few more questions."

"Really? You practically tossed him out of the house."

"I wasn't going to have him shadowing my every move, and the less I have to do with the spook brigade, the better I'll like it. But since Heather Carmello has decided that I'm not to be her significant other, I feel like I'm on a roll. I can afford to let Caleb into closer quarters. And I need to know about that goblet. It seems to be a part of the ritual, and I want to know what the omission means."

"I'll call him. When do you want to see him?"

"Tonight. I should be through with the paperwork by six. Let's meet him at Rico's Restaurant near the precinct. I'll get back to you later." He hung up.

Eve slowly pressed the disconnect before she said to Jane, "Heather Carmello. No goblet. He wants to ask Caleb if there's any significance."

"Well, you said Béla Lugosi usually took the blood straight from the source. Maybe Jelak thinks he's moved up in the world."

"Guesswork again. We need to know." She reached in her pocket and took out the card Caleb had given her. It was heavy plain paper with only the cell number scrawled on it. "So let's see if Caleb can tell us."

Before she could place the call, her phone rang.

Montalvo.

"I saw the Heather Carmello murder on the news. I would have liked to have heard it from you. Purely in the name of co-operation."

He was obviously not pleased. She probably should have told him since she couldn't discount the information he'd given them. Well, she just couldn't help it. She was having enough problems. "I've been busy."

"Then don't close me out, and you won't be so busy."

"Montalvo, I won't have you out here disturbing Joe. He has enough problems. Keep out of it."

He was silent a moment. "Very well. I won't be on your doorstep, but I do want to help. Tell me how I can do it."

He wasn't going to give up. She tried to

think. "My mother. Sandra Duncan. She lives in a condo downtown. I don't believe she'd be a target for Jelak, but we should have some protection for her. Will you do that for me, Montalvo?"

"Your mother. You've never talked about her very much. You're not close?"

"It's been an up-and-down relationship. I don't see much of her these days. At one time, we were very close."

"When your Bonnie was alive?"

"Yes. Will you make sure she's safe?"

"You can be sure of it." He paused. "You can always be sure of me, Eve." He hung up.

Eve turned away as she hung up the phone. "I guess I'd better call Sandra and tell her that she's going to be under surveillance for a while. Or maybe not. Montalvo will be careful, and I don't want to alarm her."

"I've never gotten used to you calling her Sandra."

"It was her choice when I was growing up. It made her feel younger. It still makes her feel young. That's important to her since she's on her fourth marriage."

"You never called her Mother?"

"No, but Bonnie called her Grandma. She didn't mind. She didn't mind anything Bonnie did." She looked down at the card Caleb had given her. "And now I guess I'd better make that call to Caleb."

"I'll do it. You probably want to get to work." Jane took the card. "I think I'll go out on the porch. I need to relax for a few minutes. It's been quite a morning."

Eve watched her as she went out the door before she turned to the reconstruction. She did want to get to work, but she was feeling on edge and distracted.

Montalvo?

No, not Montalvo. It had been talking about her mother and Bonnie. It had brought back too many memories. From the day Bonnie was born, it had been a golden time for Eve and her mother. Her little girl had seemed to bridge all the bitterness and resentment that Eve had felt toward a mother who had been a crack addict from the time Eve could remember. It had been Bonnie who had held that fragile relationship together by the sheer love they had both felt for her. It was Bonnie who had spurred her grandmother to suffer through painful withdrawal just so she could be with her grandchild. Even on that last day in the park, Eve could remember how Sandra had glowed with happiness while she was pushing Bonnie in the swing.

■ ■ ■ ■

"Enough." Sandra stood back and wiped her forehead. "I'm getting too old for this. Go get your mother to push you, Bonnie."

"That's okay. I'm ready to get down." Bonnie slipped out of the swing. "Thanks, Grandma." She ran up to Eve, who was sitting on the bench. Her cheeks were blazing pink with happiness, and her eyes were shining. "Did you see how high I went? We should make up a song about swings and going up, up, up."

"I'm sure someone already did. But we could make up another one."

"And about the sunshine, and the trees, and . . . oh, everything."

"That will be a very long song. But we'll take a stab at it tonight. It's almost time to go home, baby."

"Not yet." She threw herself into Eve's arms. "Ten more minutes, Mama. Please. Please. Please. I want to go and get an ice cream."

"Where?"

"Right over there. That booth by that big tree."

Eve caught a glimpse of a white stand with red lettering through the shifting crowd of parents and children. "Okay. Let's go."

"I can go by myself." Bonnie was already running toward the ice-cream stand, darting in and out of the crowds. "Grandma already gave me the money. I'll be right back."

Eve smiled at Sandra. "Grandma already gave her the money? Grandma is spoiling her rotten."

Sandra shook her head. "Not possible. What's an ice cream?" She smiled. "I love her in that Bugs Bunny T-shirt. I was wondering if maybe we could afford to take her to Disney World this year."

"I'm pretty strapped for cash." But the thought of Bonnie's face when she was confronted with all that magic was very tempting. "Maybe if I could get a second job . . ."

"Only for a little while. I know you're working hard at school too," Sandra said. "But she'd love Cinderella's Castle."

Not only love it, but be dazzled. A dazzled Bonnie was too much to resist. "We'll work it out."

"I can't wait to tell her," Sandra said, her gaze going to the ice-cream stand that had once again come into view as the crowds shifted. "Will you let me do it, Eve?"

She was as childishly excited as Bonnie had been when she'd dashed for the ice-cream stand. "Okay, but don't give a date. I have to see what I can —"

"Where is she?" Sandra interrupted. "I don't see her."

"What?" Eve frowned, her gaze flying to the ice-cream stand. "But she was right there. I saw her a minute ago in front of the stand."

But she wasn't there now. No little girl in a Bugs Bunny T-shirt and wild red curls.

Eve jerked to her feet in a panic.

"Bonnie!"

Keep calm. Even now the memory of that moment of terror was bringing back all the horror of the nightmare.

Get busy. Eve whirled toward the reconstruction of Matt on the pedestal. She began to work swiftly, frantically. "Help me, Matt." Her fingers started smoothing the clay. "And I'll help you."

"We've got it patched." The burly Georgia Power repairman was coming toward Patty with a clipboard in his hand. "Sorry it took so long." He held up the wire. "I had to cut it and splice in a new wire."

"No problem." Patty couldn't take her gaze from the remains of the wire coiled in his hand. "You did a neat job."

"That's not my work. It was severed where it reached the house." He shook his head. "It was cut through."

She stiffened. "How?"

"Don't ask me, lady. Whoever did it knew what they were doing, or they would have been electrocuted."

"Someone cut it?" She shook her head. "I thought it was caused by the storm."

"We didn't have any outages last night in this area."

"That's what they told me when I called your office to report the power loss," she said absently, her gaze on the wire.

"You should have believed them." He handed her the clipboard and a pen. "Sign there."

She signed her name and handed him the board. "You're sure? Couldn't something have fallen on it? Maybe a branch that would tear it and —"

"It was snipped clean as a whistle," he repeated. "It might not be a bad idea to call the police and make out a report on this." His gaze went across the street to the park. "Some bad things are happening around here lately."

"I may do that."

"Do you want this?" He held up the coiled wire.

"No." Good God, it was actually reminding her of a serpent. Silly. That wasn't like her. No one was more practical or less imaginative than she. "Just throw it in the garbage can on your way out."

"Right."

She watched him go out the gate before she slowly followed him. She should get back to Granddad. She'd already been away from him too long. There was little doubt she'd be in for one of his tantrums.

The coiled wire was on top of the trash as she reached the front of the house.

Some bad things are happening around here.

She shivered. Yes, they were. And for the first time she felt as if those bad things were creeping close to her.

Stop standing here staring at that damn wire. She lifted her shoulders as if to shrug off that heavy burden. Just go inside and soothe down Granddad and make his supper, then think about what she should do.

If that crazy son of a bitch was trying to make her a victim, then she'd find a way to blow him out of the water.

Seth Caleb was already waiting in the reception area at Rico's when Eve and Jane walked into the restaurant.

He smiled. "This is an interesting place. Sombreros on the walls and policemen at every table."

"The food is good, and it's close to the precinct," Eve said. "Joe should be here any minute."

"He's here now," Joe said from behind her. "I would have been here sooner, but Ed Norris stopped me when I was leaving." He hailed a white-aproned waiter. "A table, Marco."

Marco smiled. "Right away, Detective. Only one minute."

"Why meet here?" Caleb asked. "Am I supposed to be intimidated by all this display of legal might?"

"If you have reason to be," Joe said. "But I didn't want to wait until I got home to question you. There's a chance I might have to go back to the precinct to check out something you tell me."

"What trust." Caleb gestured for Jane and Eve to precede him as the waiter led them to a table. "But at least you think I have something to contribute." He waited until they were all seated and had ordered drinks before he continued, "Tell me about Heather Carmello. The information on the news was very sketchy."

"We weren't hiding anything from the media. She was a prostitute who usually worked the bars on Peachtree. Same MO as the Norris killing."

Caleb stared him in the eye. "Except?"

"No goblet. Does that have significance?"

"Oh, yes."

"Then what the hell does it mean?" Joe said through his teeth, when Caleb didn't elaborate. "Do I have to pull it out of you?"

"No, I wouldn't be here if I didn't intend to tell you what you need."

"He's pissed at you, Joe," Jane said bluntly. "He wants to give you a few needles before he lets you have what you want."

"Exactly." Caleb smiled at Jane. "How perceptive you are." He turned back to Joe. "But I'm through with that for the time being. What do you want to know?"

"Tell me about Jelak in Fiero. Tell me about the ritual. Tell me about the goblet."

"In what order?"

Eve had had enough. "Don't play games with us," she said curtly. "A woman was killed last night. You think Jane may be on his list too. I won't have her in danger because we don't know enough."

"You don't mention that you're his prime target." Caleb smiled. "I find that curious."

"Tell us," Eve said. "Everything."

Caleb shrugged. "There are people fascinated with vampires all over the planet. Your United States is particularly fond of the concept. Movies, best-selling books, TV series. It's no wonder Jelak became so obsessed with them."

"It's entertainment," Jane said. "No one believes they actually exist."

"People believe what they want to believe. Particularly if they're unstable to begin with. I'm sure you've found out by now that Jelak has always had an affinity for blood. He collected vials of blood from the time he was a boy."

"We just recently found that out. How did you know that?" Eve asked.

"I had an extremely violent discussion with Jelak's teacher, Master Franco Donari. Jelak had bared his soul to Donari while he was teaching him."

"Teaching him what?" Joe asked.

"The way to win the game," he said softly.

"You mentioned a game before. What the hell do you mean?" Eve asked.

"Blood Game. The path that would lead Jelak to his heart's desire." He glanced at Joe's impatient expression. "I'm getting to it. Give me a little time." He took a sip of the margarita the waiter had set before him. "Franco Donari was a member of a cult group located in Fiero, Italy. It was a fairly small group, a dozen or so, whose members bragged that they were of the true blood and had all kinds of rituals and ceremonies to glorify themselves."

"They actually thought they were vampires?"

"Yes, or on their way. They conveniently forgot the stories about the effects of garlic, or crosses, or melting in the sunlight. That would have been uncomfortable. But they embraced the power and the fear."

"Ridiculous."

"I can't argue with you there, but they'd bought into the idea and developed it along the lines they wanted it to go. They looked upon themselves as scholars above the rest of humanity. When Jelak discovered them, he thought he'd found a home. But to his chagrin he found that it wasn't that easy. He couldn't just join the fraternity. He had to earn his way."

"Killing?" Jane asked.

He nodded. "And the ingesting of the blood. The cult doctrine preached that eternal life and godlike powers could only be attained by taking the life and blood of many truly exceptional victims. That way he could gain all their strength and power until he reached his exalted state. It was supposedly an odyssey that could take years."

"He killed a prostitute last night," Joe said. "That wasn't very selective."

"No, that may have just been a gesture of

defiance. Or he could have reached out and took her to soothe the hunger."

"Hunger?" Eve said.

"Donari says that after years of continuous blood taking, Jelak probably developed an appetite that had to be appeased. That's why Donari told Jelak that he should find a host that would provide him with basic sustenance and free him to search out his exceptional kills." He took another drink. "Jelak told him that he had someone in mind. He didn't give him a name, or I'd have been able to locate Jelak a hell of a lot sooner."

"Kistle," Eve said.

"Probably. I'd bet that he was hovering around Kistle like a vulture." He met her gaze across the table. "He let Kistle do his work for him. When Kistle made a kill, he'd follow him and take the blood he needed from the victim. Of course, it was only an appeasement. I understand Kistle was big on killing children, and they usually don't have time to become exceptional."

She flinched. "I disagree. Every life is exceptional."

He nodded. "I'm speaking from Jelak's point of view."

"It's a hideous point of view." She looked down into her drink. "So he was stirred into moving when we went after Kistle?"

"You killed his host, and that was a major inconvenience. He'd have to do his own basic feed killing, and that would keep him from concentrating on reaching his ultimate goal."

"The goblet," Joe reminded him.

"The goblet was part of the cult ritual. The man standing before the table was the one who took the gift of life. The other men at the table represented the stages that the candidate would have to go through before he reached his goal. The goblet was to be used only for specific purposes. A truly exceptional kill or perhaps a warning. It was never used on one considered unworthy."

"The goblet in my refrigerator," Eve murmured.

"A warning," Caleb said. "And so was the death of Nancy Jo Norris. He considered you very special and wanted to make sure you made the connection. But he must have found Nancy Jo's blood superior because he left her the goblet."

"And the prostitute in the park?"

"Not worthy of full ritual."

"This Donari gave you chapter and verse about his cult, didn't he?" Jane asked.

"With a good deal of persuasion. Yes, he was very helpful."

"You said he was Jelak's teacher. What did he teach him?"

"Burglary, lock picking, the art of choosing a host, how to slit a throat in two seconds. Any number of other skills."

"All very good skills for his chosen career." Jane was studying Caleb's face. "And where is Donari now?"

"He's no longer with us." He met her gaze. "Neither are any other members of the cult. After Donari died, they took off from Fiero in quite a hurry. It took me years to track them all down."

"You said there were a dozen in the cult," Eve said.

"Yes." He lifted his drink to his lips. "And they stood by and let Jelak experiment with Maria Givano. I thought it time that we said good-bye to that particular cult."

He's a powerhouse.

Eve remembered Jane's words as she gazed at Caleb. Power and deadliness and relentless energy.

"Then the goblet was omitted because Jelak didn't consider Heather Carmello worthy," Joe said.

"More than probably. You can be sure if the victim had been our lovely Jane that we would have found a goblet."

"Be quiet," Joe said. "That wasn't necessary, Caleb."

"No, but it bothers you more than it does Jane." He lifted his glass to Jane. "Which I admit might have been my intention. Well, have I told you all you want to know, Quinn?"

"Maybe. Except about yourself."

His brows rose. "I thought I'd been very frank."

"Perhaps too frank. You're not stupid, and yet you as much as admitted to multiple homicide."

"You'd have to prove it. And as you say, I'm not stupid enough to let you do that. I just wanted to give you —"

Jane's cell phone rang, and she glanced at the ID. "I'm sorry, I have to answer this. It's Patty Avery." She pushed her chair back. "I'll take it in the bar."

Joe watched her cross the restaurant before he turned back to Caleb. "What did you want to give me?"

"The knowledge that I'm totally committed to getting Jelak." Caleb leaned forward, his dark eyes glittering and intense. "What do you say, Quinn," he said softly. "Let's go hunting."

Damn, he was persuasive, Eve thought. She couldn't keep her gaze from his face. At that moment, his intensity was almost hypnotic.

Evidently not to Joe. He leaned back and shook his head. "I plan on going hunting. But you're not invited."

"Yes I am. Or you wouldn't have brought me here tonight. You said you wanted information. I gave it to you. Now let me help you find him."

"So that you can kill him. We don't want the same thing, Caleb."

"Actually, we do. I've done my research on you, Quinn. Ex-SEAL, former FBI agent. That's an odd balancing act. Violence and law. With which are you most comfortable?"

"None of your business."

Caleb smiled. "Never mind. I think I know."

"How?" Joe asked sarcastically. "Do you feel it? Like you do Jelak."

"No, I can't do that with everyone. I'm just a student of human nature." He looked up and watched Jane coming back across the restaurant. "But it doesn't take an expert to know that your Jane is a little upset."

More than a little, Eve thought, as Jane reached the table.

"Is something wrong with Patty?"

Jane nodded. "I'm going over to see her.

She found out her power line was deliberately cut last night. She doesn't want to involve the police because she knows it will upset her grandfather. I'm going to have to convince her to do it anyway." She picked up her purse. "I'll take a taxi. I'll see you at home."

"No, I'll go with you," Eve said.

Jane shook her head. "It will be difficult enough for Patty having me there. You saw how her grandfather behaved. He doesn't like anyone in the house. I'm not letting you in for a tantrum."

"This is your friend, Patty?" Seth Caleb asked. "It happened last night?"

"Patty Avery. Yes."

"Curious."

Eve's gaze narrowed on his face. "What are you thinking?"

"I believe in connections. And definitely not in coincidences. Is that the only thing that happened to her last night?"

"Yes, she thought the power outage might be the storm."

"But now she's worried?" Caleb said.

"She lives across the street from Piedmont Park," Eve said.

"Connections," Caleb murmured. He tilted his head. "Jane, will you call her back and ask her to do something?"

"What?"

"Look in her refrigerator."

Eve felt a chill. "And what is she to look for?"

"You know," Caleb said softly. "He didn't think the kill was worthy. We have a missing goblet. Would he have thought your friend worthy? Is she strong, clever?"

"Yes," Jane said.

"Go ahead. Call her," Joe said curtly.

"Your faith is touching." Caleb smiled. "Do you believe in connections, too, Quinn?"

"I believe in the process of elimination."

"I hope you're wrong." Jane was already dialing. "Damn, I hope you're wrong." She spoke into the phone. "Hi, I'm on my way, but I'd like you to do me a favor. Would you take a look in your refrigerator and tell me if you find anything? Thanks." She waited, and when Patty came back on the phone, she smiled. "That's good. Are you sure?" She had a thought. "Check in the back, maybe a lower shelf."

She waited again.

"Shit." She drew a deep breath. "No, don't touch it again. I'll tell Joe, and he'll send someone to come and get it. I'll be there myself in fifteen minutes." She paused. "Lock your doors, Patty." She hung up and looked at Caleb. "Gold goblet with carvings. Blood residue. How did you know?"

Joe muttered a curse and reached for his phone.

Caleb shrugged. "A guess. Connections. He wanted vindication and revenge. He couldn't hit at you, so he went after your friend, Patty." He shrugged. "But something went wrong, and he couldn't get to her either. So he took another kill and used the goblet as a threat. Would you mind if I came along and took a look?"

"No." Joe was on the phone talking to the precinct, and he glanced up to say, "This is now an official police investigation."

"And there's nothing official about me," Caleb said. "But I found your lost goblet before he had a chance to refill it with the target of choice. Doesn't that count for something?"

"It counts for a hell of a lot," Jane said. She looked at Joe. "Patty is my friend. She may be in this trouble because of me. You do what you like on an official level. I'll take help where I can get it." She turned back to Caleb. "I don't care if you can hear him or smell him or feel him. Any way you can get Jelak is fine with me."

"I assure you I can't hear or smell Jelak. Feeling is bad enough. May I drive you to your Patty's house?"

"Yes." She looked at Eve. "It's okay. Can't you see? He's brimming with hate, but it's not for anyone but Jelak."

"But he'd offer any of us up as a sacrifice to get him." Eve rose to her feet. "I don't care about her grandfather. I'm coming with you. Her house is going to be teeming with police and forensic people anyway." She glanced at Caleb. "You can follow us."

"Fine." He got to his feet. "We'll see you there, Quinn."

"You certainly will," Joe said grimly as he hung up the phone. "And you'll stay out of my way."

"By all means; I'm just happy to be allowed to trail along."

Eve shook her head. She was remembering Caleb, all power and intensity, inviting Joe to go hunting. If Caleb was "trailing" along, it was a deceptive move that was only designed to get him what he wanted.

Jane was gazing at Eve, reading her expression. "We don't have to trust him. He can help Patty. That's all that matters, isn't it?"

Eve nodded. "That's all that matters."

NINE

"I didn't expect you, Eve. It's bad enough that I bothered Jane with it." Patty made a face as she opened the door. "Sorry about this."

"So am I," Eve said. "And there's nothing to be sorry for. We may have brought this down on you." She turned to Caleb, who was coming up the steps. "This is Seth Caleb. He's something of an expert on Jelak, and we thought you wouldn't mind if we let him come."

Patty frowned. "You mean he's a sort of profiler?"

"Sort of." Caleb smiled. "I won't be long. Joe Quinn will be arriving shortly with his tech crews, and he won't want me bothering him."

"Great," Patty said dryly. "Techs running all over the house. Granddad will have a cow."

"It's best," Jane said. "You know that, Patty."

"I was hoping just to fill out a report on that power line." Patty looked at Caleb. "But that goblet screwed me up, didn't it? It's the same man who killed those women?"

"It's a very good possibility. Could I see the goblet?"

She jerked her head in the direction of the kitchen. "It's on the counter next to the refrigerator." She moistened her lips. "How did he get into the house? I locked the door last night."

"Jelak was trained to get past locks." He moved toward the kitchen. "I'm just wondering why all he did was leave the goblet."

"You mean you're wondering why he didn't slit my throat?" Patty shivered. "I've been wondering that too."

"Was there anything different about your routine last night?"

"I talked on the phone for quite a while before the power went off. That was a little different. Granddad didn't like it. Then he was nervous because of the power outage and wanted me to stay with him."

"How long?"

"All night. I slept in the chair by his bed."

"You didn't leave the room to get him anything?"

"No, he'd already had his medicine." She gazed at him. "You think that murderer

Jelak was in the house waiting for his chance, don't you?"

Caleb nodded. "I think if you'd left your grandfather's room anytime during those first few hours, you'd have been the victim and not Heather Carmello."

"Why didn't he come into Granddad's bedroom and try to kill us both?"

"That's not according to ritual. He would have considered it crude. It has to be one-on-one. He probably stayed until he thought you were in there for the night, then went after someone else."

"What about the goblet? There was blood . . ."

"He came back, didn't he?" Eve asked. "He took the chance of coming twice. After the kill, he wanted to show how easily it could have been Patty."

"Dear God," Jane murmured.

Caleb nodded. "It was a gesture of bravado. He had to make a statement this time." He paused at the kitchen door. "And he probably wanted to check to make sure Patty was still with her grandfather. Usually, he'd limit the kill to one a night. The ingestion isn't pure otherwise. But in this case, he wouldn't have minded another ritual. He didn't take Heather Carmello's blood for himself."

"You're so damn casual," Patty said. "It's *my* blood you're talking about."

"I'm not casual," Caleb said. "I hate the idea of what Jelak is doing. I'm just trying to answer your questions. You can't fight him if you're ignorant of what he is."

"You certainly know what he is. You must have studied him for a long time," Patty said.

"Long enough. The kitchen is that way?"

They followed him as he went into the kitchen and squatted to look at the goblet on the counter. He stared at it for a long time. "It's Jelak. And it's the same."

"But you knew it probably was him," Jane said. "And what do you mean the same? Were you expecting something different?"

"You're very observant." Caleb rose to his feet. "There's a possibility that the goblet could have been different. Though I wouldn't expect it, considering Jelak's actions."

"What kind of difference?"

"The number of the men at the table. The ones that represent the twelve stages that Jelak has to pass through before he reaches his final goal. That could change."

"Patty!"

"Granddad," Patty said wearily. "I have to go to him and explain before Joe and the forensic techs get here. Lord, I don't want to deal with this right now."

"Would you like me to take care of it?" Caleb asked. "I've had training in this kind of thing."

"I thought you were a profiler?"

He shrugged. "It all has to do with psychology."

"No one's trained to deal with Granddad," Patty said. "He's going to raise hell. I wouldn't put anyone through it."

"Let me try." He headed for the door. "Sometimes a stranger has better luck than a family member. I wouldn't want Quinn to have a bad time when he gets here. Which room?"

Patty hesitated. "Second bedroom off the hall."

"And what's his first name?"

"Marcus."

He nodded and disappeared down the hall.

"I shouldn't have let him do it," Patty said. "It's my job."

"Then he should know that within a few minutes," Jane said. "I'm glad that he's going to try. You look beat."

"It scared me," Patty said. "The idea of anyone being in the house and me not knowing it. It's like a horror movie I saw once." She paused. "And this guy belongs in a horror movie, doesn't he?"

"Yes," Eve said. "Jelak qualifies."

Patty shuddered. "Do you think he's right about Jelak killing me if I'd left Granddad's room that night?"

"I wish I could say he was wrong," Jane said. "But he seems to know Jelak."

Patty nodded. "Those details were pretty —" She stopped. "I think I hear cars outside. Joe must be here." She grimaced. "And that means your Seth Caleb didn't have enough time to explain much of anything to Granddad. I'm surprised I haven't heard him screaming for me yet. I'll go and let Joe in and try to run interference when he goes in to talk to Granddad."

"Joe can take care of himself," Eve said, as she and Jane followed her toward the front door. "Stop trying to shoulder everything yourself, Patty."

"It goes with the territory," Patty said. "Just because I called you for help tonight doesn't mean I have to saddle anyone else with —"

"Be quiet," Jane said. "We're friends. We'll do what friends do. Support. Now, do you have a couch where I can sleep? I'm going to move in with you for a few days. Your grandfather can just get used to me."

"No way," Patty said flatly. "No one is going to hover over me and hold my hand."

"Look, this may be my fault. I need to —"

"She's right, Jane," Caleb said from the doorway of her grandfather's room. "You shouldn't come here. It's what Jelak wants to happen. You'll be more vulnerable than you would be with Eve and Quinn." The doorbell rang, and he smiled. "And, even as we speak, there's Quinn. I'd better prepare to make my departure. I tend to annoy him." He moved toward the door. "I think Marcus will be okay for a while. I didn't have much time, but he seemed willing to cooperate."

"Cooperate?" Patty repeated. "Granddad?"

"No guarantees," Caleb said. "But since he really cares about you, there's a chance." He stepped forward and opened the door. "Hello, Quinn. I was just leaving. You'll be glad to know I didn't disturb a thing. Ask Eve."

"I'll do that." He looked at Patty. "Are you okay?"

She nodded. "A little uneasy. No, dammit, big-time scared." She glanced at the four forensic techs coming up the steps. "And they make it seem too real."

"We'll be in and out as quick as we can." He paused. "We'll need statements from both you and your grandfather."

"He doesn't know anything."

"I'm sorry. We have to get a statement." Joe stepped aside for the team to enter. "Where's the goblet?"

"In the kitchen."

"I'll show you." Jane started across the room toward the hall.

"And I'll go prepare Granddad," Patty said. "It's not going to do any good, Joe. He'll rave and rant at you, and there's nothing he can really tell you."

"I have to do it, Patty."

"Whatever." She shrugged and moved toward her grandfather's room.

"Good-bye, Eve," Caleb said. "I'm sure I'll see you again soon." He turned back to Joe. "Jelak is nowhere near here, Quinn. I thought perhaps he might be. He was trying to draw Eve and Jane into the web and using Patty as bait. I wasn't sure if he could resist making contact or at least being near them. But I can't sense any trace of him. He's not here."

"That's why you wanted to come here?"

Caleb nodded. "And I had to check out the goblet." He moved out on the porch. "Call me if you need me. I'll be in touch."

He strode down the steps and toward his car, parked across the street.

Joe turned back toward Eve. "Was he telling the truth?"

"About not disturbing anything?" Eve nodded. "Except Patty's nerves. He told her a little too much more about Jelak than she was comfortable with." She added, "And he examined that carving on that goblet very closely. He was looking for something. He said something about the number of the men changing."

"What?"

She shook her head. "He said that it was still the same. Then Patty's grandfather called her, and Caleb didn't mention anything else about it."

"A teaser?"

"I don't believe Caleb would —" She shrugged. "He's pretty up-front. Probably because it suits him to be. But he didn't appear to be trying to hide anything." She looked at him. "And he didn't want Jane to stay here with Patty. He said that was what Jelak wanted."

"He's right. It would be the worse possible move. I wouldn't let —"

"He's ready to see you, Joe." Patty stood in the doorway of the bedroom. "Anytime you're ready."

"Now." He strode toward the door. "It's only a preliminary, and I'll be through in a few minutes, Patty. We'll have to ask him to sign a statement later."

"Okay." Patty nodded and stepped aside as he entered the bedroom.

"Patty?" Eve's gaze was on Patty's face. She looked dazed. "What's wrong?"

"Granddad."

Eve stiffened. "Is he all right? Did Caleb hurt him?"

"I . . . don't know," Patty said. "Maybe."

"What do you mean?"

She gazed at Eve in bewilderment. "Granddad smiled at me."

Two hours later, Eve walked Joe to his car parked on the street.

"I'll be home as soon as I get my report written out," Joe said. "And I'm leaving one of the squad cars here to escort you and Jane back to the cottage." He said curtly, "Don't let her stay here, Eve."

"Patty wouldn't let her do it." She smiled. "Neither would I. Stop worrying."

He shook his head. "That's not going to happen."

Eve didn't speak for a moment. "You had no trouble getting a statement from Patty's grandfather?"

"No, he was very cooperative. He didn't know anything, but he was patient, even pleasant."

"Really. That's unusual."

"Yeah, I know Patty says he's difficult. Maybe he was having a good day." He shrugged. "Anyway, it made my job easier."

"That's what Caleb said. He said he wanted to try to make your job easier."

"So he talked the old man into giving me a break?" Joe asked skeptically. "He was a stranger to him. I doubt if he'd have any influence."

"And he was only in the room for a few minutes." Eve paused. "Weird."

"*He's* weird," Joe said. "And I'm tired of dealing with weirdos." He shook his head. "But I guess someone could call me that, couldn't they?"

"Not anyone who had a good sense of self-preservation," Eve said. She watched him get into his car. "But, yes, Caleb is definitely a little bizarre." And she was tired of dealing with the bizarre too. She wanted a return to the norm. She was desperately missing their steady, down-to-earth, day-to-day routine.

What was she thinking? Any steadiness that they'd had in these years had been fleeting at best. And it had always been her choices that had thrown them into turmoil. She stepped away from the car. "I'll see you back at the cottage."

He nodded as he pulled away from the curb. "I've decided I'm going to release a photo of Jelak to the media. I can only say we want him for questioning in the killings since we don't have a damn bit of proof. But I'll feel better about having his face out there for everyone to recognize."

"I will too."

"And I'm leaving a squad car here at the house for Patty."

She smiled. "Can you arrange for Charlie Brand to take the first watch? She'd feel safer."

"I'll put in a request."

"Do that." She watched his car until it rounded the corner before turning back to the house. Jane was just leaving and saying good-bye to Patty on the porch. Patty waved to Eve, then turned and went back into the house.

"I still think I should stay with her," Jane said as she walked toward Eve. "But she won't have it."

"Neither would Joe and I," Eve said. "Caleb was right. That's what Jelak would want you to do." She got into her car. "And Patty will have protection. There's no problem now that there's proof she's involved in the case."

"No, I'd say that's a definite." She shivered. "The idea of him sitting only a room away just waiting like a spider in his web for her to come to him gives me the creeps." She paused. "Again, if Caleb is right about that happening. We're just taking it for granted that he is."

"He's very convincing."

"He managed to convince Patty's granddad." Jane got into the passenger seat. "She's freaked out about it. She said it's almost as if he's not her grandfather."

"That much difference?"

Jane nodded. "He took her hand and told her that she had to take care of herself. She said she couldn't remember a gesture of affection from him all the time she was growing up."

"Sad."

"She was used to it. She's not used to warmth and caring from him. She's wondering if he's had a stroke or something."

"Or something."

"It's as if Caleb hypnotized him."

Eve remembered that moment in the restaurant when she'd thought Caleb's intensity was almost hypnotic. "Not likely. It takes time to induce hypnosis, and he was only in that room for a few moments. Maybe what he said to the old man just struck the right note."

"He said something about her grandfather really caring about her. If that's true, you'd never know it from the way he treats her."

"Sometimes people can't show how they feel." Eve started the car. "Maybe he's one of them."

"Until Caleb walked in and had a talk with him," Jane said. "Crazy . . ."

"Yes," Eve said. "But what hasn't been crazy since Jelak appeared in our lives? We just have to deal with it."

"I'm on my way home," Joe told Eve, when she picked up the call at the cottage two hours later. "I just left the precinct, so it will be forty minutes or so. Is everything okay there?"

"Yes, I'm working, and Jane is out on the porch with Toby. Have you eaten?"

"I grabbed a sandwich from the machine." He paused. "Charlie Brand will take over surveillance tomorrow morning. I couldn't get him tonight."

"Good enough," Eve said. "It will be like having a friend out there. Patty needs all the friends she has around her right now. I'll see you soon." She hung up.

Eve had sounded abstracted, Joe thought as he hung up. But then she was always abstracted when she was working. After the first measurements of the skull, she became totally engrossed in the process of turning clay into a perfect replica of the face of the victim. It was a combination of scientific exploration and sheer instinct and creativity. When she'd finished putting on her tissue depth markers, the skull resembled a voodoo doll. Then she started taking strips of plasticene and building up the spaces between the markers and lastly came the smoothing and working of the clay. She always told him that there was no such thing as perfection in forensic sculpting, but Eve came very close. He always thought that her instinct became almost magical as the face grew beneath her fingers.

At any rate, he was glad that she was doing something that would keep her mind off Jelak. The bastard was coming closer every minute and touching people they both cared about. Patty had been a part of their lives for years and that goblet was —

"He didn't want Patty," Nancy Jo said. "Eve is the only one he wants."

That car swerved as he glanced at the passenger seat. She was sitting there, next to him.

"No!" He drew a deep breath, his hands tightening on the steering wheel. "I thought I was rid of you. What are you doing here?"

"You didn't come back to the lake. I had to come to you." She frowned. "It wasn't easy. I didn't know how to do it. Someone had to teach me."

"Then you should have stayed there. I'm doing everything I can do."

"He's still alive. He still has my blood. And Daddy is getting impatient. I can feel it."

"Then go get someone to teach you how to reach him. Your father is damn persistent. I'm not going to be able to stop him."

"I know." Her blue eyes were full of tears. "He won't give up. He has someone following you right now."

"What?"

"The blue Camry in the next lane. It's someone he hired to keep an eye on you. He didn't like it that you wouldn't take a bribe."

"You seem to know a lot about what's going on."

"I'm learning. I have to learn. No one is helping me . . . except her."

"Except who?"

"The little girl."

He stiffened. "What little girl?"

"The one who taught me how to come to

you. She said I should get away from the place where it happened. She said if I was going to stay, I should go away somewhere and begin to heal."

"She appears very knowledgeable about this kind of situation," he said.

"Yes, she said it happened a long time ago for her. I liked her. She wasn't like the others. She didn't try to push me. She just sat with me and told me she knew what I was feeling. She was quiet, and yet she made me feel . . . good."

"And does she have a name?"

"Of course. Bonnie."

He had been expecting it, but he still felt the shock. "And when did she come to you?"

"The night after you came with that Megan person. Bonnie wasn't like the others. She knew I had to stay."

"Because of your father."

"She said that if their need is too strong, then you have to help them." She moistened her lips. "She knew how I felt."

"Yes, she would." He looked at her. "And you know why, don't you?"

"She didn't tell me. But I felt it. It's Eve. She's trying to save Eve, isn't she?"

"Yes." His lips twisted. "We're all trying to save Eve."

"Me too. Because if he takes Eve's blood,

then everything is going to change. He may be too strong. It will be harder to kill him."

"What are you talking about? All this crap about blood making him stronger. You sound like Caleb."

"It does make him stronger. I made him stronger. Not as much as Eve would, but I gave him some strength he would never have had." She looked away from him. "And it's not crap. Ask Seth Caleb. Make him tell you."

"I've heard enough from him. He said that this cult group Jelak belonged to had certain beliefs. Even Caleb didn't say they were valid."

"Make him tell you," she repeated. "He's not what you think."

"I have a suggestion. Why don't you go visit Caleb and ask him to team up with you to go after Jelak? You seem to have similar thoughts on the subject."

She shook her head. "There's too much darkness all around him. I couldn't get near him. I have to rely on you."

"Great."

"I don't like it either." She paused. "But I may be able to help you. I found out that I may be able to tell where Jelak is."

"How?"

"I can feel him."

He snorted. "Now you do sound like Caleb."

"It's true. I don't know how he feels Jelak,

but with me it's the blood. It's my blood in him that calls to me."

Joe was silent. "Then do you know where he is right now?"

"No."

"Then I can't say that you're a reliable source."

"I'm the most reliable source that you have," she said. "I thought I felt him last night. He was excited, and his blood was pounding. It went on for a long time."

The time when he was killing Heather Carmello?

"I didn't know about her," Nancy Jo said as if he'd put the thought into words. "Not until you started thinking about her."

"She's not one of your buddies in the afterworld?"

"Stop being sarcastic. I don't even know if we can have friends. I hope so. I hate being this lonely."

"I imagine there's some provision for them." He paused. "What about Bonnie?"

"She was nice to me, but I think she wanted to rush me along so that I would be able to help Eve. Is Eve her mother?"

"Yes."

"My mother died a long time ago. I only have my dad." She added unevenly, "And he only had me. He's not happy, and I don't know how to help him."

"I think you have to let him find his way himself."

"I will not. I need to help him. I'll find a way." She looked at him. "Are you Bonnie's dad?"

"No, I never knew her."

"She knows you. She said I could trust you." She glanced out the window. "The Camry has dropped back. They must know you're going to get off the freeway here."

"Why is your father having me followed? I'd turn any information I found in to the department."

"He found out about the goblet that Jelak put in your cottage. He knows about Eve. He thinks that if he's close to you, he may get close to Jelak."

"Evidently, someone did take one of his bribes."

"You can't blame him," Nancy Jo said fiercely. "He's hurting. Someone has to help him."

"And you've elected me."

"Yes. Why not? There must be some reason why you can see me when no one else can. It must mean that you have a special job to do."

"Not that I'm just unlucky?"

"I don't think so." She smiled sadly. "But I could be wrong."

He felt again that rush of sympathy mixed

with exasperation that he always felt with her. "Maybe you're right. I don't believe in fate, but then I didn't believe in ghosts either. Anyway, I'll ride with it." He turned down the lake road. "So are you going to go hunting and let me know if you run across Jelak?"

"I'm not good at hunting. I never did anything like this before."

"Then what help are you going to be to me?"

"I don't know. I thought maybe — I don't know." She frowned. "Stop acting like a cop, Joe."

"It's what I am. It's why you turned to me."

"I turned to you because I had no one else." She was silent a moment. "But I'm glad it was you. You can be difficult, but I think you can help me if anyone can."

"I'm only difficult when assaulted by ghosts."

She smiled. "I don't believe that's true. I bet you can be difficult about a lot of things. I think I would have liked you if I'd met you before Jelak. I may even like you now."

"What a concession. Is that why you came looking for me?"

"No, I had to let you know what Daddy was doing. And to make sure you knew I could help you . . . maybe."

"Well, that's definite."

She was silent a moment. "And maybe I was lonely." She added quickly, "Though I wouldn't bother you just because of that."

"That's good. And you also wanted to tell me that crap about Eve's blood putting Jelak over the top?"

"It's not crap."

"Who told you?"

"No one. I know it."

"Then I believe we'll differ. You're a fledgling ghost in training. I can't put my trust in you, Nancy Jo. Come back when you've had some experience." He pulled up to the driveway in front of the cottage. "Now, is there anything else? If not, I'd like to go in to Eve and Jane."

"No." Her gaze was fixed wistfully on the lights in the windows of the cottage. "We take so many things for granted, don't we? Lights in a window, people we love waiting for us . . . Then it's all gone." Her gaze shifted to his face. "Don't you take it for granted, Joe."

"I don't."

"No, you've probably seen too much of death. I was too young. I thought it would go on and on. I thought I'd live forever."

"We all do at your age."

"But I didn't get a chance to grow out of it. He took that away from me." She met his eyes. "I keep wanting to cry. I'm not usually weepy. I'll have to get over it. That little girl, Bonnie, wasn't sobbing and wringing her hands. There was a sort of golden serenity about her."

"She's had a little time to come to terms."

She nodded jerkily. "I'll get there." She looked back at the house. "Go on. They're waiting for you."

"Are you going to just sit out here?"

She smiled. "You don't want to be impolite and leave me by myself. That's pretty silly, isn't it?"

"Ridiculous." But that's how he felt, he realized. "But I don't know the protocol of dealing with ghosts."

"I won't be here long. I know the trick now. Bonnie showed me."

"Then I'll say good night." He got out of the car. "As usual, it's been a different experience, Nancy Jo."

"But I don't believe you dislike it as much, do you?" She added, "You're not afraid of me any longer?"

"I was never afraid of — Well, maybe those first few minutes."

"But not now?" She was looking at him like a lost puppy.

"I'm not afraid, and I don't dislike you." He made a face. "I guess I'm getting used to you."

"And I'm getting used to you," she said eagerly. "That's part of being friends. Are we friends, Joe?"

He gazed helplessly at her. He could no

more reject her than he could a child in need. He said gently, “We’re friends, Nancy Jo.”

She smiled brilliantly. “Thank you.”

He turned and went up the porch steps. He glanced back when he opened the screen door.

She was gone.

She had learned the trick.

TEN

Jane's cell phone rang at two thirty in the morning, waking her from a deep sleep. She didn't recognize the ID.

She did recognize the voice.

"Sorry to wake you," Caleb said. "I couldn't sleep."

"And I was sleeping very well." She got up on one elbow. "It couldn't wait until morning?"

"Probably. But then I'd have to run the gauntlet with Eve and Quinn. I want to talk to you."

"So talk."

"Meet me on the porch in five minutes."

"Why?"

"I want to see your face, your expressions. I don't like telephones."

"Why choose me? Why not Eve?"

"You're more open to me. I could tell that the moment I met you."

"You mean you think you could talk me

into something."

"No, I wouldn't make the attempt. I pick and choose."

"What did you do to Patty's grandfather?"

"Meet me outside, and we'll talk about it."

"If you come near the porch, the police officers in that squad car will stop you."

"I'll drop by and have a talk with them. I'll show them how harmless I am."

"You'll get your ass shot."

"Five minutes." He hung up.

She slowly hung up. She should stay in bed and ignore Caleb. He was a disturbing influence, and Joe was right in treating him warily.

To hell with it. She had never been afraid of disturbances. They were what made life interesting. And Caleb was a disturbance that would have a gigantic payoff if she could find a way to use him to help Eve. He was right, she was open to him, to anyone who could end this hellish situation.

Besides, she was curious. He was an enigma, and she wanted to know more about him. She threw back the covers and got out of bed. She drew on her terry robe and headed for the door. Toby was running ahead of her as she tried to move quietly through the house.

Caleb was sitting on the top step of the porch when she opened the screen door.

"Turn on the porch light. It will make the cops in the squad car feel better. And I'll be able to see your face." He looked at her and smiled. "It's beautiful up here. You must love to visit. Come sit down."

She switched on the light and glanced at the squad car. "I can't believe they didn't stop you. The least they could do was to call us and check."

"I told you, they could see I was harmless."

"Yeah, sure." Even leaning casually against the porch rail, he looked anything but harmless. She dropped down beside him, then had to shift over as Toby squeezed between them. "Did Patty's grandfather think you were harmless?"

"You won't let that go. It must have upset you."

"I don't like puzzles. What happened with her grandfather was a puzzle."

"And I like puzzles. It keeps the wits sharp. That's important."

"Patty's grandfather," she prompted.

He smiled. "I just talked to him. I reminded him what a wonderful granddaughter he had in Patty. I suggested he mellow out and enjoy life a little more."

"That's all?"

"That's all."

"And he accepted your suggestions even though you're a stranger to him?"

"Sometimes it happens like that."

"You're not telling the truth."

"Actually I am."

"Not all the truth."

"You do dig deep." He chuckled. "No, not quite." He looked out at the lake. "I told you I was a hunter. I have certain talents that make me valuable in that area. I'm very persuasive."

"What does that mean?"

"To find someone, you have to have people willing to tell you what you want to know. I have no problem with accomplishing that end. I can make people want to please me."

"Hypnosis?"

"I guess you could call it that if you wanted to generalize. It's a little more abstract and complicated."

"Against their will?"

"Sometimes. Or you could say it wasn't against their will if they wanted to do it. Isn't that right?"

"No."

He laughed. "You're absolutely correct. By every moral standard it's wrong. That's why I had to develop my own code of choices and limitations."

"But they're your choices. You could change them to suit yourself. That could be an awesome power in the wrong —" She stopped. "Good God, I'm accepting all this crap as if I believe it."

"You do believe it. You see things that aren't clear to other people. That's why I'm talking to you tonight."

"There could be another perfectly logical reason why Patty's grandfather turned into a reformed Scrooge."

He didn't answer.

"*If* you're telling the truth, is the change permanent?"

"No, I didn't have enough time. All the selfishness will come back in a day or two. But I think he'll remember that he cares about her."

A memory of love was a wonderful thing in itself, Jane thought.

"I didn't hurt him," Caleb said. "I chose to help Quinn, and perhaps it helped Patty and her grandfather too."

"Out of the kindness of your heart," she said sarcastically.

"No, that's not what this is all about. It's about hunting down Jelak. I wanted to make it simpler for Quinn and leave a little thread to make you curious."

And he had succeeded. Lord, he was clever. "You haven't convinced me."

"It will take time. I've been through this before. I think it helps that Eve believes in Megan. There's no one you trust more than Eve."

"Yes." She was silent again. "Is that how you convinced those policemen to let you come on the porch?"

He nodded. "They think they're doing you a service. After all, no one is safer than I am."

No one was more dangerous if what he said was true.

"I could prove it to you," he said softly. "I could make you think that I was your best friend, even your lover. It would be difficult because you're so strong, but I'm very, very good."

"I don't believe you."

"Then look at me, and I'll give you a taste. Nothing permanent. I promise." He smiled. "Aren't you curious? I dare you, Jane." He repeated, "Look at me."

She slowly raised her eyes to meet his own.

Warmth, no, heat, memories of Caleb holding her naked, driving into her body. Desire so intense and sexual that she couldn't bear it. Her breasts were firming, readying. She was melting toward him, into him.

Then he was looking away from her. "Oh, the temptation. You would be a delight."

She felt dazed, her body sensitive and still tingling. "You son of a bitch."

"Yes, I couldn't resist. Much more interesting than a comfortable, friendly interchange. But it did prove my point."

She couldn't deny that when her body was still aching. "They should keep you confined."

"They've tried over the years. But the only way to do it is to keep me drugged. And I become drug-tolerant very quickly." He smiled. "So it's up to me. I do have my code. And I don't fall from grace very often. You were just too much of a temptation, and I actually had a legitimate reason to do it."

"Rationalization."

He nodded. "Perhaps. But you weren't going to let me discuss anything until I dealt with what happened to Patty's grandfather. I had to be honest with you."

"You wouldn't have it so easy next time. I'd be prepared for you."

"And you're strong. So let's forget it and get down to the reason I'm here."

He hadn't argued with her but stepped

aside. "Why are you here?"

"To get your cooperation." He turned and looked at her again. "We both know he's going to go after Eve. That attempt on your friend was only a gesture of rage. He wants Eve, and you're the ticket he'll use to get to her."

"Why does he want Eve so badly?"

"She's the final one. He thinks her blood will put him over the top into vampire nirvana."

"Why?"

"She's extraordinary. She's extremely strong. She's old enough and experienced enough to make her blood richer than, say, yours, Jane. You're strong, but you lack the experience Eve's gained over the years. The tragedy she's gone through has made both her mind and blood the apex of richness. She's the complete package."

"Why would that make her blood different?"

"Because Jelak thinks it does. He believes it's part of the essence, the soul of her. It's what he was taught. And that's all that's important."

"It's bullshit. Tragic bullshit. And you said some of those victims were killed for no real purpose in his view."

"Except for the hunger. During this stage,

the hunger is very much present. He won't be able to keep himself from taking frequent victims. After he reaches his final goal, then everything changes."

"And Eve is that goal."

"Yes," Caleb said. "And you're the path that leads to her. You can see where I'm going."

"Eve said that you'd serve up any of us on Jelak's altar. You want me to be your bait."

"Yes."

"And that was why you didn't want Eve and Joe around when you told me."

"It would have been awkward."

She looked at him and started to laugh. "That's one way of putting it. Joe would have thrown you into the lake."

"I could probably convince him that wouldn't be a good idea."

She remembered that moment at the restaurant when he'd been trying to persuade Joe to go hunting with him. He had been intense but not totally mesmerizing as he had been with her. "Why didn't you try that before? Doesn't it work with Joe?"

"I don't know. Probably. I prefer not to interfere with free choice when it may involve the death of the subject."

She shook her head. "You're incredible."

"Yes, I am. Now let's get down to business. I promise to keep you alive if you decide to help me catch Jelak."

"With all my blood intact?"

"That goes without saying. We can't have one without the other. I won't bring you into the picture until I have a scenario I can control."

"I'm not sure I'd trust you."

"Of course not. But you'll probably do it anyway. You love Eve enough to do anything for her. I wouldn't tell them about our talk if I were you. It would only worry them." He got to his feet. "Think about it. I'll let you know when I can arrange it. First we have to find him."

She stared at him. The light was illuminating the deep planes of his face and that beautifully sensual mouth. Power and intensity and the alluring magnetism that was even stronger than she had imagined. "You're a very ruthless man, Seth Caleb."

"You have no idea." He started down the steps. "But you will, Jane." He stopped to smile and wave at the two officers in the squad car. They waved back, and he continued down the steps and strode toward his car.

Jane got to her feet and started toward the front door. Yes, she would very likely plumb the incalculable depths of Caleb before this was over.

She wasn't sure that she wanted to discover what lay beneath.

The woman was perhaps thirty-five, dressed in a dark suit, and was frowning thoughtfully as she crossed the CDC parking lot.

Serious and responsible, Jelak thought. She was everything he had been hoping for when he had staked out the building. Old enough to be experienced, and her job with the Centers for Disease Control reflected intelligence and perhaps the qualities that, at least, made her a candidate to permit him to ingest her blood.

And perhaps more. Perhaps another step closer.

She was unlocking the door of a tan Toyota and getting into the driver's seat.

Sensible car, again reflecting that maturity that was so important to make the feeding tolerable at this stage of his development.

Yes, it was going to be all right. He knew it. Relief poured through him. She would give him the strength he needed to endure until he could take that final goblet from Eve Duncan.

He started his car and followed the tan Toyota out of the parking lot.

■ ■ ■ ■

It was four thirty in the morning when Joe's cell phone rang.

Ed Norris? What the hell?

"I suppose I don't have to ask how you got my cell number, Norris."

"Another one," Ed Norris bit out. "When are you going to stop it? When are you going to catch him?"

"As soon as I can. What are you talking about?"

Eve was sitting up in bed, looking at him.

"I just got word from my informant at the precinct that there's been a killing in midtown. Margaret Selkirk, researcher with the CDC. Body found in the backyard of her house by her daughter. Throat slit. You let him do it again, dammit."

"I haven't heard anything about —" But a call was coming in now from Gary Schindler. He punched over to the call. "What's happening?"

"Margaret Selkirk. Killing. Throat slit. Seems like the same MO as the other murders." Gary paused. "There was a goblet in her hand."

"I'm on my way." He switched back to Norris. "I'm heading for midtown. Keep your damn spies out from under my feet."

He hung up and got out of bed. "Another victim. Margaret Selkirk, a researcher with the CDC. Ed Norris is raising hell. I feel like raising hell too. It's pissing me off that he's finding out about Jelak's moves before I do."

"Bribery?"

"No doubt about it."

"Any change from the Heather Carmello murder?"

"They found a goblet." He headed for the bathroom. "I'm sure that bastard, Caleb, would be able to interpret the significance of that."

"It wouldn't be a bad idea to ask him." Eve slipped on her robe. "I might as well make coffee, then get to work. I won't be able to go back to sleep."

"Sorry."

"I'm not." She headed for the door. "Actually, I'd go with you, but you'll have enough to contend with dealing with Norris."

"I don't want you at the crime scene. I don't want you anywhere near those victims."

"Because you think Jelak may be hovering? Caleb said he probably wouldn't have stayed at Piedmont Park after the killing."

"I don't want you there," he repeated. "I don't care what Caleb said."

"Okay, for now." She added quietly, "But I can't bury my head in the sand. Three victims, and Patty could have been one of them if she hadn't been lucky. I seem to be the eye of the storm. It has to stop, Joe."

"It will stop." He closed the bathroom door behind him.

Eve stood on the porch watching Joe's Jeep go down the drive.

She clasped her arms across her chest as she felt chill at the thought of that poor woman who had died tonight. Margaret Selkirk, who had done nothing but happen to cross Jelak's path.

It will stop, Joe had said.

But how long would it be? How many victims would Jelak take before they'd manage to bring that monster down?

Joe would do his job with his usual intelligence and efficiency, but he wouldn't tolerate even a slight risk to her.

But that risk might have to be run eventually. In the meantime, they'd have to explore every single avenue.

Starting with Margaret Selkirk's death.

She turned and strode back into the house.

■ ■ ■ ■

"Her fifteen-year-old daughter found her," Schindler said, when Joe arrived at the small, white house on Peachtree Circle. "The kid is almost hysterical. She said she's a restless sleeper and woke up because she thought she heard a car start outside."

"What time?"

"Two forty. She got up and noticed her mother's door was open and her bed hadn't been slept in. Her mother had been working late for the past two weeks, but she thought she'd heard her come in. So she started looking for her."

"And found her in the backyard?"

Schindler nodded. "Naked. By the garden shed at the end of the yard." He was leading Joe around the house. "With the goblet in her right hand. The kid called 911, then went upstairs to take care of her little brother and keep him from seeing their mother."

"Good move on her part. Did you call any of their relatives to come for the kids?"

"Margaret Selkirk has a sister in Helen, Georgia. She's on her way." He opened the gate. "And that expert you sent arrived about five minutes ago. He's with forensics examining that goblet."

"Expert?" Joe frowned. "What expert?"

"Seth Caleb," Schindler said. "Good man. We should have had him on the case earlier. Where did you get him? FBI?"

"What?" Joe's gaze flew across the yard to the man standing over the body. "He told you I sent him? You believed him?"

"Of course I believed him," Schindler said. "What's wrong? Are you trying to keep it confidential?"

Schindler was not easily deceived, but he had obviously been taken in by Caleb's story. Even now he didn't want to believe anything but the lie Caleb had told him.

"Oh, yes," Joe said grimly as he moved quickly across the yard. "Caleb's connection with the case is definitely confidential."

"Quinn." Caleb was turning away from the body. "I'm glad I arrived before you. I had a chance to examine the goblet. It's Jelak's calling card. And I think he completed the ritual."

"What are you doing here?" Joe asked.

Caleb turned to Schindler. "Do you mind staying here and seeing if forensics turns up anything new? I need to talk to Quinn about that goblet."

"No, glad to do it." Schindler knelt beside a tech. "Take your time."

"We'll only be a few minutes." Caleb glanced at Joe. "Come on, we'll talk while we walk back to the house. Selkirk's kids are in rough shape. I want to spend a few minutes with them before I leave."

"I'm not going to let you near them," Joe said. "I don't know how you managed to con Schindler, but I won't have you manipulating those children."

"I didn't tell the whole truth, but I didn't exactly lie to Schindler." He smiled. "I am an expert, and I was brought into the case. Only not by you."

"How did you know about the murder?"

"Eve called me. She was upset by Margaret Selkirk's murder. She said to tell you that if you wanted her to stay out of it, you had to use every resource. She thinks I'm a resource."

"So you hotfooted it over here and tried to —"

"I took advantage of an opportunity," he interrupted. "Now you should do the same. You've been very reluctant to use me except when you need a particular bit of information. I've had to waltz around you. I know why, but it's time the dance stopped."

"Just what do you know about me?" Joe asked warily.

"Nothing specific. But it wasn't difficult

figuring it out. Even though Renata wouldn't break Megan's confidence by telling me anything but that she was contacting them about you. But you're fiercely resentful about the idea of anything to do with psychic gifts. Since I'm the closest representative of that dislike, you automatically rejected anything to do with me." He tilted his head. "Now why would that be?"

"I'm sure you're going to tell me."

"Certainly. You recently discovered you were one of the chosen, or should I say, one of the condemned. You resent it in yourself but have to accept it. But you're trying your damnedest not to have to accept it in anyone else."

"And just how have I been condemned?"

Caleb shook his head. "That's your business. I may be curious, but I'll never ask you."

"How kind."

"And it doesn't matter unless it interferes with me getting Jelak. Eve is on my side in this. She doesn't want any more deaths, and she thinks I can help. I could use that, use her, but I don't want to do that." He looked him directly in the eye. "Now, I'll ask you again. Will you go hunting with me?"

Joe was silent. He could still feel the simmering anger and resentment he'd experienced when he'd walked into this yard today. Some of it had been earned, but how much was the anger at Caleb and how much at his own condition?

A hell of a lot was at Caleb, dammit.

"Don't you ever lie to anyone working one of my cases," Joe said curtly. "I don't know why Schindler didn't send you on your way."

Caleb smiled. "He likes me. I remind him of his brother."

"What?"

"Never mind. Schindler is a nice guy. I wouldn't have tried to con him if I hadn't wanted a look at that goblet. I wasn't sure that you'd let me examine it." He added, "Because I'd already decided that I wasn't going to con you."

"You pick and choose?"

"Yes, I do. I can do that." He opened the kitchen door. "I hope you find that you can too."

"What are you talking about?"

"Codes. Are you going hunting with me?"

Joe hesitated, then slowly nodded. "I believe I am."

"Good," Caleb said. "Now you can go back to Schindler and do all the things you have to do as a fine upstanding man of the law. I'll go up and talk to the Selkirk kids. They'll need understanding and strength if they're going to get through this."

"And you're going to furnish it?"

"I can help bridge the gap until some of the pain goes away."

"What a great humanitarian."

"No, I just believe in balance. It doesn't hurt me to take a little time and devote it to doing something worthwhile. It lightens my core. I do a good many things that people perceive as evil. If a soul becomes too black, then it rots."

"An unusual philosophy."

"Not really. Actually, very ancient."

"Well, you can't give a fifteen- and ten-year-old enough understanding of this ugliness. Hell, *I* don't understand it."

"I do," Caleb said as he went inside the house. "I'll share it with you. After you finish here."

The blood was fine, wonderful.

Jelak could feel the clear zing of strength and endurance through his veins. The Selkirk woman had been as strong as he'd hoped. He'd chosen well. He'd been afraid when she'd fought with such fierceness that the blood might not be as mature as he'd hoped.

Children and young people usually were the ones who were frantic in their struggles.

Age usually mellowed and caused death to come easier. But he'd found out to his delight when the woman was begging him to let her go that she had two children. Mothers usually fought desperately to keep close to their young, and motherhood only added richness to the Gift. At any rate, the blood was exquisite.

He went to the closet, pulled out his black Croco case, and set it on the bed. He hummed a little as he opened it and gazed down at the goblets he'd carefully wrapped in red velvet.

Three left.

But he wouldn't need all three.

Margaret Selkirk had been better than he had hoped. He had expected her to give him strength to see him through until Jane MacGuire. She had given him more than that, and he might be able to go directly to Eve Duncan. He would know by tomorrow if Selkirk's blood stayed strong in him.

He unwrapped one of the goblets. It shone in the lamplight, and he held it up. Jane MacGuire. That would make eleven guests at the table. If he needed to take her.

"I'm getting close," he murmured. "Soon I'll be one of you."

He reverently unwrapped the last goblet.

The perfect twelve.

He lifted the goblet and felt the blood pounding through him as he looked at the carving. No single figure begging to be admitted. Complete. Together.

The perfect twelve at the feast.

"Do you feel me, Eve?" he murmured. "It's your gift that's going to save me. I'll drink deep, then we'll be together forever. You'll like it. I know you've been waiting for me."

His tongue touched the rim of the goblet, imagining the coppery taste of her blood.

"Just a little longer . . ."

Blood.

Eve suddenly tensed, her fingers hesitating on the clay of the reconstruction.

The dizziness had come out of nowhere, followed by that sinking, whirling sensation.

Then had come that weird feeling of being . . . drained.

She drew a deep breath.

It was gone.

Perhaps it had never been there, only brought on by her obsession with the thought of Jelak.

And blood. Always blood.

"Eve."

She turned to see Joe at the front door. "Oh, I didn't hear you drive up."

"That's pretty obvious." His gaze was searching her face. "I'm used to you being absorbed in your work, but you look a little strange."

"I'm fine." She picked up her cloth and wiped the clay from her hands. "I just had a sudden chill." She braced herself. "I thought you'd call me. I knew you wouldn't like it that I sent Caleb down to Selkirk's crime scene."

"Not one bit."

She shrugged. "I believe he can help. I couldn't stand the thought of another woman being murdered. I heard on the news that she had two children."

"A fifteen-year-old girl and a boy, ten."

"And he didn't care if he left them orphans. How are they holding up?"

"Not good. But Caleb had a talk with them, and they're better than they were."

Her eyes widened. "You let Caleb talk to them?"

"He was good with Patty's grandfather. Maybe he's some kind of psychologist. The kids needed someone, something."

Her eyes were narrowed on his face. "But you let him do it."

"I gave him his chance. Isn't that what you wanted?"

"Joe."

"Okay, I decided it's what I wanted too." He turned and went toward the bedroom. "So I told him to follow me home and that we'd talk. He should be here any minute. I'm going to shed this jacket and wash my face. Where's Jane?"

"She went to see Patty. She thought she might be upset when she heard about Margaret Selkirk. Charlie Brand picked Jane up and will bring her home."

"Too bad she'll miss Caleb. She was in his corner all the way."

"But you're not, are you?"

"Hell, no. I'm in your corner. I'm in the corner of all those women Jelak is going to kill if we don't catch him." He looked over his shoulder. "But I don't have to be in his corner. He's not going to stay in that corner for very long. We're going hunting."

ELEVEN

"I'm sorry your Jane isn't here. She always brings an electricity to any occasion," Caleb said as he pushed back his chair at the table. "Delightful meal."

"Hamburger Helper?" Eve said. "Hardly. It was just fast."

"Hearty, flavorful, and substantial. That's all that's necessary to make it good."

"Then food must not be that important to you," Eve said.

"Sometimes. Not usually." He smiled. "But I appreciate you serving me under your roof. It shows a certain acceptance." He looked at Joe. "And trust?"

"Conditional," Joe said. "How about Kevin Jelak? Is food important to him?"

"At this point, not at all. It probably makes him ill after only a few bites. He's living on blood."

"He couldn't," Eve said. "That's impossible."

"It's possible for a little while longer. He'll grow thinner, but his energy level will carry him through." He turned to Joe. "Why did you ask me that question?"

"I wanted to know how deeply Jelak has bought into this bullshit."

"All the way." He glanced at Eve. "Could we have coffee on the porch? I've grown very fond of your wonderful views."

"I suppose we could." Eve got to her feet. "As long as you're not trying to evade our questions."

"Perish the thought. I'm encouraged that Quinn is thinking that I can be useful in digging into Jelak's psyche." He got to his feet. "I have a call to make. I'll meet you on the porch."

"Sidestepping?" Eve said to Joe as Caleb left the room.

He shook his head. "I don't think so. We'll know later." He got down the tray and carafe. "Because I'm going to ask him a boatload of questions."

Caleb was just finishing his call when they joined him on the porch. "You'll be glad to know that Jane is fine. They'd just finished the dinner that Charlie Brand had cooked." He smiled. "And it was not Hamburger Helper."

"You called Jane?" Eve asked. "Why?"

"I like to keep track of her," Caleb said as he took the cup Eve handed him. "Jelak thinks she's important. I do too."

"I'm surprised she didn't hang up on you," Eve said.

"She knows I want the best for her. She was impatient, but not angry. She's a very smart woman." He sat down on the top step and gestured to the swing. "Sit down. I'm sure you're impatient too, Quinn. You want answers. I just wanted to be sure about Jane."

"So do we," Joe said. "But there's an officer with her."

"And that was probably enough of a deterrent. However, Jelak is getting closer to his time and may get desperate." He took a sip of his coffee. "You were asking about Jelak and food." He chuckled. "You've been thinking back about all the trashy movies and novels you've read about vampires and the traditional profiles. Let's see, vampires never eat."

"You've just said that Jelak doesn't," Eve said.

"Not at this point. According to what his master, Franco Donari, taught him when he was in training, he should have no hunger except for the blood when he was coming near to his completion. Since he's completely sure that he's right around the bend from that august state, he's convinced himself that he has every sign he should have to support that fact."

"In other words, he's sold himself a bill of goods," Joe said. "What happens when he doesn't reach this completion? He'd starve to death."

"Not for a long time. The mind can do amazing things."

"I thought you said this vampire cult Jelak belonged to only believed the more palatable things connected with the legends. Starving seems pretty extreme."

"But only in the last stage of his resurrection."

"Resurrection? You've never mentioned that word."

"Didn't I? Perhaps it sounded too pretentious." He leaned back against the railing. "What else, Quinn?"

"Does he believe he can't go out in daylight?"

"No, but he's a night creature because it's easier to prey. Very sensible. I've always wondered if that's how that legend got started." He smiled. "And he doesn't think garlic or onion or holy crosses will make him powerless. A stake in the heart? At this stage he thinks a bullet would do the job.

That's why he's wary."

"At this stage?" Eve repeated. "What about when he goes through this resurrection? What does he think it's going to bring him?"

"He's certain it's going to give him everything that he wants in the world." He took another sip of coffee. "It's going to make him a god."

"Even a nut like Jelak couldn't believe that," Joe said.

"He believes what he wants to believe. According to what the cult taught him, when he reaches his final transformation, he'll receive powers beyond belief. There will be nothing that he can't reach out and take. No one who will be safe from him."

"Easy promises," Eve said. "And ones that would appeal to a monster like Jelak."

He nodded. "And like all gods, he'll be invisible to mortal man."

"Oh, for heaven's sake."

"I never said that it wasn't totally irrational. But you can see how that would make an unbalanced man try to gain all the rewards promised by the cult."

Unbalanced? Eve thought. Jelak had to be totally insane to believe that he could make himself a supreme being by spreading this trail of blood and death. "And I can't understand how he'd ever believe in that cult. It's too outlandish. You said that he'd gone to several countries before he went to Italy and linked up with that group."

"This one suited him," Caleb said. "It told him what he wanted to hear. And the cult had the cachet of having been in existence for hundreds of years. I'm sure Jelak thought that he'd found the true stronghold of the vampire. There were all kinds of wild tales about how it started. It was believed to have originated back in the fourteenth century because the people of the village of Fiero had seen dark magic performed in their midst by two brothers who had recently come to their town."

"What kind of dark magic?"

"Blood. Power. Death. The villagers were terrified. For decades they were made practically into servants by the Ridondo brothers and their descendants. But they were also fascinated, envious, and set about to study and copy them. Hence the cult was born."

"You're saying the Ridondo family were vampires?" Jane asked skeptically.

"I'm saying that the legend connects their dark arts with blood." He shrugged. "And that Jelak believed the legend."

"And you haven't told us one thing that

could help us nail Jelak," Joe said.

"You understand him better now," Caleb said. "You know he thinks he's got to keep on killing to keep himself alive. You know he's feverishly trying to reach his goal of resurrection now." He paused. "You know he's close to it."

"How close?" Joe asked.

"Selkirk was a good find for him." He reached into his pocket and brought out his digital camera. "I'm sure you noticed the goblet was different." He handed the camera to Eve. "He knew right away that he'd found a gem."

Eve looked at the viewer. At first it appeared the same as the other goblets but when she looked closer . . . "There are ten men sitting at the table instead of nine."

Caleb nodded. "Margaret Selkirk was a step in the right direction. Her blood was strong enough not only to feed him but to give him a step toward resurrection. He only has two to go." He looked at Eve. "I think that may mean your friend Patty may be off the hook."

"Patty." She immediately caught the omission. "Not Jane."

He shook his head. "And not you. He has to have two that will be sure things. And quickly. He doesn't have time to hunt down another quality kill. He got lucky with Margaret Selkirk."

"If he doesn't get his hands on either one of them right away, will he get reckless?" Joe asked. "If we do a stakeout, could we catch him?"

"Maybe," Caleb said. "Or maybe he'll keep killing to feed until one of you gets careless. That would be a form of triumph for him. How many deaths are you willing to give him?"

"None," Eve said flatly.

"Then we'd better find a way to get him quickly. If he's frustrated, then he'll start killing randomly. To prove how smart he is, to prove he's near to being a god right now." He met Joe's eyes. "What's the best way to trap a tiger, Quinn?"

"Don't even think about it," Joe said.

"I can't think of anything else. Can you?" He got to his feet. "We can make it safe." He started down the steps. "You're going to get angry now, so I'd better leave. I'll call you in the morning." He stopped as he reached the bottom of the stairs. "I see headlights up the road. It must be Jane." He stood, waiting until Jane was dropped off by the squad car and came toward him. "Hello. Have a good evening?"

"Not bad. Charlie Brand is a good cook. Patty's grandfather wasn't unbearable and even seemed to like Charlie. Patty wasn't too nervous about the killing." She shrugged. "On the whole, it could have been a lot worse."

"And how do you feel about the Selkirk murder?" Caleb asked.

"How do you think I feel?" Jane looked up at him. "You know damn well how I feel, Caleb."

Eve suddenly tensed as she looked at the two of them. The bond between them was almost visible. What kind of bond? And how had it been forged? Whatever it was, she wanted it broken. She said quickly, "Jane, there's coffee in the carafe."

Caleb glanced at her and smiled. "Yes, give her a cup of coffee. It's beginning to be a little chilly. Good night, Jane. I'm glad everything went well for you." He smiled at Eve. "Good night, Eve. Thank you for bringing me into the fold. You won't regret it."

"I hope not," Eve said. "But I've always found if I make a mistake, I can just smash it down and start over."

"On your reconstructions?" He nodded. "I can see you doing that. You wouldn't tolerate anything but perfection in a task so important." He waved as he set off for his car. "It obviously works for you. I'll have to see if it does for me."

Jane stood watching him walk away before turning and starting up the stairs. "He seems right at home. Things have obviously changed. You'll have to fill me in about your evening."

"I will," Eve said. "We know more about Jelak and his vampire obsession than I want to know. You'll find it as bizarre as we did."

"And did you find out any more about Caleb?" She poured herself a cup of coffee. "He's a little bizarre himself."

"Do I detect a note of resentment?" Joe asked. "Good. Keep it. We've agreed to use each other to get Jelak, but don't trust him."

"There may be a time when we have to trust him," Jane said. "I'd like to know more about him. You said you were going to check him out."

"I did. No criminal record. Thirty-seven years old. Parents dead. Born in Lucerne, Switzerland, but grew up in Edinburgh, Scotland, with his uncle, Rolf Mardell, now deceased. He was left a sizable fortune by both his parents and Mardell. He spends a lot of time traveling about the world."

"Hunting," Jane said softly.

Joe nodded. "Hunting."

Jane turned to Eve. "You're being very quiet."

"I'm thinking that I should get back to work." She stood up. "I didn't get enough done before Joe brought Caleb home." She gave Jane a level look. "I can control my work. I'm having trouble with everything else at the moment. I'm not sure what's happening with either you or Joe."

Jane said quietly, "Anything that's happened is because we care about you."

"Not good enough. I don't like being an outsider because you think it will make me safer." Eve didn't wait for an answer. She went into the house and strode over to her studio corner.

She took the towel off the head of the skull. "Hello, Matt. I'm relieved to get back to you. It's much simpler when it's just the two of us."

The little boy's face was beginning to take form beneath her fingers. All the painstaking measuring of tissue depths was vitally important, but it was the actual molding that was Eve's special domain. She relied on accuracy but also her instinct. At this stage she was always absorbed, almost mesmerized by the creative process. She had been in that state earlier in the evening when that sickening panic had struck her. It had been all the more frightening because it had jarred her away from the work that was her passion.

Could an obsession as strong as Jelak's have had the power to reach out and touch her?

She didn't know, she thought wearily. Stranger things were happening all around her.

Give a face to this lost child. Bring him home. Let his parents have closure at last.

Close Jelak out. Close out Caleb, who was almost as disturbing.

Close out the thought of the blood.

"We think we've located Jelak's car," Schindler said, when Joe walked into the squad room the next morning. "It looks like the same one that the security camera caught at Perimeter Mall. An old Lincoln Town Car. Maybe '93."

Joe stiffened. Dammit, a break at last. "Where?"

"Don't get excited. GBI found it on the side of the road near Kennesaw Mountain about an hour ago. It was apparently abandoned."

"That doesn't mean he didn't leave something in it that we could trace. Is forensics there yet?"

Schindler nodded. "They're going over it with a fine-tooth comb. Do you want to go or wait for the report?"

"I'm going." He turned and walked out of the squad room. He was reaching for his phone as he reached the car. He dialed Caleb. "They've found Jelak's car abandoned. Will you be able to tell anything about his whereabouts from it? You said you could feel him."

"Doubtful just from the vehicle. But I can try."

"Damn right, you can." Joe pulled out of the parking space. "Kennesaw Mountain. I'll give you exact directions when I'm closer." He hung up and glanced at his rearview mirror. Blue Toyota. He was being tailed again. Ed Norris probably knew everything that he knew. What the hell. Joe probably wouldn't know that much that the world didn't. Caleb had not been encouraging, and Joe was probably an idiot for using spook tactics to try to find Jelak.

At this point, he'd use anything he could to get a line on the bastard.

Forensics was still going over the massive gray car when Joe arrived at the park.

Caleb was standing to one side, watching them.

"Well?" Joe asked.

He shook his head. "All I know is that he's nowhere near here."

"What good is that going to do us?"

"Not a damn thing." He grimaced. "What did you expect? That I'd touch the steering wheel and get a vision of him? Sorry, it doesn't work like that. If he's within two miles, and there's low interference, I can feel him, track him. Otherwise, I'm blank."

"Some hunter."

"Shut up, Quinn. I could call Renata and see if she could send someone who can do the touchy-feely stuff. But it will take her a while."

"And by that time Jelak will have moved on." He was gazing at the huge car. How many times had Jelak used it to stuff bodies in that trunk or in the backseat? "Those forensic boys are probably getting a hell of a lot of fiber evidence."

"For the trial," Caleb said. "Which is never going to happen. He used that car when he kidnapped Nancy Jo Norris, didn't he?"

Joe nodded. "He picked her up in it at Perimeter Mall." He stiffened as a thought occurred to him. "Are you sure you can't trace him?"

Caleb nodded, his gaze on Joe's face. "I

told you, I'm not touchy-feely. Why?"

Joe didn't answer. He turned on his heel and strode back to his car.

"Answer me, Quinn." Caleb was standing by his driver's seat as Joe started his car. "You're up to something, and I'm not going to be left out in the cold."

"Then follow me. I don't give a damn."

"Where are you going?"

Joe backed up the car. "To find someone who's touchy-feely."

The yellow tape was gone from the crime scene at Allatoona. There were no longer media trucks parked out down the street.

Thank God, Joe thought. It was broad daylight, and the last thing he needed was for some reporter to come running up to him with a barrage of questions.

He got out of the car and started across the glade toward the woods.

He looked over his shoulder as he heard a car pull in behind him.

Caleb.

"Stay there. You're not invited."

"Whatever you say."

"Right." He had almost reached the woods, and he dismissed Caleb from his mind. He didn't care if Caleb camped out there all day as long as he didn't get in his way. The reason he was here was absurd and slightly mad, but it was on a par with the way the rest of his life was going.

He stopped inside the shadowy confines of the trees and looked around. No one. No slim, blond girl in a red sweatshirt. Hell, she had said that Bonnie had told her to get away from the place where she had died. She might not even be around here. But he didn't know what else to do.

Okay, go for it.

"I'm here, dammit. Where the hell are you?"

No answer.

"If you think I'm going to stay out here yodeling for a damn ghost, you're mistaken. Either show up, or I'm out of here."

"You don't have to be rude."

He whirled to see Nancy Jo only a few yards away. "I feel rude," he said curtly. "And like a blasted idiot. How did I know you weren't tripping the light fantastic in the Great Beyond?"

"I told you I wouldn't leave Daddy. He needs me." She was gazing searchingly at him. "And I think you need me too. Or you wouldn't be here. Is it something to do with Margaret Selkirk?"

"No." He added, "Though I'm not surprised you know about her. You belong to the same club."

"Yes, we do," she said sadly. "My heart aches for her."

"But evidently she decided to cross over and not stick around. I wasn't honored by her presence."

She shook her head. "You're wrong. She's still here."

"Then thank God I don't figure in her afterlife. I didn't see her."

"If you'd gone upstairs with Seth Caleb, you'd have seen her. She was with the children."

Joe felt as if he'd been kicked in the stomach. The idea of walking into that room where the children were grieving and seeing their mother with them was shocking even in retrospect. "How do you know?"

"I was there too. I was trying to help her. I know how lonely and scary it is at first," she said. "But she wouldn't listen to me. She kept trying to get through to the children. Then Seth Caleb came and it got a little better. But she can't leave them until she knows they're going to be all right."

"Another woman with a mission," Joe said.

"Stop trying to be hard," Nancy Jo said. "I know that you're hurting for her just as I am. Daddy will survive if I can get him through this. But those children will be scarred."

"Hell, yes, I'm hurting." Joe's hands clenched

into fists. "And I'm confused and sorry and scared shitless. I've got to get Jelak before he does this again."

"And you think I can help you."

"So you're suddenly a mind reader?"

"Why else would you have come bellowing for me like a cow in labor?"

He made a face. "You could have chosen a more appropriate comparison, Nancy Jo."

She smiled faintly. "But not one more accurate. You like me. You want to help me. But every time we're together, you're fighting it. So yes, you do bellow."

"Maybe," he said. "You said you could sense Jelak, that you thought you could find him. If you had some of his possessions would that help?"

"I don't know. Perhaps."

"All I'm getting is maybes and I don't knows," he said in disgust. "Caleb came up with zilch."

"Which sent you bellowing to me," Nancy Jo said. "What did you find that belonged to Jelak?"

"His car. Probably the one he used to bring you here to Allatoona."

She stiffened. "The car. I've been thinking about it lately. It was as big and heavy as a hearse. Do you think that Jelak made that connection?"

"It wouldn't surprise me. It's parked at Kennesaw Mountain right now. After forensics gets through with it, they'll tow it in to the impound yard. Will you come and look at it before they do?"

"Of course." She moistened her lips. "I've got to look at it. I've got to see it, touch it. Right now, it's not even real to me. It's just part of the nightmare."

"That's probably a mercy."

"I've got to get rid of the nightmare. Bonnie said that, and I didn't understand, but now I'm beginning to see what she meant."

Bonnie, again. Eve's daughter seemed to be moving in and out of Nancy Jo's awareness as she did Joe's.

He turned. "Then let's see if we can use that damn car to hang the bastard. Coming?"

She smiled. "I don't need a lift, Joe. I can find you with no problem."

He glanced back over his shoulder. "That's right, you know the trick. I wish to hell I did. I wouldn't have had to come here bellowing for you."

"Maybe someday I can teach it to you."

"Not if it means I have to be a ghost. I'm not ready for that."

"Neither was I."

No, nineteen years old and full of life and all that the future held. A beautiful life, and the longer he was with her, the more glimpses he was seeing of the extraordinary woman she would have become if Jelak had allowed her to live.

He was suddenly furiously angry. "Then, dammit, let's go get the son of a bitch."

Kennesaw Mountain

"Why did you send the forensic team away?" Caleb asked. "They didn't seem pleased."

"Too bad. They can do the rest of the tests later." He watched the last van go down the hill. "Why don't you go back to the precinct and wait for —"

"I wouldn't think of it." He leaned against his car and crossed his arms across his chest. "I'm too interested in all this erratic behavior you're showing me."

"It's not erratic." Where the hell was Nancy Jo? He'd been hoping that he'd be able to get rid of Caleb before she arrived on the scene. It wasn't going to happen. Caleb was sticking closer than glue. It didn't really matter. At this point, he didn't give a damn if Caleb thought he was nuts or not.

"Maybe erratic wasn't accurate. Then unusual."

"I'll grant you unusual." The van had gone around the turn of the road. Where was she? "But that's the pot calling the kettle."

"He's much blacker than you, Joe," Nancy Jo said. She was standing in front of the big Lincoln, staring at it in fascination. "It frightens me. Why should it frighten me?"

"I don't know. Memory?"

"Memory?" Caleb repeated. "What are you talking about?"

Joe made an impatient gesture and turned away from him. "Let's get it over with, Nancy Jo." He opened the trunk of the car. "He probably stashed you in the trunk after he put you out. Do you have any recollection?"

"No." She put her hand on the rust-colored carpet lining the trunk. "It seems strange not to be able to feel things. Bonnie said if I stay long enough some of it will come back. Sunlight . . . rain . . ."

"You don't sense anything?"

"Nothing about him." She shuddered. "But I wasn't the only one Jelak stuffed in this trunk. One, two, three . . . Five. I think there were five. Four of us were unconscious but Kerry was still awake, and she fought, her nails were bloody from trying to get out." She reached out and touched a tiny brown stain on the carpet. Tears rose to her eyes. "I feel her, but I can't help her."

"You have sensation when you touch the blood?"

"Yes, but I can't help her."

"It's all right, Nancy Jo." He closed the trunk. "She doesn't need your help anymore." He went to the driver's door and opened it. "Get in and see if you get anything."

"He sat there." She came to stand beside him and stared at the seat. She swallowed, hard. "Dear God, I don't want to do it."

"You said you couldn't feel anything."

"I can remember," she said fiercely. "I can remember his face."

"You won't do it?"

She drew a deep breath. "Of course I'll do it. Give me a minute."

"All the time you need."

Two minutes later she slowly slipped into the driver's seat. She closed her eyes. "He was in this car the night he killed Heather Carmello. After that, he decided it wasn't safe to keep it. He'd have to steal another car and abandon this one."

"What kind of car?"

She shook her head. "He hadn't decided. He liked big American cars, but he was leaning toward a smaller foreign job. He kept thinking about Seth Caleb and the way he'd tracked him at the lake cottage. He doesn't want to admit it to himself, but he's afraid of him." She opened her eyes. "May I get out now? I feel as if he's here with me. I can almost hear his heart beat."

"Just a little longer. I need to know where he is."

"I can't tell. All I know is how he was feeling the last time he was in this car."

"Run your hand along the dashboard."

She hesitated, then lifted her hand and ran her fingers along the leather dashboard. "Nothing."

"The cup holder and the passenger seat."

She took a deep breath and touched the cup holder. She snatched it back as if burned. "Heather Carmello's blood. He had the goblet in the holder when he took it to Patty Avery's house. It was only a short distance, and he was in a hurry."

"Try the passenger seat."

She didn't move. "When can I get out of this car?"

"After the passenger seat."

"Dammit, Joe." She swallowed and reached out her hand to touch the dark fabric. "It had better be worth this —" She gasped and bent double. "No!"

"What is it?"

"Oh, my God. Oh, my God. Oh, my God."

"What is it? Talk to me."

"Oh, my God."

"Nancy Jo."

"I *see* him." Her fingers were pressing on the fabric of the passenger seat. "I see him. I feel him. No, I don't feel him. I feel *me.*"

"What?"

"My blood pounding in him." She looked down in horror at her hand touching the seat. "When he got back in the car that night, he still had a little of my blood on his hand. He'd been very careful to clean up the area, but he had blood on his hand from the goblet. He . . . licked his finger, then wiped it on the seat. He wasn't worried. He could always clean the seat later. He knew how to do that. It had happened before." She shook her head. "But even though he couldn't see it, the blood is still there. *My* blood."

"Focus. You said you could see him."

"Dammit, stop being a cop. I'm trying to focus. You try to think when you can feel your blood pounding in that murderer's body and —"

"Okay, I'm sorry. When you touched the bloodstain, you felt a connection with Jelak?"

"I feel it right now. And if I wasn't trying to focus, then I'd take my hand off this damn stain. I've changed my mind. I don't want to feel anything. Not sunlight. Not rain. Not if this is in the package." The tears were running down her cheeks. "I don't want to be part of him. Make it stop."

"That's what we're trying to do." Joe knelt beside her in the passenger seat. He wished he could touch her, comfort her. “We’re going to make it stop. Tell me what you see, Nancy Jo.”

“Goblets. He’s looking into a black Croco case that has those gold goblets arranged in three neat rows. He’s reaching out and stroking one of them.” She shuddered. “I know those goblets. He put one to my throat after —”

“Where is he? Look around.”

“It looks like a motel. A bed with a cheap-looking flowered cotton bedspread. There’s a desk. A red door.”

“Red door? Bathroom door or exterior?”

“I don’t know. No, exterior. I see one of those plaques that give the room rates hanging on the door.”

“Can you see the name on the plaque?”

She shook her head.

“Try.”

“I can’t see it,” she said through her teeth.

“Anything else? Newspapers?”

She shook her head. She was starting to pant. “I can’t stand it. I have to leave him.”

“Just another minute. The desk. Is there stationery on the desk?”

“Just a leather folder.”

“With the name of the hotel?”

“No.” Her chest was lifting and falling with the harshness of her breathing. “No.” She tensed. "But there's a telephone book on the desk. It's the yellow pages. It's thin . . ."

"Atlanta?"

"No, Roswell. Roswell yellow pages. I can't see anything more. Jelak is closing out everything but the feel of the goblet in his hand. No, he's thinking about her. The way she's going to taste, the triumph she's going to bring him." She shook her head. "Don't let him do it. Don't let him do it. Don't let him do it again."

"Who is he thinking about?"

"You know. Eve. It's always Eve. None of us really mattered to him. I do matter. My life mattered."

"Yes," he said gently. "Let go. Get out of the car, Nancy Jo."

"I *do* matter."

"You matter very much. Now get out of the car."

She nodded jerkily and her hand slowly left the fabric of the passenger seat. She slumped against the steering wheel like a broken doll. "It hurts. It makes me feel sick and scared. I can't do this again, Joe."

"I won't ask you."

"You will if it would save Eve." Her lips twisted. "But I don't think I could do it." She got out of the car. "I just hope that —" She broke off and moved toward the front of the car. "It was very hard. I don't remember ever going through anything as terrible as that. Don't let it be for nothing."

"I promise that I —"

She was gone.

TWELVE

"Am I to assume that you're finished?" Caleb asked. "I don't wish to interrupt, but my curiosity is off the charts. Considering, I believe I've been very patient."

Joe had almost forgotten Caleb was there. He turned and braced himself. "Well? Say it. Not that I give a damn."

"Don't be on the defensive. Who could understand better?" He smiled. "And now I know what Megan confided in Renata about you. Ghosts? Very interesting. But not a talent I'd like to have."

"Neither do I." He paused. "But I'm beginning to accept it."

"And use it. Touchy-feely?"

"Nothing so light. She went through hell."

"Nancy Jo Norris?"

"Yes."

"And was it worthwhile?"

"I'd better make sure it is." He headed for his car. "I'll call forensics and get them back here, but I need to get on the computer."

"Am I invited this time?"

He nodded. "I may need you. I don't know his exact location. Nancy Jo said he's probably in a motel somewhere in Roswell. That's about forty minutes from here. Sparse furniture. Flowered cotton bedspread."

"Not very helpful."

"Exterior door is painted red."

"Better." He got into Joe's car. "You drive. You know the city." He reached for Joe's computer on the seat. "I'll search for any motels in Roswell with red doors."

It was time to move, Jelak thought, as he reluctantly put the goblet back in the case. Perhaps a hotel somewhere outside the city. He'd always thought that losing himself in the center of a city was safer, but everything was changing now. That photo Quinn had released to the media was dangerous. He might be recognized. He'd been forced to make very public kills, and not only Joe Quinn but Seth Caleb was after him.

But he'd shown them both they couldn't stop him. Margaret Selkirk had been a triumph, and soon he'd be beyond this running. Soon no one would be able to stop him.

He gave the perfect twelve goblet a final caress before he slowly shut the case. He could almost feel the power it was radiating.

Do you feel it, Eve?

You will.

"Red Door Inn." Caleb looked up from the computer. "It's a chain. There's one on Holcomb Bridge Road in Roswell."

Joe's hands tightened on the steering wheel. "Anything else similar?"

"Not so far." He was flipping through the hotels. "Not in Roswell."

"Then let's go for it." He reached for his phone. "I'll call the desk and see if I can find out which room by giving a description of him."

"It's a one-story motel," Joe said as he hung up. "The clerk said Jelak may be in room 24. He registered under the name of Ted Jonas two days ago. The clerk couldn't recall his face, but remembers noticing that he had biceps like a weight lifter."

"Yes," Caleb said. "How far?"

"A couple miles." He looked at Caleb. "Get out here."

"What?"

"You said that you could feel him. Well,

by the looks of those tire tracks Jelak left in the mud, he must have been able to feel you too. Isn't that right?"

"Yes, but the circumstances are different. We're in the middle of the city. There's so much interference from other people that it's doubtful that he could sense me."

"Screw doubtful. I'm not having you blow it for me."

"Dammit, I won't blow it. We go in fast, and it won't matter if Jelak knows we're coming."

Joe pulled over to the curb. "Get out."

Caleb muttered a curse and opened the door. "You're making a mistake. I can *get* him."

"So can I. If you don't send up any red flags." Joe pulled out into traffic again. "I won't take that chance."

"I'm not going to give up."

Joe knew that he wouldn't. Caleb would do anything he had to do. He could only hope that he could find Jelak before Caleb managed to get to the motel.

Room 24 had to be on the far side of the U-shaped structure. Joe cruised slowly along the parking area, his gaze on the red doors.

The late-afternoon sun highlighted the

faded brilliance of the chipped paint and the brass numbers on the doors.

Room 18.

A cleaning woman was opening the door of the room.

A stocky man in a Braves baseball cap was loading up his gray Honda at the end of the row of rooms. He opened the driver's door and shoved a black Croco case into the passenger's seat.

Goblets in a black Croco case.

He was going to change to a smaller car, maybe a foreign job.

And that man in the baseball cap wasn't stocky, he was muscular.

Jelak.

Joe stomped on the brakes.

Jelak's head lifted at the screeching sound. Fury twisted his face as he saw Joe jump out of the car. "No!"

He threw himself into the Honda.

Joe drew his Magnum. "Stop. You're under arrest, Jelak."

"The hell I am."

Joe saw the dull luster of metal in Jelak's hand and hit the pavement.

A bullet splintered the red door behind him.

Jelak was barreling toward him in the Honda.

Joe rolled out of the path of the tires as the car skidded by him.

He lifted his Magnum and got off a quick shot.

He saw Jelak jerk as the bullet hit him. Fierce pleasure tore through him.

But the bastard didn't stop. He rounded the corner of the motel and headed for the street.

Joe jumped in his car and did a U-turn.

Jelak was already on the street and heading for the freeway when he got around the building.

And Caleb was running down the block toward the Honda.

Shit. Jelak would pick him off. Joe aimed at the Honda's rear tire.

The Honda swerved as the tire blew.

Caleb was alongside it and grabbed for the open window, his feet bracing against the side of the car.

Jelak was lifting his gun.

"Caleb, jump, dammit," Joe called.

Caleb released the window, fell to the street, and rolled to the curb.

Jelak was on the freeway, riding on the rim of the blown tire.

Joe called for backup as he entered the street. Jelak couldn't go far with that tire. They might have the bastard.

Caleb was up, running toward him, jumping into the passenger seat. "You screwed it up," he said through his teeth. "You should have let me —"

"Shut up," Joe said as he entered the freeway. "He has a bullet in him and a blown tire. I've called for backup. We'll get him. And what the hell were you trying to do jumping on his car like a damn monkey?"

Caleb ignored him, his gaze on the cars whizzing in the lanes ahead of them. "I don't see him. I don't feel him. I think he's already off the freeway. Take the next exit."

It would make sense, Joe thought. That tire alone would have made Jelak try to get off the freeway as soon as possible. He exited the freeway at the next exit and started to double back.

"We've lost him," Caleb said. "Dammit, it would have to be in the middle of the city. I can't *feel* him."

"I shot him. Maybe I got lucky, and the bastard's dead."

Caleb shook his head. "He's not dead. I'd know it."

Joe didn't think he was dead either. He didn't have any special insight like Caleb, but he was sure that all of Nancy Jo's efforts had been wasted. If he'd been lucky, he would have found Jelak in that motel room instead of ready to fly the coop. He'd almost had him. "You're probably right. Then we just keep on looking."

He was staggering, Jelak realized, as he clutched the black Croco case tighter under his arm. He was getting weaker, and he had to find a place to rest, to heal. After he had abandoned the car behind that deserted warehouse, he must have walked miles. Twice he'd had to hide in the brush when a squad car had cruised slowly by.

And the blood was trickling out of the wound, Jelak thought, outraged. Precious blood. Nancy Jo, Margaret Selkirk, all the others . . . Blood that would give him the prize that he had striven for so long to gain. It wasn't a strong loss, but even a little was too much. He'd tried to bandage it, but the blood was still seeping around the handkerchief he'd used as pressure.

The wound itself didn't worry him. He didn't think Quinn had hit a vital organ, and he was close enough to the divine state of resurrection that his strength would carry him through. But if he lost too much blood, then he would have to delay the final victory. Even Eve would not be able to send him over the top.

So he had to stop the blood, find a way to

get to a doctor and get the wound stitched. Fury tore through him. Damn Quinn to hell. How had he found him?

Seth Caleb? More than likely.

It didn't matter. Quinn had to be punished. He'd thought that Caleb was the main threat, but Quinn had found him. Quinn had shot him. He had to show him he couldn't do this to him.

There was a BP gas station up ahead with the usual snack and convenience store. He could hear country music pouring out of the radio of the Ford truck parked by the pumps and saw a teenage girl with long, shiny brown hair filling up her Mazda.

He couldn't afford to wait longer. He had to stop this trickle of blood.

He'd wait until there were no customers inside the snack shop and make his move.

Ed Norris was sitting in the passenger seat of a dark blue limousine when Joe walked out of the precinct that evening. "I want to talk to you, Quinn."

"And I don't want to talk to you. It's been a very bad day, and I have no desire to listen to your guff."

"I'm not going to give you any guff." Norris got out of the limousine. "And I don't think it was a bad day if you managed to put a bullet into my daughter's murderer." He shrugged. "I could have wished you were a better shot and blown his brains out."

"I was off-balance. He'd just tried to run me down."

"Jelak did kill my daughter?"

"I believe he did. It's early days. We have no proof."

"Was that what you were doing at Allatoona earlier today? Looking for proof?"

"Yes. Of a kind."

"What proof?"

"You have people following me all the time. I'm surprised you don't know."

Norris smiled. "I'm surprised I don't either. Someone slipped up."

He was actually being likable, Joe thought. He was getting a glimpse of the charismatic politician who was on his way to the White House.

"I was looking for evidence connecting the car Jelak abandoned to your daughter's crime scene." That was true at least.

"And you found it?"

"I found it."

"And you were able to locate Jelak from it."

"Yes. Much good it did me."

"But you almost had him."

Joe tilted his head and gazed curiously at

him. “Almost isn’t good enough. I thought you’d be ranting and raving.”

“You have a right to that opinion. I’ve given you a hard time.”

“Are you apologizing?”

“Maybe.” He looked Joe in the eye. “I felt like I was being crucified, and everyone was taking their turn with the hammer and nails. I’ve dealt with red tape and bureaucracy, and I couldn’t stand the thought of Nancy Jo’s death being buried in it. You were a prime target, and I let loose.”

“I noticed,” Joe said dryly.

“And I’ll still be after you. I just wanted you to know that you’re the only one I’ve seen who’s brought in results. You found Jelak once; I think you’ll find him again. You don’t have to worry about one of my employees tailing you any longer. If you see a car behind you, it will be me. When you find him, I want to be there.” He paused. “If I didn’t have to keep on your ass, I think I’d like you, Quinn.” He added, “And I believe my Nancy Jo would have liked you too.”

“I know I would have liked her, Senator.” He turned away from him. “And now I’m going to go home and soothe my wounds and prepare for the next foray. I wanted to get Jelak. I’ve *got* to get him.”

"Because of your Eve Duncan."

"Because of Eve and your daughter and Margaret Selkirk and all the other women who Jelak is victimizing. They're all important." Nancy Jo had said something like that, he remembered. He strode toward his car. "They all matter."

"You could talk about it." Eve turned over in bed and laid her head on his shoulder. "You're lying there stiff as a board and staring into the darkness."

"I should have caught him," Joe said. "Caleb said I blew it, and he was right."

"He was wrong. Caleb is a fanatic, and you shouldn't listen to him."

"It's hard not to listen to him. He insists on making himself heard."

"You almost got Jelak. That's more than he did."

"Almost, again. If you finished one of your reconstructions and stepped back and realized that you'd almost got it right, what would you do? You know the answer. You'd smash the clay and start again."

She chuckled. "Okay, no more comforting bullshit." She paused. "But you never told me how you found him in the first place."

He was silent. "Nancy Jo. She can connect with him."

"How?"

"Blood. Her own blood that he took from her."

She shuddered. "I'm sorry I asked."

"No, you're stronger than that. As strong as she was when she was trying to find him for me." He pulled her closer. "She's desperate. She wants to protect her father, but it's more than that. It's something to do with the blood he took from her. It's like an obscene bond that links them together even though she's no longer alive."

"Blood." She had a sudden memory of that suffocating moment when she had been working on the reconstruction. "I can understand how she feels."

"I felt . . . sorry for her. She was touching the blood on that seat and trying to help me, but she was hurting. I didn't know how to help her, so I just kept asking her questions, hammering at her." He added in frustration, "I don't know how to handle any of this. At first, I was afraid of her. Then I just wanted to get rid of her because she was disturbing my life. But gradually I began to change. I can't look upon her as anything but the person she was when she was alive. She's still that person."

"Is she?"

"Except that she's learning, changing. I

never thought much about life after death. I never expected to have to — I don't know the rules any more than Nancy Jo does. Was I right to go to her and ask her to help? It hurt her. Shouldn't I have left her in peace? They always talk a lot about rest and peace."

"If you didn't force her, then it was her choice."

"Yeah, some choice. She's scared that Jelak is going to kill her father. She'd do anything to keep that from happening."

Eve got up on one elbow and shook her head as she looked down at him. "Only you, Joe."

"What?"

"For a man who was mad as hell that this thing had happened to him, you've taken a giant leap. Now you want to protect her rights even from yourself. I suppose I should have expected it. It's how you are, what you do." She kissed him gently. "You've tried to protect me from the moment you met me."

"I had no other option. I knew from the beginning that protecting you was protecting myself." He pulled her back down and cuddled her close. "And you can't tell me that if you were faced with this craziness that you wouldn't try to figure it out and make it better for everyone."

Bonnie.

If Eve had accepted that Bonnie was a spirit instead of trying to tell herself that she was a hallucination or dream, would she have been able to put her little girl's soul at rest? The thought was unbearably painful. Joe was searching, trying to find answers, trying to set everything right for Nancy Jo. All these years Eve had only taken comfort, love, and survival from Bonnie. She had thought bringing her home was the one true answer, but what if it wasn't? What if she could find some other way to give Bonnie what she needed? What if the solution had been there all along, and she had ignored it? Joe wasn't ignoring anything, he was probing, questioning. "You're a better person than I am, Joe. I believe I'd have a tendency to hide away from a truth as uncomfortable as this. Just do what you think is right. That always works for you and everyone around you."

"Easy to say. The rules may be different." He paused. "And I can't make any mistakes now. He's getting too close." He shifted in bed. "Go to sleep. Staying awake and listening to me trying to sift through this thing isn't going to do any good."

"It's doing good for me," she said. "I'm learning what a fine man you are, Joe. I always knew it, but reinforcement is always welcome."

"And it took a ghost to show you what a sterling character I am."

"No, it took your response to the situation." She pressed her lips to his shoulder. "And the knowledge that I'm still learning from you. Good night, Joe."

He didn't answer. His hand was gently stroking her hair, and he was still staring into the darkness.

Thinking, she realized. Trying to solve the puzzle. Trying to make everything come out right . . .

As he had tried to make everything all right for her all those years ago when she had been spiraling downward into a depression from which there probably would have been no return.

But there had been a return, and it had started that night over a year after she had lost Bonnie. She had gone to bed, and Joe had called her on her cell phone.

"I'm fine, Joe. It's just a little cold."

"A little cold that's lasted over a month," Joe said grimly. "Not surprising since you've practically stopped eating. You must have lost ten pounds in the last couple weeks."

"You're exaggerating. Maybe a few pounds."

She wished he'd just hang up. She was so tired. All she wanted to do was close her eyes and go to sleep. She knew Joe meant well, but he kept at her all the time. To eat, to get more rest, to stop the constant frantic work, any work, that filled her days and kept her sane.

"If you're not better tomorrow, I'm taking you to a doctor."

"No, it's just a cold, Joe." She paused. "Any news?"

"Do you think I wouldn't have told you right away? No news. We haven't found her."

Yes, she shouldn't have asked the question. She knew it hurt Joe to have her do it. Yet she had to ask it every time. The question dominated every moment of her life since Bonnie had been taken over a year ago. "I'm sorry. It's not that I think she's alive and you'll find her and bring her back to me. I've accepted that my Bonnie is dead." But it still hurt to put that acceptance into words, and she had to stop for a minute. "It's just that every night I'd put her to bed, tuck her in, and kiss her good night. It hurts me to think of her thrown away somewhere, out there all alone."

"We'll find her, Eve."

"I know you will . . . someday. I want to go to sleep now, Joe. I'm very tired."

He muttered a curse. "I'll be over at ten to

pick you up and take you to the doctor."

"We'll talk about it tomorrow. Thank you for everything, Joe. Good night." She hung up.

She set her phone on the bedside table and turned out the light.

Go to sleep. There was no pain when she just let go and let the darkness carry her away. She was beginning to welcome, embrace, that darkness.

"But you can't have it, Mama. You have to come back."

Bonnie's voice, Eve realized hazily. She was feverish. It couldn't be Bonnie. Bonnie was lost . . .

"I'm not lost. I'm here with you. I'll always be with you, Mama. Open your eyes and look at me."

Eve slowly opened her eyes. Bonnie was sitting on the window seat with one leg tucked beneath her. She was wearing the Bugs Bunny T-shirt and jeans in which Eve had last seen her. "See?" Her smile lit her small face. "I'm here. Why are you so sad? We're still together."

"No, you're —" She couldn't say the word. Not when this Bonnie was so glowingly alive. "You're a dream."

"Am I? I don't feel like a dream. But maybe you're right. Does it matter?"

"No." Not as long as she could see her

smile, hear her voice. "I've missed you, baby."

"I've missed you, too, Mama. But we're together now. You should have known we'd be together. It just took a little while." She leaned back against the alcove wall. "But Joe is scared you're going to get really sick. You'll have to get better so that he doesn't worry so much."

"I know. But sometimes it doesn't seem to matter."

"It matters to me. Everything you do matters to me." She smiled. "So I know that you'll do everything you can to get well and strong. Just like you used to tell me, Mama." She chuckled. "Eat your vegetables. Wear your sweater. Don't jump into puddles."

Eve found herself smiling. "I promise I won't jump into any puddles. And you didn't pay attention to me as much as you should have, young lady."

"But I always knew that everything you did was to keep me happy. You always wanted me to be happy."

"I still want that, baby."

"Then stop looking so sad. You've got to be happy too." She tilted her head. "I don't want to talk about vegetables and puddles. Would you like to sing a song with me?"

"I'd like that very much. 'All the Pretty Little Horses'?"

"No, that's not my favorite now. I like the one about wishing on a star. It's happier. It's all about dreams coming true. Do you remember the words?"

"Yes, I remember every song we've ever sung together, Bonnie."

"Your voice sounds kind of funny. Maybe I should start."

"Maybe you should." She leaned back, her gaze fixed on her little girl, on her Bonnie.

It was a dream, but let it go on.

Let Bonnie not go away.

Bonnie's voice came softly from the darkness. "When you wish upon a star . . ."

Eve didn't know at what point she drifted into a deep sleep that night. When she woke the next morning, she expected to return to that same profound depression.

It didn't happen. She felt a strange serenity and optimism that came as a complete surprise.

And what she thought were dreams of Bonnie became part of her life. They didn't come every night, but frequently enough so that she never lost that feeling that on some level Bonnie was still with her.

And with that knowledge she had begun to function, to slowly come alive again.

Came alive and turned to forensic sculpting, a work that filled her life, and to Joe, who became the reason to live, to go on.

She moved closer to him.

"What's wrong?" he asked. "Can't you sleep?"

He was still trying to fix her problems, heal her.

"I'm fine." She kissed him on the chin and put her head back on his shoulder. "Nothing is wrong, Joe."

Dahlonega, Georgia

The teenage girl's blood was worse than useless, Jelak thought in frustration as he got into the Mazda that was parked in front of the brick office with the small sign on the door: R. J. BAKER, M.D. Nicole Spelling's blood had fed him but not given him anything more to replace the precious and quality blood he had lost. She had been too young, too shallow.

Oh, well. She had proved useful. He'd forced her to drive him to this small burg outside Atlanta to find a doctor who could take care of his wound. He'd been careful to choose an M.D. with a practice on the edge of town, and all had gone well.

It was about time. Joe Quinn had ruined all his plans for a quick finale to his glorious quest. He had put him on the run and forced him to take that inadequate Nicole Spelling just to survive.

Suppress the anger and hatred. He'd get his own back. What do you care about, Joe Quinn? What can I take from you that will punish you enough?

The answer was clear, and every bit of the blood in his body was pounding in response to it as he drove away from the office and headed back to Atlanta.

"A BP gas station was robbed and Calvin Hodges, the attendant, murdered," Schindler said as he came into the squad room the next morning. "It was on Hawthorne Street, a few miles from where we located Jelak's car last night." He paused. "There was a CLOSED sign on the door, and they didn't discover the body until this morning, when Hodges's wife drove out to check on him. The attendant was killed with a knife thrust to the heart. But there was blood on the floor near the door. It's probably not Hodges's."

"Any vehicles missing?"

"No, the attendant's car was still parked in the back," he added grimly. "But the last credit card to be entered into the gas pumps was for a Nicole Spelling."

"So?"

"Her parents reported her missing last night."

"Shit."

"Age sixteen, just got her license, driving a red Mazda her parents gave her for her birthday," Schindler said. "They said that she had a date to celebrate with her boyfriend. She'd bought a new dress and was very excited. That's why they were so worried when she hadn't come home on time."

"Sixteen."

"Yeah, sucks doesn't it?" Schindler said. "We've put out an APB on her and the car, but nothing yet."

And there probably wouldn't be anything good, Joe thought. Another Nancy Jo.

No, Nicole Spelling was even younger, almost a child.

His phone rang. Caleb.

"No, we haven't caught him," he said when he picked up. "But he's been busy. We have a dead gas-station attendant and a missing sixteen-year-old girl."

"It's logical. He'd want to replace the lost blood."

"I'm not in the mood for logic right now."

"I can understand that. So I'll go right to what's important. He's going to be angry and frustrated. There's no telling what Jelak will do. Expect anything."

"I always do." He paused. "Particularly from you."

"That's very intelligent of you. I hate to be predictable. But remember that I'm a very good ally. You may need allies soon." He paused. "What about enlisting a little help from your friend in a better place? It worked before."

"It was difficult. She told me not to ask her again."

"But you may anyway. Isn't that right?"

A teenager celebrating her sixteenth birthday. "Yes."

"And so you should. Priorities, Quinn. Call me when you find out something."

Priorities.

His job was keeping people alive. Keeping Eve alive.

Any way he could.

And now he had to bite the bullet and call Eve and tell her about Nicole Spelling.

THIRTEEN

"But you're not sure," Eve said. "She could still be alive."

"It's not looking good, Eve." Joe was silent a moment. "Damn, I didn't want to tell you."

"No, I had to know," she said numbly. "You always try to shelter me. Let me know when you find out for sure." She hung up.

Nicole Spelling. Sixteen years old. All her life before her.

Stop thinking about her. Go on with her own work.

She turned back to the reconstruction. It was almost finished. She could see the curve of the little boy's lips and the plumpness of his cheeks. "We'll find your home," she said softly. "We're almost there, Matt."

But that young girl would probably never go home again. What horror had she gone through?

Her cell phone rang and she tensed. Joe

again to tell her they'd found Nicole Spelling?

No, not Joe. She didn't recognize the ID.

"Hello, Eve." She didn't recognize his voice either. Thick, deep, a slight Southern accent. "This is very unusual for me. But I felt I had to allow myself the pleasure. I deserve it since that son of a bitch that you're screwing has put himself between us."

She stiffened. "Who is this?"

"Your master, your partner. Gift to Gift, Eve."

"Jelak?" she whispered.

"I haven't heard your voice in a long time. Perhaps five years ago when you gave that TV interview on *20/20.* You were magnificent. All the qualities that I look for in a kill. But there are so few women who can bring those to me. I knew that you'd be the final piece that would assure that I'd win the game. But I wasn't near enough to the end then to come and take you. But I kept my eye on you."

"While you were murdering all those other women." She added, "And children. You murdered children, didn't you?"

"And that does bother you. Actually, very few. Children are only good to feed, and I had a host to furnish me with that."

"Henry Kistle."

"Yes. I followed him when he left Atlanta. I knew what he was and how he took his pleasure. There were so few individuals who I knew would be able to help me with the blood. Even then, I was aware of the hunger though I didn't know what it meant. When I came back from Fiero, I knew my destiny and my place in it." He added scornfully, "The fool didn't even realize I was shadowing him, taking my fill. He'd do the kill, and I'd follow and take the blood. It went on for years. I might have had to reveal myself at some point, but then you came back into his life. Competition. I couldn't allow him to kill you. I was saving you for the final ritual. If you hadn't killed him, I would have had to do it. It would have been a pity. After all, I did owe him a debt for all those years of saving me from making those boring kills."

"You're a monster."

He chuckled. "They've been calling us monsters for centuries. At the same time they worship our power."

"Vampires? You actually think you're a vampire?"

"Not what those fools call vampire. They have no idea. But you'll know soon. You'll feel the beat of our hearts, the flow of the blood. Gift to Gift, Eve."

Dear God, she could feel it now.

Imagination.

"You're mad."

"That's not nice." He was silent, then said softly, "You didn't ask me if I'd fed on your Bonnie after Henry Kistle killed her."

She felt as if he'd stabbed her. "He didn't kill her. I know he didn't kill her. We didn't find the body."

"But you're not quite sure, are you? As I said, I wasn't entirely certain of my destiny back then, but I knew Henry and the blood always fascinated me. You probably know that by now."

"Yes," she said hoarsely.

"Pretty Bonnie. I didn't realize then that children were almost useless to win the game."

"You're just saying it to hurt me."

"I do want to hurt you. I wanted the ritual to be quick and triumphant, but Joe Quinn changed all that. I'm very angry, Eve."

"It didn't happen. Not to Bonnie."

"You'll know soon. You'll feel her, join with her. Gift to Gift."

"Stop saying that."

"I've upset you? But then you shouldn't have been ugly to me. I'll always win, Eve."

"Why are you calling me?"

"I needed you. He shot me. He took my blood. I was afraid I'd lost too much. But now I feel strong again."

"Did you kill Nicole Spelling?"

"But of course. But she was almost useless. Like a child." He paused. "Like Bonnie. I'll see you soon, Eve."

He hung up.

Her hands clenched the edge of the table until the knuckles turned white.

She felt dizzy with pain.

Bonnie.

The ugliness of the picture Jelak had drawn was beyond belief. A child being fed on by that monster.

Her baby.

Oh, God, the tears were running down her cheeks.

It was a lie. He'd only wanted to hurt her. It had to be a lie.

"Eve?" Caleb was standing in the doorway. "You didn't answer my knock. I saw the squad car was still here, and I was worried that you — What the hell is wrong?" He was across the room in four strides. "You look sick."

"I feel sick." She wiped her damp cheeks with the back of her hands. "Jelak."

"What about him?" He took his handkerchief and gently wiped her eyes. "Other than that the bastard might have killed two other people. Though that's enough."

"There's no might about it. He killed the gas-station attendant. He killed Nicole Spelling." She drew a shaky breath. "Though she was useless to him. Like a child." Her voice broke. "Like Bonnie."

He stiffened. "You've seen him? Talked to him?"

"He called me." Lord, she had to pull herself together. "He wanted to hurt me."

"I should have expected it." He took her hand and led her toward the couch. "Sit down. I'll get you a glass of water."

She wasn't about to argue. She dropped down on the couch. "Why should you have expected it?"

"He would be furious at Joe Quinn for what happened. He'd want to strike out and hurt him. He knows he can hurt him by hurting you." He handed her a glass of water. "And it appears he succeeded."

"Bonnie." She took a swallow of water. "He told me she was one of the —" She couldn't say it. She couldn't even think it. "It wasn't true. I knew when he was saying it that it was flimsy — but he — it could be true. I don't know."

"And that's what he's counting on." He knelt in front of her and was carefully wiping her face with a cool, wet cloth. "You don't know. What you don't know can twist and cut and hurt you."

"You don't have to do this." She reached up and took the cloth from him. "You're being very kind, but I'm okay now. I'm sorry I was being so childish."

"I'm not." He sat back on his heels. "I'm sorry he hurt you before I managed to kill the bastard." His eyes met her own. "And in the most painful way possible. You're trying to block it out, but it will come back when you least expect it. When you're working, before you go to sleep . . . I don't think we should let him have that victory. Do you?"

She tried to smile. "No, I won't let him do that to me. It will take a little while, but I'll —"

"I don't want it to take a little while. It would worry me. I don't like to be worried." He took both her hands. "Listen, Eve, it didn't happen. Jelak never knew your Bonnie. He never touched her. You know that. In your heart, you're absolutely certain."

As she met his eyes, she felt a tremendous surge of relief. Of course she knew that. She just hadn't been able to see beyond that load of agony that had been heaped upon her. It was so clear now. "He never touched her."

"And if he ever tells you that again, you'll realize immediately that it's a lie." He smiled. "He can't hurt you. Not with Bonnie."

She nodded, then suddenly stiffened. "Are you doing something that — I'm not Patty's grandfather."

"Not in the least. I'm not changing anything about the way you think or even your perception. I just did a little reinforcement. When you're raw, you need a little bandage to make you stop thinking about the wound."

And she was still aware of that hurtful wound, but it was anger, not agony that she was feeling. Anger at Jelak. "You're a dangerous man, Caleb."

"Not to you." He got to his feet. "Well, yes, I should probably qualify that. Not intentionally. I'll make us a pot of coffee. Where's Jane?"

"With Patty again. I'm not much company when I'm finishing up a reconstruction." She got to her feet and went over to the skull. "Don't tell her or Joe about the call. If he wanted to hurt Joe through me, I'm not going to let him do it. Why are you here, Caleb?"

"I wanted to check to make sure you were

okay. I've been uneasy since Quinn shot Jelak. It opened a whole new spectrum of problems."

"Jelak's still after basically the same thing."

"But just the fact that he called you indicates that his mindset has changed. He was being moderately cautious before. That's gone."

"But if he's careless, that may be good for us."

"He won't be careless. He's smart, he's been trained by an expert, and he's had years of experience. Bold doesn't mean careless."

"He was enraged at Joe." She shivered. "Ugly rage."

"Quinn is standing in his way."

"The way to me."

He nodded. "His whole focus for years has been on this final ritual. Now he's not sure if he might have to delay it if the blood he lost was important to his resurrection."

"How would he know?"

"He might suspect by the way he feels. No way to be sure until after he takes you." He smiled without mirth. "Then if he doesn't become a god, he'll know he has to keep on with the rituals until he feels the power."

"Which means that he could be killing

indefinitely. Particularly if his definition of power is the ability to become invisible."

He nodded. "But he'll go first for a known power source."

She knew where he was going and it terrified her. "Jane."

He held out the coffee cup to her. "She's definitely a powerful woman. She'd be on his list. Either before or after. You knew that."

Yes, she had known, but the thought still frightened her. Caleb wanted her to be frightened, she realized suddenly. "My Lord, you're devious. First, you set me up by making me feel better about Bonnie, then you make me afraid for Jane. You're trying to manipulate me."

He nodded. "But I really didn't mean to bring Bonnie into the mix. That was an impulse Jelak triggered. But I did come out here to prepare the way."

"For what?"

"In the end it's going to come down to you, Eve. You're the prize that Jelak's got to have. Quinn will let it go on forever if it means putting you or Jane in danger. I knew that the minute I saw Quinn with you."

"But not you, Caleb," she said. "You don't care if either one of us is at risk."

"I care."

"That's hard to believe." She remembered something else. "You came here to 'prepare the way' with me. But you'd already done it with Jane, hadn't you? I wondered why I felt as if the two of you had a kind of bond."

"Very perceptive. You might say that was true." He smiled. "We did share an experience."

"You were covering all your bases."

"That's what a hunter does," he said simply. "And I could have behaved much more dishonorably than I did."

"So what happens now?"

"Nothing. Both of you know what you should do to save lives. You know that I'm ready to help you." He set his cup down on the counter. "And it may all be for nothing. Quinn may be able to bring Jelak to his knees without me involving you as bait. It would be a wonderful and welcome solution."

"You won't be involving me or Jane," Eve said. "We won't allow you to manipulate us, Caleb. You may have set us up, but that's as far as it goes. Any action we take will be our decision."

"I didn't expect anything else." He turned and moved toward the door. "But you have my number, and you know I'm here for you when the time is right."

"You're very sure, aren't you?"

"Yes." His smile disappeared, and she could see an element of regret in his expression. "I've been a hunter for a long time. I can see the pattern."

Eve stood there for a moment after he had walked out the door. It was exasperating that she couldn't dislike him. She wished she could attribute it to that strange persuasive ability Caleb seemed to possess, but she believed him when he had told her that he could have been more dishonorable. He was probably being as ethical as he could be considering he was such a ruthless bastard.

And what a hell of a dichotomy that was.

But she'd have no trouble at all disliking him if he did anything but tread delicately in his attempt to manipulate Jane. She'd go after him with guns blazing.

"I'm on my way to Dahlonega," Joe said when he called Eve. "They've found Nicole Spelling."

"Dead?" Eve asked.

"Yes. She was found in the examining room in a doctor's office there. Dr. Baker was killed too. Jelak probably forced him to treat him, then murdered him. Nicole was clearly a ritual murder."

"Sixteen. So young . . ."
"Yes. Just a kid."
"It just goes on and on. When are we going to be able to end it?"
Joe didn't answer. "I'll call you from Dahlonega and let you know what's happening there." He hung up.
She had been expecting that Joe would tell her Nicole was dead from the time she'd gotten the call from Jelak. It didn't make the news any less shocking.
When would they be able to end it?
Joe hadn't answered her. How could he? Jelak seemed to be able to go on forever. He thought he was some kind of Monster Superman, and the way he was running roughshod over the world she could almost believe it.
"Bad news?" Jane had just come in the front door.
Eve nodded. "Nicole Spelling. Her body was found in Dahlonega at a doctor's office. Joe's on his way there now."
Jane shook her head. "Ever since I heard about her disappearance, I've been hoping . . ."
"Me too," Eve said. "Hoping doesn't seem to do any good." She turned to face her. "But that's all we have unless we try to do something about it."

"No," Jane said sharply. "I can see where this is going." Her eyes narrowed on Eve's face. "Caleb's been talking to you."

"Yes."

"Dammit, he should have left you alone."

"But he didn't. Just like he didn't leave you alone. Did he?"

"No. I would have told you, but I didn't want —"

"You didn't want to involve me, you wanted to protect me. For heaven's sake, Jane, we've always worked through things together. You let Caleb convince you to close me out."

"It was your life," Jane said. "Caleb couldn't have convinced me of anything if I hadn't been scared shitless." She shrugged. "And he didn't make me commit to anything. It was just a sort of oblique suggestion."

"That you allow yourself to be used as bait." She added, "Yes, 'oblique' is the word."

Jane's gaze flew to her face. "That son of a bitch. You?"

"Divide and conquer," Eve said dryly.

"I'll cut off his balls," Jane said.

"He's obsessed. He wanted bait. He didn't care which one of us he had to use."

"Well, I care," Jane said. "You're out

of it, Eve."

"You've already decided that you're going to let Caleb use you." She shook her head. "What on earth did he do to you? He said that you'd 'experienced' something together."

"It has nothing to do with that," Jane said. "If I thought it had, I'd really be after his balls."

"He's very persuasive." She added quietly, "No, Jane." She held up her hand as Jane opened her lips to protest. "I won't let it happen. I know how you feel." Her lips thinned. "But I won't let him push either one of us into something until we decide it's right. Though God knows that news about Nicole Spelling is a pretty big push on its own."

Jane nodded soberly. "Jelak just keeps coming."

Should she tell Jane about the call from Jelak? At first, she had wanted to protect her from that ugliness, but she couldn't keep silent after reprimanding Jane for not confiding. They had to face everything together as they had since Jane had come into their lives.

"And he's coming nearer to us all the time." She paused. "He called me today." She held up her hand to stop Jane's flow of questions. “Sit down. I’ll tell you all about it. Everything has got to be out in the open. Even a few things I was waiting for Joe to tell you.”

Nicole Spelling was stretched out naked on an exam table in the cold, sterile room. Her hands were crossed on her breasts. There was no goblet in her hand.

Schindler shook his head. “God, I was hoping we weren’t going to have to tell her folks that son of a bitch had done this to their kid.”

Joe nodded. “I know.” He had known that this job was going to be rough. He had dreaded it all the long drive to Dahlonega. And it appeared that the case was still squarely in their laps. He had talked to the local sheriff, and they were more than eager to turn over jurisdiction of the case. It was too ugly for this quiet town. “The authorities here are going to send Dr. Baker to their own county morgue. They want to keep him here. He’s served this town for nearly forty years. But after forensics gets through here, we’ll have Nicole Spelling taken to the morgue in Atlanta.” His lips twisted. “And then we get to talk to her parents and get a final ID. I guess we should feel lucky that the doctor was alone in the office when Jelak made his visit. We only have two bodies to deal with." It was hard to feel lucky after seeing that kid lying on the table and white-haired Dr. Baker crumpled on the floor of his office.

He started for the door that led to the waiting room. "I'll make some calls to the precinct while I'm waiting for forensics to finish. You don't have to stick around. I'll take the kid home."

Take her home. The phrasing had been unconscious. Eve's phrase. Perhaps it was because Nicole was so young that he identified her with Eve's lost children. "And I'll talk to her parents."

"Thanks, Joe." Schindler headed for the door. "I'm not about to refuse. This one is tough."

And so was Schindler, but there was always a case that hit too close to the heart. He was probably identifying Nicole with his twelve-year-old daughter, Cindy. "Yeah. But you're not off scot-free. I'll let you do the paperwork."

"No problem." Schindler was already heading for the parking lot.

Joe dropped down in a waiting-room chair and wearily stretched his legs out before him.

No goblet. Nicole hadn't been found

worthy. Son of a bitch.

For some reason that omission was pissing Joe off. He almost wished that Nicole would pop out of that exam room so that he could tell her that she was worthy, and loved, and all the other good things to which a young girl had a right.

How long he'd come in such a short time. Now he was wishing for a ghostly visit? No, but it wouldn't blow him away if it happened.

Evidently it wasn't going to happen. Maybe Nicole was happy to move on. Good for you, kid. Maybe you could have a few words with my friend Nancy Jo.

And in return she could tell you that you shouldn't pay any attention to that murdering bastard.

You're damn worthy.

Nicole Spelling was proving worthy after all, Jelak thought as he watched the medical examiner's van drive away from the doctor's office. Not in the most splendid sense but still very useful.

It was what he had planned, but plans often went awry.

Not this time.

He watched Joe Quinn get in his car and drive out of the parking lot. He'd accompany Nicole to the morgue as if she were someone of importance instead of a mere trifle.

Go on, Quinn. Do your duty. Be her honor guard.

I'll be right behind you.

No use hurrying, Joe thought. He'd let the M.E. van get to the morgue and the techs ready Nicole Spelling for the final visit from her parents.

Neither Joe nor Nicole's parents would be eager for that final confirmation.

He took his foot off the accelerator and braked to slow down.

Nothing happened.

He pressed the brake again.

Nothing.

Shit.

No brakes?

Joe stomped on the brake again.

Nothing. Completely gone.

Okay. No reason to panic. He wasn't driving through the hills any longer. It was pitch-dark out here in the country, but he could barely make out dirt on the far side of the road. No deep gullies or ditches. He'd wait until he came to a level stretch, then drive off the road into the dirt that bordered it.

There. Up ahead.

He eased the car off the road and bumped along the rough dirt, gradually slowing. Then he swerved and came to a stop.

He sat there for a moment, getting his breath. The situation might not have been life-threatening, but it hadn't been pleasant.

And it shouldn't have happened.

There had been no problem on the drive up here. He kept the cars in great shape, and there should have been no —

"Need a lift?"

He tensed. His gaze shifted to the man walking toward him in the darkness. He could see only a dark silhouette framed against the headlights of the car parked several yards away.

"I'd say you might." Ed Norris smiled as he got close enough for Joe to identify. "Judging by that vehicular swan dive I saw you pull. It looked like your brakes are shot. You should really have them examined regularly. I could give you the name of my mechanic."

Joe got out of the car. "Should I ask what you're doing here, Norris?"

"I told you that I'd be the only one tailing you from now on. When I heard about Nicole Spelling, I naturally decided I had to see what was happening."

"And you didn't by any chance tamper with my brakes?"

Norris's smile vanished. "Hell, no. Why would I do that?"

"I don't think you did. It's not your style." His gaze searched the darkness behind Norris. "So it might be a good idea for us to get in your car and get the hell out —"

A motion behind Norris in the darkness, black on black.

"Down!" Joe pushed Norris to the ground.

A bullet tore past Joe's ear as he dropped on top of him.

The second bullet didn't miss.

Eve was still up working when her phone rang at eleven forty that night.

Joe? He'd called earlier to tell her he'd be late.

It wasn't Joe.

"Eve, Caleb. I'm going to pick you and Jane up in fifteen minutes. Be dressed and ready to go."

"I've already told you, I'm not taking any orders from you. I've discussed it with Jane and we're not at all pleased about the way you —"

"Don't argue. I'm taking you to the hospital. Damn, I guessed wrong. I never thought he'd go for Joe."

Her heart stopped. "Joe? Joe's in the hospital?"

"No. I'll explain on the way. Get Jane and be ready." He hung up.

She wanted to murder him. Throwing that out about Joe, then hanging up. She didn't know if Joe's not being in the hospital was bad or good.

She was scared to death it was bad.

She headed down the hall to wake up Jane.

"Tell me about Joe," she said, as she and Jane got into Caleb's car. "Now."

"I don't have anything to tell. I wish I did." He pulled out of the driveway. "I've been in contact with Detective Schindler at the precinct. He came back early from Dahlonega to do paperwork. Quinn was accompanying the body to the morgue later. They got a call from Georgia State Patrol that Joe's car was found at the side of the road about ten miles out of Dahlonega. Ed Norris was lying near it. He'd been shot. His car was nearby too."

"What about Joe?" Jane asked.

Caleb shook his head. "No sign of him. They took Norris to Northside Hospital for treatment. Shoulder wound. He was unconscious, but the EMTs didn't think the wound was life-threatening."

"Joe," Eve said. "If Norris was there, he has to know what happened to Joe. I have to talk to him."

"That's why we're on the way to the hospital," Caleb said. "I knew that would be your first reaction. I already checked with the hospital. They're not allowing anyone to see him yet. And he has a whole platoon of security camping out in the hall to protect the great man."

"I have to see him."

He nodded. "I'll see to it. Let me go in first."

"Dammit, we've got to talk to him," Jane said. "You have to make it happen, Caleb."

"I said I'd do it. Have a little faith." Caleb glanced at her. "I want to find Quinn as much as you do."

"No way."

"Perhaps not for the same reasons, but I'm very heavily invested in Quinn's well-being. I promise we'll find out everything Norris knows within a few minutes of getting to the hospital."

"Providing he's not still unconscious," Eve said.

"Then it may take a few minutes more," he said absently.

Eve stared at him, startled.

"I won't hurt him," Caleb said, as he

noticed her expression. "Trust me."
She had to trust him. She had to know about Joe.

FOURTEEN

"He's awake." Caleb was whisking Eve and Jane through the crowd of security and police in the hall outside Norris's room.

The crowd was parting like the Red Sea, Eve thought. Smiling at Caleb as if he was their best friend and politely at her and Jane. One of the aides even opened the door and stepped aside to let them enter.

Ed Norris's shoulder was bandaged, and he was very pale. His gaze fastened on Eve's face. "You're Eve Duncan. I've wanted to meet you ever since I heard about that goblet that bastard left at your place. He wants to kill you too."

"Where's Joe Quinn?"

He shook his head. "I don't know. I stopped because Quinn was having car trouble. He asked me if I'd tampered with his brakes, then told me to get back in my car."

"You were shot. Was Joe shot too?"

"I wish I could tell you. He saw someone behind me and told me to get down. Then he pushed me down and dropped on top of me." His lips tightened. "The bullet hit my shoulder on my way down. If he hadn't pushed me, it would probably have been a chest or heart wound. He saved my life."

"But what happened to Joe?"

"I passed out almost immediately." He paused. "I thought I heard another shot."

Eve inhaled sharply.

"I'm sorry. I'm not sure," Norris said. "Damn, I feel helpless. I've got to get out of this hospital."

Eve felt helpless too. Helpless and scared and panicky. "Thank you." She turned toward the door. "If you remember anything more, call me."

"I will." He added as she reached the door, "It was Jelak, wasn't it?"

"Yes, I'm sure it was."

She left the room and let Caleb carve a path for them through the crowd to the elevator. She didn't speak until the doors of the elevator closed behind them. "It had to be Jelak."

Caleb nodded. "That goes without saying."

"He stalked Joe and shot him," Jane said. "Revenge for the bullet he took from Joe?"

"He was terribly angry with him," Eve said. "He said Joe was in his way."

"Not revenge. At least not the major motivation." The doors opened, and Caleb stepped aside for them to exit. "Which may be a lucky break."

Eve's gaze flew to his face. "What?"

"Jelak may want him alive." He was leading them through the reception to the parking lot. "Norris said he heard a bullet. It didn't necessarily have to be a fatal bullet."

"You think he's still alive?" Eve stopped to look at him as they reached his car. Desperate hope was soaring through her. "Why?"

"Get in the car. Let's talk this out."

"Why?" Jane repeated, after they'd settled in the car.

"Jelak was stalking you to lure Eve into a trap. Quinn put all kinds of safeguards around you to keep that from happening." His lips twisted. "And I was working around those safeguards to pull Jelak into a trap."

"I noticed."

"But Jelak decided to go around a different way to get what he wanted."

"Joe," Eve whispered.

Caleb nodded. "You've been with Quinn a long time. He's important to you. If you thought his life was in danger, he'd have his bait."

"Then he wouldn't kill him," Eve said quickly. "He wouldn't be able to get what he wanted if Joe was dead."

"If you're right," Jane said.

"Quinn was taken from the scene. Why? Unless Jelak intended to use him for something."

"Or make us think he was alive and still use him," Jane said.

"That's true. I won't deny that's a possibility. We'll have to see."

"You expect him to call me," Eve said.

"Oh, yes. I don't think there's any doubt about it." Caleb started the car. "But since we don't know when, I'll take you home to wait in comfort."

"Comfort? Not likely."

"Comparatively speaking. May I wait with you?"

Why not? Caleb might be able to help if worse came to worst. "As long as you don't try to move us all like puppets."

Caleb shook his head. "The pieces are in place through no manipulation by me. I'll just try to keep them in play and help you survive."

"Help Joe survive," Eve said fiercely. "I'm not going to let Jelak kill him."

"And that's what Jelak is counting on."

She knew that, but it didn't matter. "He's not going to die, Caleb."

"I hear you." Caleb drove out of the parking lot. "And Jelak will be delighted to hear it too."

"Be quiet, Caleb," Jane said curtly. "We know what you're saying. We know what you want. We'll work it out."

"I'm sure you will. That's why I want to be on-site to watch you." He looked away from her. "But I'll try to keep my own counsel while I'm doing it. Mum's the word."

"Go to bed, Eve," Jane said gently. "It's almost dawn. I know you can't sleep, but you could stretch out and rest."

"Why doesn't he call, dammit?" Eve shook her head. "I couldn't lie down. I feel as if I'm wound so tight that I'm close to breaking."

"Then work for a while. At least it will keep you occupied."

Eve nodded jerkily. "Okay. You're right." She moved across the room to her work area. "It won't keep my mind from going into high gear, but it will keep my hands busy."

Jane watched her for a few minutes before she turned and went out on the porch.

Caleb was coming down the lake path toward the cottage. Toby was trotting beside him. It was odd how Toby had taken such a liking to him.

"What were you doing?" she asked, as Caleb came up the steps a few minutes later.

"Walking. Thinking. Guarding." He sat down on the top step, and Toby plopped down on the porch above him. "Keeping out of your way so that you and Eve can comfort each other. I'm not a very comforting person."

"You have quite a few edges." She sat down beside him. "Guarding?"

"It would be like Jelak to stage an elaborate scenario, then hit hard when you weren't expecting it. I was just making sure he was nowhere around."

"But you weren't expecting him."

"No, I'm expecting Eve to get a call." He looked out over the lake, which was mirroring delicate pink and gold. "Dawn's breaking. He's making her wait a long time."

"Bastard."

"Smart bastard. The longer you worry, the more eager to pay the price."

"You said his taking Joe was a complete surprise to you. You're not easily surprised, Caleb."

"I was expecting it to be you. I was almost

certain that he'd try until he got you. He would recognize Joe's value on a cerebral level but not on an emotional one. Jelak operates almost entirely on his emotions."

"Why doesn't he feel that Joe's valuable?"

"He's male."

Her brow knitted. "So is Jelak."

"Not really. He's a vampire god in training. Or so he perceives himself."

"And men have no value for him? Why not?"

"The blood. It's too dominant and aggressive. He can't take the elements he needs from it. A woman's blood is smooth and complex, and the strength will blend like a river running to the sea."

She gazed at him. "You seem to know a hell of a lot about how he thinks."

"He thinks how the cult taught him to think, and I've made a study of the cult."

"When you're not hunting them down to kill them."

"But I had to know all that in order to hunt them down." He smiled. "Which makes me valuable to you because I can tell you how Jelak thinks."

"Why does he think that becoming a god is possible? Did this teacher that you told me taught Jelak claim he was a god?"

"Donari? No, he called himself master,

but he was a student like Jelak. But he was much further along on the path and saw in Jelak a bright light. He wanted to mold him."

"A cult composed of students and based on a flimsy legend. It would take a nutcase like Jelak to be drawn into it. I can't understand how it even existed at all, much less for hundreds of years."

"Power can be an amazing beacon. That's what's held the vampire legend intact since it began."

"You said it started because two brothers with supposed magical dark powers showed up in their village?"

"Yes, the Ridondo brothers. They evidently had a lot of charisma as well as their vaunted magical powers. They convinced the entire village that they weren't only vampire elite themselves but able to teach others how to attain that power."

"And what happened to the Ridondos?"

"They lived the high life for a number of years. Why not? They acted like kings, and everyone was afraid to oppose them. One of them, Jaime Ridondo, was even mayor of the town for over twenty years. One of the rules they laid down for the villagers was that no one was ever to speak of their power. That allowed them a certain degree of protection and permitted them to live normal lives."

"Normal?"

"Normal for them. They married, had children, but eventually moved away from the village."

"So that no one could ever prove they weren't the mythical creatures they claimed to be."

"It would have been the clever thing to do."

She shook her head. "And the legend lived on and made superstitious people like Jelak find their way to it."

"Yes, it's not surprising."

"It's surprising to me." She wrapped her arms around her knees. "I can't imagine that many ugly people rushing to embrace more ugliness."

"That's because you don't have the ugly gene. Jelak was born with it and just went looking for a place to plant it and make it grow."

She was silent a moment. "Jelak hates Joe. He won't let him live even if he thinks he's going to get what he wants. Isn't that right?"

"Not if he sees any way out."

"We can't let anything happen to him," she whispered. "It would kill Eve."

"And not you?"

She nodded. "He's been my friend for all the years I've been with them. It was difficult for me to get close to anyone during those first years. Eve was easier. She was like me. We'd both grown up on the streets. Joe was different. He was tough, but he'd never experienced what Eve and I had. I guess I was a little jealous of what Eve felt for Joe. I knew how hard it was for her to love anyone. Her whole focus was Bonnie. But she loved Joe and, heaven knows, Joe loved her. I'd watch him looking at her, and it made me feel lonely. I never let either one of them see it because I was grateful to have whatever Eve could share with me." She shrugged. "But Joe and I both knew that we had to get along, or one of us might lose Eve. It was never spoken, but the thought was always there. Neither one of us could stand the thought, so we gradually began to open to each other. But Joe never pushed me. He was just there whenever I needed him."

"That's pretty impressive."

"He is impressive, in every way." Her lips tightened. "And we can't let anything happen to him. There aren't that many good guys in the world that we can afford to let one of the best go down the tubes." She looked out at the dawn, which was now a bold and flaming statement. "And if Jelak doesn't call soon, I'll go crazy. I'm going to go in the house and see Eve trying not to show how much this is tearing her up." She got to her feet. "And I'll want to kill Jelak. If you can think of a way that we can arrange that, I'm ready to listen."

He murmured. "I assure you I'm working on it . . ."

She opened the screen door. "Work harder."

Eve's phone didn't ring until after two that afternoon.

She saw Jane and Caleb come to attention on the couch across the room. She braced herself and punched the button.

"Have you been waiting for me?" Jelak asked. "I would have called earlier, but I had a few arrangements to make. You're very special, and I had to prepare for the final stage of my transformation."

"You shot Joe."

"Of course, he had to be punished. He shed my blood. It could have been a terrible inconvenience. But I've faith in myself. No one could ever tell me the exact amount of true blood I'd need for my resurrection. Donari could only say my mind would tell me when I was ready. In spite of the slight loss, I still feel very strong. With you, I'll be ready. I have no doubt of it."

"I don't care about your damn blood. Is Joe still alive?"

"Yes, I had no intention of killing him yet. But I would have been able to be more accurate if Nancy Jo's father hadn't shown up and gotten in the way. That was completely unexpected. I had to hurry because I was afraid some of his aides might be hovering around him."

"How badly is Joe hurt?"

"A crease in his temple. Not nearly enough blood spilt to satisfy me after what he took from me. Though pain is nearly as good."

"I want to talk to him."

"Presently. We have negotiating to do. A gift for a gift."

"You're not going to release Joe no matter what I do."

"How can you be sure? I've had my revenge. He's not important to me. I'm sure Caleb has told you that he'd be no good to me even to feed. On the other hand, he could give me what I want most in the world."

"You're a monster. I can't trust a monster."

"But you have no choice." His voice

lowered to persuasive silkiness. "And in the end, wouldn't the possibility give you an excuse to take what you want?"

"I don't know what you mean."

"I've studied you for years. Your phrasing when you answer questions. Your expressions to given situations. That's how I knew that you were perfect for the final resurrection."

"So?"

"You want this. You're tired of searching for your Bonnie. You want it over. You want your life over. That's why you're so perfect for me. There will be joy when you come to me."

"You're mad."

"No, my mind is keen and sharp because I'm so close to the resurrection. In your heart of hearts you know that it's true. I only have to give you a reason to do it."

"Give me a reason. I want to talk to Joe."

He sighed. "Unfortunately, I can't do that yet. He's being very stubborn. He won't talk to you. I've hurt him exceedingly, but he said he won't let himself be used."

"He's already dead."

"You see? I knew you'd think that I was lying. That's why I'm irritated with Quinn. I didn't want this delay. I suppose I could send a photo to your phone, but you'd assume it was doctored. No, I have to find a way to convince him he has to talk to you."

"Yes, you do. I have to hear his voice, and he has to mention something to me that no one but the two of us would know."

"That should be no trouble. There are so many secrets that exist between a couple with your history. All he'd have to do is mention one episode." His voice was annoyed. "I did think that pain was the answer. He has amazing endurance. I'll just have to work out some other way. I have a few ideas."

"Let him go. You know the entire police force will be hunting for you. Cops look out for their own."

"It will be too late for Quinn. No, you're his only hope. Make up your mind to it." He paused. "Is Caleb there with you?"

"Yes."

"I thought as much. Tell him I'm not afraid of him any longer. Soon I'll be able to meet him face-to-face." He added, "I'm going to hang up now. I have to get busy finding a way to convince Quinn to do as I wish. I think I've found the key to him."

"Don't hurt him. I won't do anything you want me to do if I find out you've hurt him again."

"I told you, I'm going down another road.

Good-bye, Eve. You'll hear from me soon." He hung up.

"He sounded so smug," Eve said as she pressed the disconnect. "And confident. He's so damn sure of himself." She turned to Jane and Caleb. "But I think Joe must be alive. Jelak wouldn't be going to these lengths if he had nothing with which to bargain. He didn't even try to bluff."

Caleb nodded. "He has Quinn. But we have a little time to find him and try to set up a trap before Jelak goes for the jugular." He grimaced. "That was purely unintentional. I would never be so insensitive."

"You'd have to be as much a monster as Jelak to be that callous," Eve said. "And I'd like to know how you think you're going to use that time Jelak has given us."

Caleb was heading for the door. "As I told Jane, I'm working on it. I'll let you know when I do."

"I've told you all I know, Senator." Gary Schindler's lips thinned as he gazed at Norris lying in the hospital bed. "It's not as if we're not looking for Joe. He's a veteran of the department. Hell, I've worked with him myself for years. The whole department is using every means we have to locate him."

"Like you've used every means to find

Jelak before this," Norris said curtly. "He's still out there killing young girls like Nancy Jo. He shot me. He shot Joe Quinn. If there's a chance that Quinn is still alive, then you go out and find him."

"Get off my back," Schindler suddenly said harshly. "I'm doing what I can, and nothing you can say will get me to do anything differently. We've all volunteered to work extra shifts to try to get a lead, any lead." He turned on his heel. "If you want a whipping boy, go call one of those pretty-boy aides in the hall."

"Detective."

Schindler looked over his shoulder. "I mean it, Senator."

Norris nodded. "I know you do." He leaned wearily back against the pillows. "I'm feeling very ineffectual at the moment, and I'm taking it out on you. I believe in payback, and there doesn't seem to be anything I can do. Quinn saved my life."

"Do you think you're special?" Schindler said. "He saved my neck two years ago when we were taking down a drug dealer. My daughter, Cindy, would have been an orphan and grown up alone in this shitty world."

Norris didn't speak for a moment. "That would have been a terrible thing. It is a shitty world that can kill young girls. If I could go back in time, I'd surround Nancy Jo with an army every time she set foot out the door." He lifted his hand to his eyes. "I'm sorry. If you need extra labor, I'm putting everyone on my staff at your disposal. All you need to do is call."

"Thanks. I may take you up on it."

Norris closed his eyes as Schindler left the room.

A shitty world, he thought. He'd thought he was cynical before Nancy Jo's death, but now he realized there had always been that streak of idealism present. He'd had dreams of changing the world. Or, at least, the corruption that was stagnating Washington.

Dreams.

They hadn't stopped Quinn from being attacked and probably killed.

They hadn't kept that ravening beast from murdering Nancy Jo.

Screw dreams.

He could feel the moisture sting his eyes. Dammit, it was here again; the pain, the disbelief, the loneliness.

Nancy Jo . . .

Oh, God, the loneliness.

No, not loneliness, he realized suddenly.

Comfort. Warmth. Laughter.

Nancy Jo telling him that horrible pun

she'd heard at summer camp.

Nancy Jo lolling with him on the beach last summer, not talking, just sitting in silent companionship as the sun went down.

Nancy Jo standing beside him when he'd been sworn in as senator, her eyes glowing with pride.

Those memories should have been agonizing. Why weren't they?

Comfort. Warmth. Laughter.

Remember, Daddy?

What the hell was happening? Imagination?

It didn't matter. For the moment the pain was gone. That was all that was important. He closed his eyes and let the memories flow over him in a golden tide.

Memories?

No.

Nancy Jo . . .

"I've just talked to your Eve," Jelak told Joe. "I was very upset that I couldn't conclude my business with her immediately, Quinn. She reacted just as I thought she would when you wouldn't speak to her."

"So you came back to try to persuade me again," Joe said. "Screw you."

"There are persuasions and persuasions." He checked the ropes binding Joe's wrists and ankles. "I thoroughly enjoyed playing with you, but I'm too impatient to deal with your stubbornness. I've been waiting for Eve too long." He smiled. "So we're going to go to step two. I probably should have known that you'd respond to the mental, not the physical."

"I won't respond to you at all. You're not worth it, Jelak."

"You'll change your mind," he said softly. "I'm going to leave you for a while. Do you know where I'm going?"

"To hell, I hope."

"If I did, I'd rule there." Jelak smiled. "No, I was impressed by how concerned you were with my kills. Particularly Nancy Jo and Nicole. They appeared to touch you."

Joe stiffened. "I'm a detective. Your kills aren't any different from those of any other slimeballs I jerk off the streets."

"I think they are. I'm willing to put it to the test."

"What kind of a test?"

"I'm going to go and find a young girl, perhaps fifteen, or sixteen. It doesn't matter that she's not old enough to be interesting. I'm doing it for you, not me."

"For me?"

"Yes, I'll let you watch the ritual. You can decide if a young girl's life is worth not speaking a few words on the telephone."

"And those few words could mean that I'd be helping you get Eve here."

"Yes, what a problem you'll be facing. I'll be interested to see how you handle it." He turned toward the door. "What a responsibility. I must choose a very, very special girl for you, Quinn."

The door closed behind him.

It was about time.

Jane watched Caleb's car pull into the driveway in front of the cottage and went down the steps to meet him. "Where have you been?"

"You missed me? I've only been gone a few hours." He got out of the car. "I thought you'd call me if Eve heard from Jelak again."

"Where have you been?" she repeated. "I didn't miss you. But you're the only one who knows how Jelak thinks."

"And you need me."

"I need to give Eve a little hope. She doesn't have a large quantity of that commodity at the moment. Now where were you?"

"I went to talk to Megan."

"For God's sake, now? Is she going to look into a crystal ball and tell us where to find Joe?"

"Don't be sarcastic. If she could, I'd ask her to do it. We don't have many options."

"Why did you go to see her?"

"I asked her to help me contact Nancy Jo."

She shook her head. "You've lost me."

"Eve told you about Quinn and Nancy Jo?"

"Yes."

"What did you think about it?"

"I tried not to think about it. It was too bizarre when connected to Joe. I decided to file it away until Joe actually talked to me about it." She looked at him. "Why?"

"I was there when Nancy Jo pointed Quinn to the motel where we found Jelak."

"You see ghosts too?"

"No, but it was clear what was happening."

"Nothing is clear about any of this."

"Except Nancy Jo found Jelak once. She might be able to find him again. I went to Megan to see if she could help."

"What did she say?"

"That she couldn't hear or see Nancy Jo but that she believed Quinn when he said he could." He grimaced. "So she's no help to us."

"Good God, I was hoping that you'd bring up something that was verging on reality.

I've had enough of Jelak's obsession that he's a vampire. Now you're telling me that we have to send Joe's pet ghost after him?"

"No, I'm telling you that I'm hoping that we get lucky and can contact Nancy Jo." He added soberly, "Because I don't know what in hell to do if we can't."

Jane stared at him for a long moment. "You mean it."

"Yes, I may think of something else. I won't give up. But if Quinn was willing to use Nancy Jo, then that may be our best shot."

Their best shot was a young girl who had been dead for days?

"So what do we do?"

"Quinn went to Allatoona to make contact with Nancy Jo. I thought I'd start there."

"*We'll* start there," Eve said.

They turned to see Eve standing on the porch. She came slowly down the steps. "Let's go."

"It's a long shot," Caleb said. "My Lord, is it a long shot. It will be like talking to the wind. How do you know if she's listening, if she's even there? And even if she finds out what we need, how can she tell us?"

"Do we have another solution?" Eve demanded. "If you do, tell me, and we'll go for it. If you don't, then I'll take your long shot. I'll take any way I can find."

"You could let Caleb and me go to Allatoona alone," Jane said. "It could be frustrating as hell. You don't need that right now."

Eve shook her head. "I'm going. You want to help, but you don't really believe in spirits. How could you? It hasn't *touched* you. I believe in Nancy Jo. Because Joe believed in her. Who knows? That may help." She got into the passenger seat of Caleb's car. "Or it may not. I've got to try. Get me there as quickly as you can, Caleb. We don't know what's happening with Joe."

Jane stared at her for a moment before she climbed in the backseat. Eve was right. She was out of her depth. She could only offer support, not understanding. Eve might need that support if Allatoona was as nonproductive as she believed it was going to be. "Tell me what I can do."

Eve glanced at her as Caleb started the car. "Phone Gary Schindler. Tell him to meet us at the police impound yard in two hours so that we can get into Jelak's car. Joe said she had to touch the blood on the passenger seat before she made the connection with Jelak."

"Providing she'll do it," Caleb said. "And providing you can make contact with her to even ask her to do it."

"I know all the ifs, ands, and buts," Eve said. "At least we can make preparations if we do get through to her."

And how would they know if they did get through, Jane wondered. It was like blundering around in the dark. But what choice did they have? She was already dialing the precinct. "I'll make sure Gary Schindler is there waiting for us. Needless to say, I won't explain why we want access to the car."

FIFTEEN

"Quinn went into that stand of trees," Caleb said, as they got out of the car at Allatoona. "He told me that I wasn't invited to go any farther than here."

Eve was already walking toward the woods. Joe had described his meeting with Nancy Jo to her, but how did they know that this was the place that they could reach her? Who knew where she could be found? Her Bonnie had come to her in any number of places. But then Eve had had problems thinking Bonnie was anything but a dream. Did that make a difference?

She was in the shadow of the woods now. She was vaguely aware of Jane and Caleb behind her, the sound of the cicadas, the breeze blowing through the trees.

"What do we do?" Jane asked. "It's not as if we can go knocking on a door."

"Wait." Eve moved deeper into the trees. She wasn't feeling anything, she realized in despair. And she certainly wasn't seeing anything. Not that she had expected to be able to do that. But she'd hoped she'd be able to sense . . . something.

They waited fifteen minutes.

Twenty.

"Eve," Jane said gently.

"I know." She straightened her shoulders. "The only thing we can do is assume she's here and act accordingly." She moved to the center of the trees. "I'm Eve Duncan, Nancy Jo. We came to ask you to help. Joe needs you. And we need to know where Jelak is right now." She paused. "I know he said it hurt you, but Joe really needs you."

No sound but the wind.

No feeling but her own desperation.

"We're going from here to the police impound yard. You'll be able to get in his car again, touch that blood. If you'll do it." She tried to keep her voice steady. "After that, it's still up to you. I don't know what you can do. I don't know how you can let us know how to help. We're going to do everything we can. It may come down to me going to Jelak. That would be okay if I could be sure that Joe would be safe. But I don't believe he would be. We both know what a monster Jelak is."

Still nothing.

"We're leaving now." One more try. "Joe liked you. He wanted to help you. I don't see how he could feel like that if you didn't like him too. Please help us, Nancy Jo."

She turned on her heel and said jerkily to Jane, "That's all we can do. It's up to her. Let's get down to that impound yard."

"Is that all you want?" Schindler asked in bewilderment. "I thought maybe Joe had mentioned a lead or something."

"No, I just wanted to take a look at it." She gazed at the huge boat of a car as she gingerly opened the driver's-side door. Jelak had opened this door, sat in that driver's seat, she thought in repulsion. She didn't want to touch it. "Will you make sure they leave this door open tonight?"

"Why?"

Jane stepped forward. "What difference does it make? Maybe she wants to air the stench out of it." She took Eve's arm and pushed her gently toward the gate. "Just do as she asks. Okay?"

Schindler nodded, his gaze fixed sympathetically on Eve's face. "Sure. I'm sorry, Eve. There will be a break soon. We're doing everything we can to find him."

"I know, Gary." Eve didn't look at him as she headed for the gate. "Thanks for coming tonight."

"Anything you want," Schindler said. "Just let me know."

"Any problems?" Caleb asked when they reached his car, parked outside the gate.

"No," Eve said. "Other than that Schindler thinks I'm headed for a nervous breakdown. Jane was so protective when she whisked me out of there that he probably thinks she's going to have me committed."

"It worked," Jane said. "And you didn't have to make explanations. Do we wait around and see what happens?"

"No. What would we see? Caleb didn't see anything when she was in the car before. Joe is the only one who can see her. Right, Caleb?"

He nodded. "And I only heard a one-way conversation. Which was interesting but a little frustrating."

"Then we might as well go home and wait for Jelak's call. We've done all we could. Though heaven knows we have no idea what that was." Her lips twisted. "We don't know if we made contact. We don't know if she paid any attention if we did. We don't know if she'll be able to bear connecting with Jelak, much less being able to do anything that would help Joe."

"Yes, we did the best we could," Jane said.

"You said all the right things, Eve. Now we have to see what happens."

"But how do you persuade a ghost?" Eve shook her head. "This experience isn't going to bring you any closer to understanding why I would even believe she exists."

"You believe it. That's all that's important," she said. "And if you hit a home run, then I'll believe it too."

"Was I gone too long?" Jelak asked. "I had to find just the right girl to please you, Quinn. Do you know where I found her?"

"I'm sure you're going to tell me."

"She was at a Girl Scout camp near Stone Mountain. Isn't that amusing? I watched the girls around the campfire singing and telling stories and tried to decide which one would have the greatest effect on you. I chose sweet Mary Lou. I don't know her last name. She seemed quieter than the others, but she smiled a lot. She wears glasses and she's about twelve or thirteen."

"Why waste your time? You said you didn't like young girls."

"But they seem to touch you."

"You're going after her?"

"Oh, I've already got her. I waited until she went to her pup tent and took her then."

Joe tried to keep his face expressionless.

"I won't let you blackmail me like this, Jelak."

"I think you will. Though I can understand why you'd choose Eve over that adolescent. She's a bounty of riches, and Mary Lou isn't even approaching the ability to compete. However, there's a possibility that even if Eve decides to trade, you might still have a chance to save her. With Mary Lou there will be no possibility. She was brought here for one purpose and one purpose only."

"Then why would you think I'd believe you'd let her live no matter what I did?"

Jelak smiled. "I'm sure you'll think of a way to make sure I do."

Joe shook his head.

Jelak's smile faded. "You're beginning to annoy me again. But really, actions are better than words. I believe I'll let you get to know our Mary Lou. I'll bring her in, and you can see what you're destroying. She'll probably be unconscious for another fifteen minutes or so. Sedatives have a stronger effect on those closer to childhood. But you can look at her and think about what's going to happen." He headed for the door. "I'll be right back."

He was true to his word. In two minutes he returned carrying a thin, gangly girl in blue plaid pajamas. He dumped her against the wall and pushed the red-brown hair away from her face. "Vulnerable, innocent, more child than woman. But the hair color reminded me a little of Eve Duncan's hair." He turned toward the door. "I'll let you be alone with her. There's something about a sleeping child that's very appealing."

Diabolical, Joe thought, as he stared at the young girl. She was as vulnerable as Jelak had said. Just a kid. Her skin still had the glow of childhood. The son of a bitch had hit him hard and blown his defenses. What the hell could he do?

There had to be something, and he'd better think of it quick.

"Would you like some coffee, Eve?" Jane asked. "I know you're not going to sleep, so you might as well have the caffeine."

"Why not?" Eve went to the window and gazed out into the darkness. "Jelak's not in any hurry to call, is he?"

"He said he wasn't going to hurt Joe," Jane said as she scooped coffee into the coffeemaker.

"But we don't know how much he's hurt him already. Where's Caleb?"

"He decided to drive around and see if he could sense anything. He said it was a needle in a haystack, but he couldn't stand not doing something."

"I know how he feels."

"You did what you could."

"No, there's something else I can do. If Jelak would just call."

"I don't like the sound of that." Jane looked up after she turned on the coffee-maker. "Don't even think that I'd let you make a trade."

"You'd have nothing to do with it." She smiled wearily. "This is between me and Joe."

"And Jelak."

"Maybe Jelak is right. I'm not afraid, Jane. Not for myself."

"Well, I'm scared enough for both of us."

"Joe has been by my side all these years. He's given me everything. I won't let him die."

"No, we won't. We'll find a way. Not Jelak's way, Eve."

"I think I'll go out on the porch and get some air."

"Eve, I won't let you do it."

"There's no use discussing it yet. Stop worrying, Jane." She went out on the porch and sat down on the swing. She'd stay here for a while and give Jane time to calm down. She should have kept her thoughts to herself, but she was dead tired and too accustomed to sharing with Jane.

"So you told her the truth. You scared her, Mama."

Bonnie.

She was sitting on the floor by the door, with her legs crossed and her head leaning back against the wall. "You scared me too."

Eve shook her head. "You're never frightened."

"Sometimes I am. I just never let you see."

"What are you frightened about, baby?" She moistened her lips. "About . . . where you are?"

"No, I'm fine here. I keep telling you that. You scare me. I want to be with you, too, but it can't happen."

"I was almost on my way to you that first night that you came to me."

"That's why I came. I could see that you were letting go. But look what you've done in all these years. All the parents you've helped, all the children you've brought home. All the love Jane gives you. All the love you and Joe have had together. Now Jelak comes, and you think you have a reason to stop. I'm not going to let you, Mama."

"I won't let Joe die, baby."

"Of course not. I know you wouldn't. Joe has to live. He's the one who keeps you here. We'll have to work it out."

"How?"

Bonnie shook her head. "I don't know yet, Mama."

Eve was silent. "All these years I wouldn't admit you were anything but a dream. Did I hurt you?"

"How could you hurt me?" Bonnie's luminous smile lit her small face. "It didn't matter how I was with you as long as I was with you. If you needed me to be a dream, then that was fine with me."

"But it shouldn't only be what I need. How can I help you? Is there something I can do for you?"

Bonnie chuckled. "Oh, Mama, that's just like you. You decide I'm definitely a ghost and set out to change my living conditions. I don't need anything. If I said that I wanted you to stop looking for me, would you do it?"

"I have to bring you home."

"Then do it. But know that I can't feel any more at home than I am with you now. That's only a shell you're going to bring home, Mama."

"I can't be that impersonal about it. I loved that shell. I want it back."

Bonnie sighed. "We'll talk about it later. You're too emotional about Joe right now. It's throwing everything out of kilter. Perhaps when Joe is safe, you'll be more reasonable."

When Joe is safe.

The words jarred Eve back into the fear and panic. Was there a chance that Joe would be safe?

"Go in and talk to Jane and make her feel better," Bonnie said. "She's scared about Joe, and now she's scared about you too."

She didn't want to go. Her times with Bonnie were rare and special, and she didn't want to leave her.

"But you want to be with Jane too. I'll always be here for you, Mama."

"I know. Sometimes it's hard to remember." She got up from the swing and moved toward the door. It was time to go back to the world. Jane needed her. Joe needed her.

And, as Bonnie had made clear, she needed them too.

Zilch, Caleb thought, as he turned on Northside Drive.

He'd been cruising the city for hours, and he'd not come up with anything. Not a hint of Jelak's presence.

Why the hell was he bothering? The chances of his being able to sense Jelak in a city of this size were astronomical. Too many people to interfere with his focus. Even if he caught the trail, it would be blurred.

Did he have any choice? He had to go on unless Jane called him with another lead.

Jelak had hit a bull's-eye with Joe Quinn. Eve would not be held back for long from going to Jelak if she could see no other way of freeing Quinn.

The Jelak he had studied for years would not have realized Quinn's value. He'd been riveted in one direction, seeing only the blood and not the other pieces of the game. Jelak would claim that he was so close to his resurrection that his mind was open and a thousand times sharper. Caleb wished to hell that he could —

Jelak.

His hands clenched the steering wheel.

It was only a tendril of sensation, gossamer thin. He concentrated. Come on, Jelak, give me something.

A blurred wisp of recognition.

Where?

South.

He turned down the next street.

Stronger. Still blurred but a tiny bit more defined.

Then it was gone.

Dammit.

No, it was there again.

Hold on to it . . .

The young girl, Mary Lou, hadn't stirred in the last ten minutes. Joe only hoped that

Jelak hadn't given her an overdose. He doubted it. Jelak was an expert, and there was no telling how many victims he'd overcome with that same sedative. He'd be very careful. What was the use of having a weapon if you destroyed it by carelessness? Joe should be hoping the kid stayed unconscious for a little longer. The only thing waiting for her when she opened her eyes was stark terror.

And the only thing waiting for him was a choice he didn't want to make.

"You're bleeding. All those cuts . . . He hurt you."

His gaze flew to the corner of the room. Nancy Jo was huddled against the wall, her arms folded tightly across her chest as if to keep from shaking. "Yes, he hurt me. What are you doing here?"

"She . . . came. Eve. She said I had to help you."

"Eve?"

She nodded jerkily. "I didn't want to do it. It was worse than last time. It wasn't only seeing him. I knew I had to come. He's here, isn't he?"

"Probably in the next room."

She closed her eyes. "I feel him. My blood is pounding so hard that I feel dizzy. I want to be brave, but all I can think about is his knife cutting across my throat."

"You are brave. You came anyway, didn't you?"

"Yes." She opened her eyes. "I had to do it. Daddy told everyone you saved his life. I couldn't let you die."

"Your father is okay? I wasn't sure."

"He's in the hospital. He's worried about you. He's worried about everything. But I think I made him feel better. Bonnie helped me."

"Bonnie helped you do what?"

"She taught me how to make him dream. She said that's the first step. He can't see me or hear me yet, but gradually it could happen. Then he won't be so lonely," she added unevenly. "And I won't be so lonely. But Bonnie says it can't be because of me. It doesn't work that way."

Mary Lou stirred and muttered something.

Nancy Jo looked down at her. "He's going to kill her, isn't he?"

"Unless I can stop him. Unless you can stop him."

"That's why I'm here. But I don't know what to do."

"Find out where we are. Try to let someone know."

"But you're the only one I can talk to."

Dammit, he knew that and it was frustrating the hell out of him. "Okay, then just tell me. I don't see any way out from talking to Eve. I can't have that girl butchered. But I might be able to slip in a reference she'd understand."

"I'll try." She looked around her at the leather chairs and fine oak end tables. "But do you have any idea what this place is?"

"It looks like it might be the anteroom of a church." His gaze went to the arched windows and the crucifix on the wall. "So much for vampires being afraid of religious relics. He seems to be adapting just fine."

"You had me look for names on doors and phone books before at that motel."

"I've already looked around. I don't see anything."

She got to her feet, bracing herself. "Maybe I could go out there where he is. There could be something there that would tell us."

He could tell she was scared to death. "He can't hurt you, Nancy Jo. Not now."

"I know that with my mind. But I can feel the blood in him, my blood, and I forget." She moistened her lips. "But I've got to remember. He almost killed Daddy. He wants to kill you and Eve and that girl. I can't let him do that. It's got to stop."

"I couldn't agree more. Now see what you can do about it."

Her gaze flew to the door. "He's coming." Panic tensed her body. "I can't —"

■ ■ ■ ■

She was gone.

"I'm heading back to the cottage," Caleb said when Jane picked up. "I should be there within fifteen minutes."

"I take it you didn't find any trace of him?"

"I found a trace. It was in the Buckhead area of Atlanta. I thought I might have him, but I kept losing the track. I drove around there for over an hour. There was just too much interference."

"Can't you try again?"

"Yes, I thought I'd get on the Internet and try to map out the area where Jelak seemed strongest and see if I could see any pattern."

"I'll help you."

"I'll take all the help I can get." He paused. "How is Eve?"

"Holding up. She always does. She's not going to like this news you have to give her. We need something positive."

"Then we'll hit the Internet and see if we can find anything that's even remotely in that category."

"I don't like that word 'remote.' "

"Neither do I, Jane. Neither do I."

■ ■ ■ ■

"What? She's not awake yet?" Jelak looked down at Mary Lou. "I suppose I'll have to do something about that. Did you know that a knife prick acts like a shot of adrenaline?"

"I didn't find that when you were slicing at me."

"But you have a different mentality than this child." He took out his knife. "Maybe the wrist. What do you think, Quinn?"

"I think that you've won, Jelak."

He shook his head as he lowered the knife. "So easily. You're disappointing me. I was hoping that you'd hold out for a while."

"That would give you too much pleasure, and in the end it would be the same. I couldn't let you kill her."

He smiled. "Then I suppose I should call Eve and let you talk to her."

Joe shook his head. "Not until I'm sure this kid is safe. Give her another whiff of that ether and take her out of here. Just a tiny whiff. I want to see her awake once you release her. I want to see her moving away from you."

"You're being very demanding."

"I'm not giving you something for nothing. Take her back to that area where you picked her up. Let her loose and get back in your car."

"And is that all?"

"No, I want you to video pictures back to my phone. You don't have to untie me. You can set it up on the table over there. I want to see Mary Lou walking, no, running, away from you. And I want you to keep that camera on as you drive away so that I know you're not following her."

"And then when I come back, you'll do as I say?"

He nodded. "I'll talk to Eve. I'll mention something we did together that only we know about. She'll know that you didn't kill me. Wasn't that your complete list?"

"That covers it. Yet how do I know you'll keep your word after I let Mary Lou go?"

"There would always be another Mary Lou, wouldn't there? I'm not stupid enough to think that you'll not keep on playing now that you have a winning hand."

"Yes, you're not stupid at all, Quinn. Just exceptionally stubborn." He stood looking down at the girl. "It's a pity. I've never failed to complete a kill when I was this close."

"But you said she wouldn't do you any good."

"No, but it's the principle." Then he

shrugged and reached in his pocket and pulled out a small bottle. He knelt. "Just a tiny whiff, you said?"

The deal was struck, and Mary Lou would live. Now Joe had to make sure Eve would have ammunition to fight back.

And pray that Nancy Jo would help them after her panic subsided.

Neither one of those priorities was looking promising at the moment.

Eve's cell phone rang two hours later.

"I've solved my problem," Jelak said. "I know you were biting your nails worrying if Quinn was alive. Yet I must say you deserved a little anxiety since you wouldn't believe me."

"I would have been mad to believe you."

"Yes, but you've wasted a good deal of my time. After all the years I've been waiting, I resent even a little delay. That's over now. I'm going to hand the phone to Quinn now, then we'll negotiate."

Her hand was shaking on the phone.

"Eve?" Joe said. "God, I'm sorry."

It was Joe. Relief surged through her. She hadn't been absolutely sure until this minute that he was alive. "Don't be crazy. You have nothing to be sorry about. Are you okay?"

"A little sore in places but otherwise fine.

I wasn't given a choice that either one of us could accept. He decided that grabbing a twelve-year-old kid would force my hand. He was right." He paused. "He wants you to be absolutely certain that he has me before he starts his damn negotiations. He said to mention something in our past that wasn't known to anyone else." He paused. "Several years ago you went to Louisiana and you worked on a reconstruction at that big mansion that looked like Tara. I followed you down there, and we had a fight. Do you remember?"

She hesitated. "Yes, I remember," she said slowly.

"Okay, then I've complied with Jelak's damn bargain. He wants the phone back. Don't deal with him. Tell him to go to hell."

Jelak's voice came on the line. "Very noble. But you will deal, won't you? I didn't think there would be any question about that once you were sure I had him."

"I'll deal." She made a motion as Jane opened her lips. "But I'm not the suicide junkie you seem to think. I don't want to die. I'm not going to come to you and meekly present my neck for the sword like Anne Boleyn. I want a chance. Tell me how I can get it and still free Joe."

He chuckled. "If I hadn't known you were

the perfect finale for me before, I would now. Let me think . . ." He was silent a moment. "Allatoona. No one would repeat a crime in the same place only days after the first one was committed. Go into the woods and wait for me. I'll bring Quinn, but I'll keep him bound. If I see that you have a weapon, and you try to ambush me, then I'll kill him. If you escape me and can get back to him, then you can release him. If you don't escape me, then I'll go back and cut his throat. Will that give you enough incentive? And, of course, if I see police or media, he's dead."

"When?"

"It's almost midnight now. Three in the morning? That's truly the dead of night."

"Yes."

"I can hardly wait. It's been too long." He paused. "And I wasn't wrong about you, Eve. You may be trying to hide it from the people who love you, but you do want this." Jelak hung up.

"Did you hear?" Eve hung up the phone. "Three o'clock. That doesn't give us much time."

"To get to Allatoona?" Caleb asked.

"No, to find Joe before he takes him there." She flipped open the computer. "You earmarked that area where you said you

sensed Jelak, didn't you?"
"Yes, why?"
"Pull it up."
"Why?"
"Because that reconstruction I worked on down in Louisiana wasn't at a Tara-like mansion. It was a church."
Caleb gave a low whistle. "Holy shit." He bent over the computer. "Let's see how many churches we can find in that quadrant . . ."

"Seven," Jane said as she looked up from the computer thirty minutes later. "Three Catholic — St. Mark's, St. Francis, St. Catherine; two Baptist — Trinity Baptist, Peachtree Baptist. One Methodist, Jacob's Ladder. And even a Buddhist temple. Who would know that there would be that many churches in one section of the city?"
"And they're spread out all over the area," Eve said in discouragement. "How are we supposed to find the right one in time?"
"Split up," Caleb said. "And if you see anything suspicious, call me. I'll come and check it out."
"Why a church?" Jane asked. "I'd think that he'd veer away from religious doctrines."
"Jelak wouldn't care about the religious

side of it," Caleb said. "I'd bet he wants a grand temple to house his resurrection ceremony. So he's borrowing one of these churches."

"Borrowing? Churches aren't usually deserted even when there are no services. I just hope that he didn't hurt anyone."

"Don't count on it." Caleb headed for the door. "I'll take the Buddhist temple. Eve, you check out St. Mark's Cathedral. Jane, Peachtree Baptist. Look for cars in the parking lots. Or any sign of interior lights. Anything different."

"Right," Eve said. She was ahead of them as they reached the steps. Panic was racing through her. All those churches and only a couple hours to cover all of them.

And if they ran the time too close, she might not make it to Allatoona to meet Jelak at three. That would be dangerous for Joe.

Hell, everything was dangerous for Joe.

She could only move at top speed and pray.

Prayers weren't working, Eve thought in despair over an hour later.

There was no sign of any occupancy at St. Mark's. No lights. No cars in the parking lot. Not even on the streets surrounding the cathedral.

She called Caleb. "Nothing. What about you?"

"I was able to get into the temple. It's a splendid building, but Jelak gave it a pass. I just heard from Jane. The Baptist church is empty too."

"Four more to go." She checked her watch. "It's one thirty. It will take at least forty minutes to get to Allatoona." She started the car. "I'm closest to the Methodist church. I'll try there. I'll have to give it up and meet Jelak if that's a zero too."

"I'll call Jane, and we'll split up the others." He paused. "Don't go to Allatoona without me."

"Jelak will probably have to allow time to get to Allatoona too. There won't be any way to surprise him if we don't find the church right away. And I can't risk Jelak flying off the handle and doing something to Joe to punish me." She backed out of the parking lot as she glanced at her GPS. "I'll be on my way to Allatoona unless you call me within the next forty-five minutes and tell me we've found him." She hung up.

She had been so full of excitement and hope when she had realized that Joe had been able to slip in a clue to where he and Jelak were located. It had seemed as if their luck was turning.

Don't give up. They still had forty-five minutes.

Such a short time, she thought in agony.

Please let the next church be the right one.

As she reached the intersection, her cell phone rang. She tensed. Private number. Jelak?

"Eve Duncan?"

Not Jelak.

"Yes."

"Ed Norris. I'm sorry to disturb you at this time of night. I guess I woke you."

"No, I was awake."

"Because you were worrying about Quinn. I've had some sleepless nights myself lately."

"Yes, I'm very sorry about your daughter."

"She was a loving child and my best friend."

"I hear she was a wonderful girl. I don't have much time. What can I help you with, Senator?"

"I do seem to be rambling, don't I? I call you up in the middle of the night, and I can't seem to get to the point. It's because I'm feeling awkward as hell." He was silent a moment. "Okay, here it is. I had this dream. It was weird. I kept seeing this picture. Over and over. The same picture."

"What picture?"

"You've got to understand. I'm a realist. I

don't go off the deep end. Maybe I've not been quite myself lately but I'm as stable as the Rock of Gibraltar."

"What are you trying to say, Senator?"

"The picture. I think you're supposed to know about it."

"Why?"

"Hell, I don't know," he said testily. "But the picture wouldn't go away, and neither would your name. It kept pounding at me, and it wouldn't stop. So I'm telling you. And if you tell the media I'm off my rocker, I'll deny this call and sue you."

"What was the picture?"

"It wasn't really a picture, more like a stained-glass window."

Her heart skipped a beat. "Like the ones you'd see in a church?"

"Yes, a bearded man surrounded by small animals."

"St. Francis of Assisi, patron of animals," she murmured. "St. Francis! Dear God in heaven."

"I know it's crazy. Anyway, I told you."

"Thank you. Thank you. Thank you." She was quickly keying St. Francis Cathedral into her GPS. "It's not crazy. I have to hang up, Senator."

"It's not crazy?"

"The whole world's crazy, but you're calling to tell me this is the sanest act you've ever done."

"I somehow thought I was doing the right thing. And it's going to help you?"

"I hope it will. I pray it will." She hung up and called Caleb. "It's St. Francis Cathedral. How close are you?"

"Fifteen minutes. Are you sure?"

"I'm sure. I just got a call from the senator. I think Nancy Jo came through for us." She looked at the GPS. "I'm twenty-five minutes away."

"Jane is a good forty-five minutes from there. I'm not going to wait for either of you. I'll see you at the cathedral."

Sixteen

Caleb drew up a map of the interior of St. Francis of Assisi Cathedral on his laptop, scanned it quickly, then took off across town.

The interior of the sanctuary of the church appeared to be as grand and rich as Jelak could wish for his final resurrection. Choir stall facing the altar. Two anterooms leading off the sanctuary. The meeting rooms were in an adjacent building linked by a covered walkway.

So where would Jelak keep Quinn?

Quinn had known he was in a church, so it would follow that he'd been aware of religious artifacts. Meeting rooms were usually for classes and less identifiable. The chances were that Quinn had been in the main part of the church. Choir chancel. Sanctuary. Anteroom.

Which one?

He'd start in the choir chancel and work

down. It was located above the nave where the congregation sat and he'd be less likely to be noticed if he was up there looking down. Most people had a tendency to look straight ahead.

He parked a block from the cathedral and stared for a moment at the tall spires and medieval architecture.

He couldn't sense Jelak, but the cathedral was surrounded by apartment buildings. Too many people, too much interference at this distance. He'd be fortunate if he could sense him ten yards away. But, then, Jelak wouldn't be able to sense him either.

Both blind to each other. Level ground.

But they wouldn't be on level ground once he found him in that cathedral.

The excitement he hadn't allowed himself to feel was suddenly here, pounding in his veins. After all the years of hunting, Jelak was *his.*

He got out of the car and moved quickly down the block. No cars in the parking lot, but a small gray Honda was parked in readiness on the street in front of the huge doors of the main entrance.

"All set to go. You're ready to take your final kill," he murmured. "But are you ready for me, Jelak?"

■ ■ ■ ■

He was not in the choir chancel.

But Caleb found the slumped body of a priest on the stairs leading up to it. Evidently the church had not been vacant as Eve had hoped. He stepped around the body and swiftly climbed the stairs.

No Jelak. But from this vantage point, Caleb could see the golden goblet set out on the altar, which was covered in scarlet velvet. Jelak was clearly planning on bringing Eve back from Allatoona for the ritual.

His gaze wandered around the sanctuary below him.

Jelak wasn't in the sanctuary either.

Then one of the anterooms.

Which one? Left or right of the altar?

Choices.

He couldn't risk going into the anterooms from the sanctuary. He'd have to go outside and around the church to see if there were any windows in the anterooms.

Fast.

He was only ten minutes ahead of Eve, and he wanted to try to get all this over before she arrived at the cathedral. Getting Quinn safely away from Jelak was their top priority.

It was not Caleb's priority.

He had to destroy Jelak in the quickest way possible no matter who was in his way.

"It's time we left. I'll need you to walk to the car." Jelak cut the ropes that bound Joe's ankles. "I admit I like the idea of returning to Allatoona. It will bring back memories of an interesting kill. Naturally, Nancy Jo Norris wasn't anywhere near the status of Eve, but she was surprisingly rich in strength for one so young. And she was the first one of my kills they called you in to investigate. You should have some nostalgic feeling for Allatoona too."

"Nostalgia? I felt disgust that some slimeball would kill a nice kid like that." Joe flexed his ankles to get the blood circulating. He didn't have the use of his hands, but he was good with his feet. Watch for the chance, then a roundhouse kick to the belly and another to the throat. "But then I found out that you were a coward and a nutcase and that 'slimeball' would have been a supreme compliment."

Jelak's lips tightened. "Did I tell you what great pleasure I had inflicting all those wounds on you? I might keep you alive for a while after the resurrection to play with you some more."

"Resurrection? You actually believe that crap? It's all been for nothing, Jelak. If you did manage to kill Eve, you'd still be the pitiful gargoyle you've been all your life."

"You lie," he said through his teeth. "You know nothing. Caleb could tell you. He knows how close I am." He drew a breath and straightened. "I'm going to go and collect my goblet and my knife. I'm planning on bringing your Eve back here, but you can never tell what can happen. I believe in being prepared." He suddenly chuckled. "Like our little Girl Scout, Mary Lou. You do realize I'll go back for her?"

"I considered the possibility."

"It's not a possibility." He grabbed his black Croco case and headed for the door. "I'll leave you to dwell on that while I go pack my beautiful goblet."

The moment he went out of the room, Joe got to his feet. Though still bound to the chair, he half hopped to the door. He'd wait to one side and hook his tied hands over Jelak's neck and twist until —

"You look completely absurd," Caleb said as he climbed through the window. "You know your chances of taking him out are practically nil tied up like a Thanksgiving turkey."

Relief poured through him. "Then untie

me, dammit."

"I'm in the process." Caleb took a knife out of his pocket as he glided across the room. "But cutting you free is more practical. I need you to be out that window in just a few minutes to stop Eve from coming to your rescue." He was sawing through the ropes as he was speaking. "Damn, you're cut to pieces. You look like a pincushion. Some of those wounds will need stitches."

"Do you have a gun?"

"Yes, but I'm not giving it up. I don't have time to argue. I can sense Jelak, and he's damn close. He's probably not reached a stage of sensitivity that will let him sense me with all this interference around us, but I can't be sure." He stepped back when Joe was freed. "Go out that window and find Eve."

"Not when I'm this close. Jelak will be coming through that door any minute." He added grimly. "And I'm no longer tied like that turkey you mentioned."

"You're being troublesome, Quinn."

"Tough."

Caleb slipped the gun from his jacket pocket and pointed it at him. "Get out, Quinn. Find Eve before Jelak does. She should be here any minute. I won't have you in my way." He met his eyes. "I won't kill you, but I'll make sure you won't be a bother to me. Don't think I won't use it."

"Oh, I don't doubt that." He hesitated, then ran to the window and slid his legs over the sill. "I'll find Eve. I'll make sure she's safe, then I'll come back. And I'm not sure who I'll take out first. Jelak or you."

Eve noticed Caleb's car immediately when she pulled up at St. Francis.

It was parked across from the cathedral.

He had said he wouldn't wait for her. He must be inside. She hesitated, then swiftly climbed the steps to the massive doors of the entrance. Try to slip inside as quietly as she could if the door was open.

It was open. Was Caleb or Jelak responsible? She wasn't going to worry about that now.

No one was in the vestibule.

She moved toward the sanctuary, warily looking on either side, peering into the shadows.

No one.

The first thing Eve saw when she entered the sanctuary was the golden goblet.

She inhaled sharply. In the darkness of the huge chamber, the candles on either side of the altar caused the goblet to shimmer. She couldn't stop staring at it.

She shook her head to clear it. This was no time to be caught up in all the evil that goblet represented. Where was Jelak?

Her grasp tightened on the gun in her hand.

And where was Joe?

"You couldn't wait to see me?" The muzzle of a revolver was pressed to the middle of her back. "I didn't expect you. But this is much more convenient than Allatoona. You will have to tell me how you found me. But, first, give me that gun."

"Why? If I do, you'll kill me. You'll kill Joe. Go ahead, shoot me. Then you won't have your damn final ritual."

"You're right. So instead, I'll shoot your hand, you'll drop the gun. But then you'll be wounded and won't be able to defend either yourself or Quinn."

He was right. It was better to be without a weapon than wounded. Caleb must be around somewhere. She'd have to rely on him. She dropped the gun.

He scooped it up. "And now let's go see Quinn. I have to make sure you're secured before I go looking for Caleb. I'm sure he's with you. I'm surprised he let you come in by yourself."

"You shouldn't be surprised." Caleb stood in the anteroom doorway. "It was always going to be between the two of us, Jelak. That's why you've always been afraid."

Jelak stiffened, back arched, as if struck by a whip. "I'm not afraid of you, Caleb. I'm beyond it. It's true I was counting on the resurrection, but I don't need it. I'm strong now."

But he *was* afraid, Eve could tell. He was staring at Caleb in defiance, but she could see the faint tremor in the hand that was holding the gun.

She didn't blame him. In this moment, Caleb was truly intimidating. She had become accustomed to him in the past days and was no longer constantly aware of the power she had noticed on that first meeting. But it was as if he'd suddenly shrugged off a casual cloak to reveal authority, menace, and a deadliness that shocked her. He exuded, radiated, shimmered with it.

He started to walk toward Jelak.

"Stay away." Jelak lifted his gun in panic.

"Why? You're so strong. You used all their blood to make you that way. All their strength and intelligence and will."

"You're still angry about Maria Givano." His lip curled. "She was nothing. I thought I'd get a jump start to the resurrection with her. It was too good an opportunity to miss. I had to experiment when I found out that she might have the power."

"You made a mistake."

"Yes, she had no power."

"No, your mistake was killing her. It's going to bring you down." He took another step forward. "You're still so much weaker than I am. You're shaking. Your blood is pounding. You're feeling it, aren't you?"

"No." Jelak's voice was hoarse. "I'm strong. And I'll be stronger when I kill you." His finger started to squeeze the trigger.

"No!" Eve jumped forward, jerking Jelak's gun aside.

"Bitch!" His hand swung around and knocked her to the floor.

"Keep down, Eve," Caleb called as he moved forward. "It's okay."

Okay? Jelak was going to kill him.

"Stay away from me, Caleb." Jelak was firing as he dove behind a pew.

Caleb had a gun, Eve knew. Why wasn't he shooting back?

Another shot.

The wood on the pew next to Caleb splintered as a bullet plowed into it.

"I told you that your hand was shaking," Caleb said.

A bullet suddenly grazed Eve's cheek.

"Stay away, or I'll kill her," Jelak said. "I'll do it, Caleb."

"The hell you will." Joe was suddenly beside Eve, shoving her to one side and putting his body between her and Jelak. "Stop wasting time. Get the son of a bitch, Caleb."

Joe. Safe. Alive. Her arms closed around him.

"Keep her out of the way." Caleb's gaze was fastened on Jelak. "Put the gun down, Jelak."

Two shots plowed erratically into the altar to the left of Caleb.

"Missed again. Give up, Jelak."

"I won't give up. I'll be as strong as you. Stronger."

"Well, it wouldn't matter if you gave up anyway. I'd actually prefer that you didn't. But you know what's coming, don't you? Your teacher Donari told you what to expect if I caught up with you. That's why you've been on the run."

"It won't happen." He fired again at Caleb. "That was a lie. Even if it wasn't, I'm too close to resurrection for you to be able to — stay back!" It was a scream.

Caleb kept coming. "It wasn't a lie. Donari told you many lies, but that wasn't one of them. I knew the night that you killed Maria Givano that was the way you were going to die."

"I won't die. I'll be a god."

"No, you played the Blood Game all these years, and now you've lost. It's time to give the blood back." He was within a few feet of Jelak now. "No resurrection. Never."

"No!" Jelak jumped to his feet and started running toward the anteroom. "I'll get away from you. Just a few more kills. I'll start again and —" He stopped, his hands going to his throat.

He screamed.

Eve wanted to scream, too, as she saw his face. It was contorted, flushed, and, as she watched, blood began to trickle out of his eyes like dark tears.

"Just a little blood now," Caleb said. "I want the pain to start. Convulsions, I think. Do you know that convulsions can break your bones?"

Jelak was falling, his whole body shuddering, shaking with the force of the convulsions.

"Did any ribs break yet?" Caleb asked. "They will, Jelak."

Jelak was trying to crawl away, but he started howling with pain as the convulsions increased. "Make it — stop." He looked pleadingly back over his shoulder. "I'll do anything to —"

"Yes, you will," Caleb said. "And it will

stop soon. I've no intention of a having a broken rib shatter and pierce your heart. It would be too easy. Just a minute more."

Eve flinched as Jelak screamed again. She could almost feel his agony.

"Now it's time for the blood," Caleb said.

The convulsions abruptly stopped.

"Give it all back," Caleb said softly. "All the blood you stole. All the kills, all the lives. First the blood tears, then the rush to the brain that will cause massive strokes." He was moving slowly toward him again. "Do you feel it? Oh yes, I see that you do. They're coming. Your eyes are rolling back in your head."

Jelak was whimpering.

"But you haven't given up all the blood you took. It has to be everything. Now it's the end of the game."

Jelak began to gasp as blood began to pour out of his mouth.

He was choking painfully on the blood, Eve realized. He couldn't get his breath. She wanted to look away but she couldn't take her eyes from his face.

He was trying to speak, his gaze fixed on Caleb, blood pouring from his lips. He tried to scream.

"That should do it," Caleb said. "How's your resurrection going, Jelak?"

A gurgling, a gasp, and Jelak's body was jerking, shuddering with the force of the blood leaving his body.

Caleb bent over him and looked deep into his eyes. "It's over. You're dying. No power. No immortality. You know that, don't you? I want you to know that you're nothing."

And that desperate realization of final defeat was in Jelak's eyes.

Caleb straightened. "Burn in hell, Jelak."

Jelak arched upward, then he was still.

Caleb stood looking down at him for a long moment.

Then he turned and walked out of the cathedral.

"Dear God," Eve whispered, her gaze on Jelak's body. "What happened? What did he do to him?"

"I don't believe there's any question what he did to him," Joe said. "Just how he did it."

She shuddered. "No wonder Jelak was running from him if he thought he could do that to him."

"Personally, I enjoyed the hell out of it." Joe got to his knees. "I wanted him dead, and Caleb obliged. Though I'd rather have done it myself."

"Joe . . ." She had suddenly become aware

of the multitude of dagger cuts all over his torso. She put her hand out to touch one on his shoulder. "He did that to you . . ."

"I'm okay."

"You're not okay." She saw a two-inch cut in the flesh on his upper back that looked as if it had been hacked out. Just the pain he'd undergone for that wound alone must have terrible. "We need to get you to a doctor."

He nodded. "Let's get it over with. Those stitches may hurt as much as Jelak's carving."

"I don't think so." She was suddenly not feeling nearly as full of horror as she stared back at Jelak. "Bastard. I wish Caleb had made him suffer more."

"It was probably sufficient. Stroke, brain hemorrhaging, and suffocation." He took her arm. "And none of it can be proved in any court of law."

"But we saw it."

"Even if we testified, which neither of us is inclined to do, we'd be laughed out of court. Jelak died of natural causes."

"Blood," Eve said. "The blood killed him."

"That's apparently the way Caleb wanted it. The final irony."

They had come out of the church, and Eve took a deep breath of the cool night air.

Only a short time had passed since she had entered the cathedral, but she felt as if she had been in there for a century.

But Joe was safe. Jelak was dead. There would be no more deaths, no more danger from a man who thought he was destined to be a vampire god.

"Okay?" Joe was looking down at her.

She nodded. "You're the one who is all cut to pieces. I'm going to call Jane and tell her you're alive and functioning and to meet us at the hospital. I know you have to call the precinct and tell them about Jelak." She took his hand. "But then can we just go home?"

"That sounds good to me. I'm afraid they'll find more bodies in that cathedral than Jelak's, but someone else can do that investigation. They can get our statements tomorrow. I'll have them send someone to the cottage." He smiled. "After all, I have an excuse. I'll have the hospital tell the department to put me on sick leave."

The sun felt warm and soothing on Joe's bare back as he stretched out on the bank of the lake. He smelled the fresh scent of pine and the good clean earth. It was a day when it felt good to be alive.

■ ■ ■ ■

"Your back still looks terrible," Nancy Jo said. "Maybe you should have plastic surgery or something."

"I don't care about whether I'm a pretty boy or not." He rolled over to see her sitting a few feet away. "But I might have to have something done to keep Eve from flinching for me every time she sees them. It's only been a few days. The scars will fade." He smiled. "It feels really good to get some sun on them."

She nodded. "I can't feel sunlight yet. Bonnie says it will take a while."

"If you decide that you want to stick around. Are you sure there's not something better around the corner?"

"I'm not sure. I don't know. But I don't think I can leave Daddy yet. He needs me."

"I needed you," Joe said quietly. "And you came through for me. Thank you, Nancy Jo."

"I couldn't let you die." She shook her head. "And I couldn't let Jelak win. It would have been horrible. I just had to think of a way to do it. It was Bonnie who showed me how."

"Bonnie, again."

Nancy Jo nodded. "She said you had to live."

"I'm glad the two of you agreed on that point." He put on his shirt but didn't bother to button it. "Are you sure your father still needs you? Or is it that you need him?"

"Probably both. But I wouldn't stay if I didn't think that it was the best thing for him. He can't find his way right now. It's important that he not go down the wrong path." She smiled. "He wanted to be president. He thought he could help people. I know he can still do it. He just needs someone to nudge him along and keep him from being lonely."

"That's an important job, but I can't think of anyone who could fill it better than you, Nancy Jo."

She smiled impishly. "I can't either. With a little help from my friends. But I might get lonely too. Do you mind if I drop in now and then to see you?"

"It would be my pleasure."

Her smile faded. "You mean that?"

He nodded. "My extreme pleasure." He chuckled. "After all, you're the perfect friend. You have very few demands."

"I demanded you get Jelak."

"That was an understandable exception."

"I can't promise I might not ask something again. I can't just stand around and watch something go wrong."

"Then we'll worry about it when you do."

She nodded. "You'd be much better off having Bonnie for a friend. But she says that there's something standing in the way." She looked at him searchingly. "And I think she's right. You're closing up, Joe."

"Am I? Then maybe she's right, and there are a few obstacles that are difficult to overcome."

"Not for her. She's a great problem solver. She's helped me along any number of times."

"Then it must be me." He got to his feet. "I'm going back to the cottage."

"Because you don't want to talk to me about Bonnie." Nancy Jo was frowning. "Why not? I'd think you'd want to talk to —"

"Nancy Jo, stop being pushy." He strolled back toward the cottage. "You know the trick. It's time to do your vanishing act."

Caleb was getting out of his car when Joe arrived back at the cottage. He stood waiting as Joe walked up the path. "You're looking better than the last time I saw you. No permanent damage?"

Joe shook his head. "What are you doing here?"

"I wanted to say good-bye. I'm going to go back to Scotland." He paused. "And I wanted to express my appreciation for your discretion in making your report. It could have been awkward."

"Discretion? I only told the truth. Jelak

attacked you, but you didn't try to defend yourself. Then Jelak had a massive stroke and hemorrhage and died. The captain thought it was a bit convenient, but the autopsy bore it out." He paused. "Otherwise, I would have hung you out to dry. I won't have Eve being under suspicion for making a false statement."

He nodded. "You had to protect her." He glanced at the wounds on Joe's body. "From Jelak, from me, from the whole damn world. I respect that quality in you."

"When you're not trying to shoot me."

He smiled. "You got in my way. I was in hunt mode. I told you I wouldn't have given you a serious wound."

"Hunt mode," he repeated. "That's quite an arsenal you used on Jelak."

"A small talent, but my own. Not anything as interesting as communing with spirits."

"Not a small talent. Very deadly. Was Jelak special, or is it your common modus operandi?"

He was silent. "I think I'll let you work that out for yourself."

"I've already started. I contacted the Italian police. In the last ten years there have been a number of massive strokes among the cult group that originated in Fiero. What a coincidence."

"But none that appeared to be anything but natural deaths. Isn't that right?"

"That's right."

"Then you have your answer." He smiled. "And now, with your permission, I'd like to go inside and say good-bye to Eve and Jane. I feel as if I've grown very close to them."

"When you weren't using them."

He nodded. "When I wasn't using them. I had to strike a delicate balance."

Joe stared at him in disbelief. "You actually mean that."

"Of course. You're a man who sees only one path and forges forward on it to the end. I have to walk many paths, and when I see quicksand, I have to skirt around it."

"And do a balancing act."

He smiled. "Exactly. Now may I go in and see Jane and Eve?"

Joe stared at him for a moment, then turned and strode up the steps. "If they want to see you. I'll ask them."

"They'll want to see me." Caleb leaned back on the door of his car. "They're two women who like to put a period at the end of an episode. Good-bye is a period."

SEVENTEEN

"I'll miss sitting here and looking at your lake." Caleb took the cup of coffee Jane handed him and leaned back against the post railing, his hand lazily stroking Toby's head. "I don't think that I've ever felt quite so peaceful as I have in those moments."

"Peaceful? You?" Jane crossed to the swing and gave Eve her coffee before dropping down beside her. "You've got to be kidding."

"I have my moments." He took a sip of his coffee. "There's a lake near Fiero that I visited when I dropped in to see Maria. It was a peaceful place too."

"Maria Givano?"

"Yes." He gazed out at Joe, who was standing on the bank of the lake several hundred yards away. "Quinn is distancing himself from our little coffee klatch. I wasn't sure he'd even let me in the cottage."

"Did you expect anything else?" Eve

asked. "He still doesn't trust you."

"But you trust me." Caleb's brows lifted. "Amazing. Since I haven't done anything to persuade you." He paused. "And what you saw in the cathedral wasn't something that would inspire you to want to draw closer to me."

"No." Eve would never forget that horrible scene. Caleb had been like someone who had stepped out of a horror story, the stuff of which nightmares were born. Yet she could not keep herself from separating that man from the Caleb she had grown to know. "And you don't want me to draw close to you. You want to stand apart. Have you ever been close to anyone, Caleb?"

He shrugged. "When I was a child. My uncle, my parents, my sister. It didn't seem worthwhile to make the effort with anyone else."

Jane leaned forward. "Because you couldn't be sure it would have been a genuine closeness? It was too easy for you to make people like you, even love you. You told me that you had trouble withstanding temptation."

"What is this?" He tilted his head. "Am I having some kind of psychological evaluation?"

"Yes," Eve said. "Because you barged into our lives and made a handprint that we can't erase. Jane and I discussed it, and we decided that we had to get a grip on you before you slipped away." She smiled faintly. "So I called Megan and asked her questions. She didn't know the answers but she phoned Renata. She knew if anyone could tell us about you, it would be Renata."

Caleb nodded. "Yes, our Renata's a storehouse of information. But she usually keeps everything she knows confidential."

"Megan and she are very close," Eve said. "Renata trusts her."

"And just what did Renata tell Megan?"

"Only what we asked her to find out," Jane said. "The killing of Maria Givano seemed to be the beginning of everything. We asked why her death was the trigger that set you hunting Jelak." She paused. "She was your half sister."

"You could have asked me."

"But you might not have told us."

He nodded. "Possibly. Because one question might have led to another."

"And it did," Eve said. "She'd married a year earlier and taken her husband's name of Givano. But her birth name was Caleb." She shook her head. "But even that wasn't totally correct. Because the family had changed their name when they'd moved away from Fiero. She would have been Maria Ridondo."

"Indeed?" Caleb asked mockingly. "Then you've put two and two together and come up with the brothers who were the scourge of Fiero, the wicked purveyors of the dark arts, who held the village in thrall for decades."

"Yes," Eve said. "How dark were their arts, Caleb?"

He didn't speak for a moment. "Very dark. Jelak wasn't far off about the vampire gods."

"And the power," Jane said. "I was thinking about what you said about Jelak believing that invisibility was part of the powers he'd attain after resurrection. That was too over-the-top for me to accept. But then I started to think about the way you could move around wherever you wanted. If anyone stopped you, then you just changed their perception. That's a form of invisibility."

"Legend has a habit of twisting truth," Caleb said. "But Jelak had enough truth mixed with legend to fuel that ambition."

"You're a member of the Devanez family Megan told us about?"

"Yes, the Ridondo brothers fled Spain during the Inquisition and settled in Fiero.

They decided that the only way they could keep themselves safe from informers to the Church was to keep the villagers terrified of retribution." He shrugged. "It worked, but how much blackness can a soul take? When they decided that they would leave the village and try to start a new life, it was almost too late. They settled, they had children, grandchildren, time passed." His lips twisted. "With only minor episodes that could be called totally wicked. But the call of the blood never entirely goes away. Neither does the knowledge that the power is there ready to be tapped. Most of the Ridondo descendants found it was safer to become hunters to expel some of that passion and leach away the darkness."

"As you did."

"As I did."

"Your sister," Eve prompted.

"I was never home much. I was always away from the time I was a teenager. My parents sent me to live with my uncle because they decided that he could handle me better than they could. He was a hunter." He shrugged. "I don't blame them. I was showing signs of being a throwback to the first Ridondos and that would have been awkward for them."

"Yes, I'd describe a tendency toward vampirism as being very awkward," Jane murmured.

"And they didn't think I'd be a suitable guardian for my sister, so before they died they set up a trust find and made arrangements for her to go to a series of private schools. I admit I resented that lack of confidence. I loved Maria. I would have seen that she had a good life. But Maria was years younger and very different from me. No darkness about her. She wanted to live life and drain every minute of pleasure from it."

"You did love her," Eve said, her gaze on his face.

"Oh, yes. As I said, there weren't many people that I did care about. Anyway, she met a young man while on vacation in Paris. Carlo Givano. Handsome, charming, hardworking, totally devoted to making her fall in love with him. He persuaded her to elope and took her back to his home, a vineyard outside Genoa." He paused. "When I went to visit her, I liked him. I went away convinced that she'd made a decent marriage."

"And did she?" Jane asked.

"No." He looked out at the lake. "Givano was a member of the cult. He'd been sent to track down members of the Ridondo family, namely, female members: the males might have proved too difficult. There were still stories being repeated in the cult of the Ridondo brothers' powers. They didn't want a confrontation, they wanted a victim."

"Why?"

"They were experimenting, trying to find the strongest bloodline to lead them to their resurrection. They thought it logical that since she was a descendant of the Ridondos, her blood would be almost magical. That it might even give them instant resurrection."

"And Givano lured her to them."

"Jelak was on the scene by then, and he couldn't wait to get his hands on her. He paid Givano to give her to him." His lips tightened. "He was clumsy. He wasn't sure what he was doing. He kept her alive a long time before he realized she wasn't going to let him win the game."

"So you set out to find Jelak," Eve said. "What about Givano?"

He turned from the lake to look at her.

He didn't need to answer, she thought. It was all there in the stark brutality of his expression. She had seen what he had done to Jelak. What he had done to the man who betrayed his sister would have been equally horrendous.

She looked down into the coffee in her

cup. "I'm sorry about your sister. I can see why you would have been so bitter."

"Can you? Yes, you know what it's like to lose someone you love." He smiled. "Well, is your curiosity satisfied? Are you ready to let me go off into the sunset?"

"No."

His brows rose. "No?"

She looked up at him. "You may have done it for your own purposes, but you saved Joe, and you saved me. I can't forget that. I feel a certain bond."

"What?" He shook his head. "You're much more clear thinking than that."

"Maybe I'm not." She got to her feet. "But I don't think that we're through with each other, Caleb. I don't know what you're going to be to us, but we're going to have to play it out to the finish."

He suddenly chuckled as he stood up. "I told Quinn that you'd want to put a period to the episode. You're not doing that, Eve."

"Just a comma." She smiled faintly. "I may have need of a hunter."

He turned to Jane. "What about you? A period?"

"I'm taking it under consideration." She added coolly, "I don't appreciate 'invasions.' "

"But you liked that one." His lips indented

at the corners. "I made sure you would." He turned and started down the steps. "But I'll respect your decision, whatever it is. That's part of the code I've tried to teach myself. Good-bye, ladies." He glanced at Jane, and he smiled. "It's been an experience I won't forget."

Jane got up and joined Eve at the steps to watch Caleb climb into his car.

"Quite an experience," she murmured. "I'm not sure that you were wise to make any commitment to him at all."

"I didn't make a commitment."

"You didn't cut him loose or turn your back. With Caleb, that could become a commitment."

She shook her head. "I told him the truth. He knows all about truth and lies. Probably no one could differentiate better." She glanced at Jane. "Could they?"

"No, I guess not." She watched him drive away. "I'm going to be leaving tomorrow. I have to go back to Paris. I let Celene Denarve, a gallery owner, talk me into another show there. It's scheduled for next week."

Eve looked at her in surprise. "Why didn't you tell me?"

"Because then you would have tried to make me go back and made it difficult for me if I decided to cancel the show." She made a face. "Almost as much as Celene would have if she'd had to postpone. She's been a good friend to me, but she's got a bit of a Gallic temperament."

But Jane would have canceled it without a thought if she'd thought Eve needed her here, Eve knew. "You bet I would have made your life difficult. Dammit, you dropped everything to fly to my rescue." She reached out and lovingly took Jane's hand. "Thank you."

"Don't be silly," Jane said. "I did it for me. I would have been a nervous wreck if I'd had to gnaw my fingernails worrying from across the Atlantic." She added teasingly, "What? Do you think I like you or something?"

"I thought there was a possibility." She reached down and patted Toby's head. "Of course, it might be that you just missed Toby." She smiled. "If this is going to be your last night here for a while, I'll ask Joe to put some steaks on the grill. You always like to barbecue."

Jane nodded. "I like the ambience more than the food. The sun going down over the lake, the smell of the charcoal, you sitting on a folding chair beside the grill watching Joe. When I'm away, I remember all those things." Her gaze went to Joe standing by the lake. "It's good that I'm going away right now. You need some time alone with Joe. Things are . . . different now."

"I can't deny that's true," she said. "When I picked you up at the airport, I never dreamed how different they were going to be. But Joe seems to be handling it well." She glanced at Jane. "How are you handling it? We threw a lot of weird stuff at you. To your credit, you never threw up your hands and told us to go to the nearest psychiatrist."

"What can I say? If you were nuts, I didn't want to be sane. So I had to go along for the ride."

"It was a rough, bumpy ride."

"But we all came through it."

Eve gazed at her searchingly. "But in what state?"

"You're asking me if I believe in Joe's ghost? I still don't know. It's hard not to believe in her after you got that call from the senator. Yet it defies everything that's solid and sure in my life." Her hand tightened on Eve's. "But you're solid, you're sure, and so I have to believe everything you believe. Yeah, I believe in Nancy Jo, but I'd believe a hell of a lot more if I could see or touch her."

Eve laughed. "That's my practical Jane." She released her hand. "Now I think I'll go down and tell Joe that a barbecue is in order."

"I'll take the steaks out of the fridge." She hesitated as she turned toward the door. "You told me about Nancy Jo. You didn't tell me if you'd told Joe that you'd been seeing Bonnie."

"No."

"Why not?"

"It would have been difficult. Nancy Jo was enough of a problem for him to face without Bonnie being thrown into the mix."

"For him to face, or for you to have to give up to him?"

"What are you talking about?" Eve asked impatiently. "Joe has grown almost antagonistic toward Bonnie in the past few years. It would have just added fuel to the fire for him to know that my obsession has grown to the point that I even dreamed about Bonnie."

" 'Dreamed'?"

"It's hard for me even now to admit she isn't a dream. Imagine how hard it would be for Joe."

"But now he has his own out-of-the-world experience with which to compare it. I'd think that would make a difference, don't you?"

Eve looked away from her. "I'm not sure."

"You don't want to give her up," she said softly. "I was wondering if you'd react like that. You don't want to share her. She's been yours all these years in a way that was incredibly secret and special. To tell Joe about it would be like giving her up to someone else. You can't stand the thought."

"Ridiculous. I love Joe."

"That doesn't mean you want to share Bonnie with him. There's nothing wrong with wanting to treasure Bonnie. You just have to realize what you're doing. It was difficult, but you understood about Nancy Jo. That must have meant a hell of a lot to Joe. This is the time when Joe might come close to understanding why you never shared Bonnie."

Eve felt stunned as Jane's words hit home. Dear God, was Jane right? Eve had thought she was protecting herself from everyone thinking she was a nutcase. She had thought she was protecting her relationship by not letting Joe know how overpowering was her obsession.

But she was actually keeping Bonnie a deep, precious secret so that she wouldn't have to share her. As selfish as a miser hoarding her gold.

"It's true, isn't it?" she whispered.

"Only you will know that, Eve," Jane said

gently. "Nothing could be more natural than for you to react like that. She's your baby. She was taken away from you in life, so you want to keep this spirit of Bonnie close and safe. But either way you have to face it so that you can handle it. As I said, things are different now." She reached over and kissed Eve's cheek. "I'm going to go in and get out those steaks and start packing."

Eve still stood there after Jane had gone inside, staring down at Joe beside the lake. His brown hair was rumpled from the breeze and his tea-colored eyes were squinted slightly from the rays of the setting sun. His shirt was open and even from where she stood, she could see the tiny wounds that scarred his chest and abdomen. Wounds that Jelak had inflicted because Joe wouldn't allow Jelak to use him as bait. He was stubborn and loyal and giving and as loving as he was tough.

Emotion surged over her as she stared at him. Dear Heaven, she loved him.

She started down the steps. "Joe!"

Joe turned to see Eve coming down the steps. She was smiling, her expression eager.

"What?"

"Jane's going back to Paris." She had reached the bottom of the steps. "I thought we'd have a barbecue for her. Okay?"

"Sure. But you didn't have to come down to tell me. You could have called me back to the house from —" He stopped, stiffening, his gaze going to the top step of the porch behind Eve.

Bonnie.

She stood there behind Eve like a loving shadow.

No, there was nothing shadowlike about the little girl on the step. She was standing straight, her legs slightly parted, all bright curly hair and eyes that shone as brilliantly as the sun on the water. Not a shadow. A guardian, fearless, vigilant, watching over Eve.

And watching over him?

"Joe?" Eve said.

Bonnie met his eyes and slowly nodded.

Then her luminous smile lit her face.

"What's wrong, Joe?" Eve had stopped on the bank in front of him.

He pulled his eyes away from Bonnie. "Nothing." He was bewildered, uncertain, and yet he was absolutely sure that nothing was wrong.

He looked back at the porch. No little girl. Bonnie was gone. What else could he expect? She was the one who had taught Nancy Jo the trick.

He tried to clear his head and remember

what Eve had said. "You didn't have to come down to get me."

"I wanted to come down. I wanted to be near you." She stopped in front of him. "Touch you."

He smiled. "Be my guest."

She reached out and put her hand on his bare chest. He could feel the warm smoothness of her palm, the strength of her fingers from years of working the clay. His heart began to beat harder as it always did when she touched him.

"And I want to talk to you," she said. "I want to sit down here on the bank and talk about all the years we've been together."

He grimaced. "Past history. Let's strike new territory. I'd rather talk about the future."

"No, first we have to talk about the past." She looked up and met his eyes. "Because then we have to talk about Bonnie."

ABOUT THE AUTHOR

Iris Johansen is the *New York Times* best-selling author of *Quicksand, Pandora's Daughter, Killer Dreams, On the Run, Count-down, Firestorm, Fatal Tide, Dead Aim, No One to Trust, Stalemate* and more. She lives near Atlanta, Georgia.

We hope you have enjoyed this Large Print book. Other Thorndike, Wheeler, Kennebec, and Chivers Press Large Print books are available at your library or directly from the publishers.

For information about current and upcoming titles, please call or write, without obligation, to:

Publisher
Thorndike Press
295 Kennedy Memorial Drive
Waterville, ME 04901
Tel. (800) 223-1244

or visit our Web site at:

http://gale.cengage.com/thorndike

OR

Chivers Large Print
published by BBC Audiobooks Ltd
St James House, The Square
Lower Bristol Road
Bath BA2 3SB
England
Tel. +44(0) 800 136919
email: bbcaudiobooks@bbc.co.uk
www.bbcaudiobooks.co.uk

All our Large Print titles are designed for easy reading, and all our books are made to last.